Doan & Carstairs
Volume 1

Norbert Davis

Holocaust House first published 1940

The Mouse in the Mountain first published 1943

Whisky Priest edition first published 2010

Typeset in Monotype Fournier by James Morrison

ISBN 978-1-4461-8695-4

Contents

Holocaust House

CHAPTER I.
WHERE WAS I?

WHEN DOAN WOKE up he was lying flat on his back on top of a bed with his hat pulled down over his eyes. He lay quite still for some time, listening cautiously, and then he tipped the hat up and looked around. He found to his relief that he was in his own apartment and that it was his bed he was lying on.

He sat up. He was fully dressed except for the fact that he only wore one shoe. The other one was placed carefully and precisely in the center of his bureau top.

"It would seem," said Doan to himself, "that I was inebriated last evening when I came home."

He felt no ill effects at all. He never did. It was an amazing thing and contrary to the laws of science and nature, but he had never had a hangover in his life.

He was a short, round man with a round pinkly innocent face and impossibly bland blue eyes. He had corn-yellow hair and dimples in his cheeks. At first glance—and at the second and third for that matter—he looked like the epitome of all the suckers that had ever come down the pike. He looked so harmless it was pitiful. It wasn't until you considered him for some time that you began to see that there was something wrong with the picture. He looked just a little too innocent.

"Carstairs!" he called now. "Oh, Carstairs!"

Carstairs came in through the bedroom door and stared at him with a sort of wearily resigned disgust. Carstairs was a dog—a fawn-colored Great Dane as big as a yearling calf.

"Carstairs," said Doan. "I apologize for my regrettable condition last evening."

Carstairs' expression didn't change in the slightest. Carstairs was a champion, and he had a long and imposing list of very high-class ancestors. He was fond of Doan in a well-bred way, but he had never been able to reconcile himself to having such

a low person for a master. Whenever they went out for a stroll together, Carstairs always walked either far behind or ahead, so no one would suspect his relationship with Doan.

He grunted now and turned and lumbered out of the bedroom in silent dignity. His disapproval didn't bother Doan any. He was used to it. He got up off the bed and began to go through the pockets of his suit.

He found, as he knew he would, that he had no change at all and that his wallet was empty. He found also in his coat pocket one thing that he had never seen before to his knowledge. It was a metal case—about the length and width of a large cigarette case, but much thicker. It looked like a cigar case, but Doan didn't smoke. It was apparently made out of stainless steel.

Doan turned it over thoughtfully in his hands, squinting at it in puzzled wonder. He had no slightest idea where it could have come from. It had a little button catch at one side, and he put his thumb over that, meaning to open the case, but he didn't.

He stood there looking down at the case while a cold little chill traveled up his spine and raised pin-point prickles at the back of his neck. The metal case seemed to grow colder and heavier in his hand. It caught the light and reflected it in bright and dangerous glitters.

"Well," said Doan in a whisper.

Doan trusted his instinct just as thoroughly and completely as most people trust their eyesight. His instinct was telling him that the metal case was about the most deadly thing he had ever had in his hands.

He put the case carefully and gently down in the middle of his bed and stepped back to look at it again. It was more than instinct that was warning him now. It was jumbled, hazy memory somewhere. He knew the case was dangerous without knowing how he knew.

The telephone rang in the front room, and Doan went in to answer it. Carstairs was sitting in front of the outside door waiting patiently.

"In a minute," Doan told him, picking up the telephone. He

got no chance to say anything more. As soon as he unhooked the receiver a voice started bellowing at him.

"Doan! Listen to me now, you drunken bum! Don't hang up until I get through talking, do you hear? This is J. S. Toggery, and in case you're too dizzy to remember, I'm your employer! Doan, you tramp! Are you listening to me?"

Doan instantly assumed a high, squeaky Oriental voice. "Mr. Doan not here, please. Mr. Doan go far, far away—maybe Timbuktu, maybe Siam."

"Doan, you rat! I know it's you talking! You haven't got any servants! Now you listen to me! I've got to see you right away. Doan!"

"Mr. Doan not here," said Doan. "So sorry, please."

He hung up the receiver and put the telephone back on its stand. It began to ring again instantly, but he paid no further attention to it. Whistling cheerfully, he went back into the bedroom.

He washed up, found a clean shirt and another tie and put them on. The telephone kept on ringing with a sort of apoplectic indignation. Doan tried unsuccessfully to shake the wrinkles out of his coat, gave up and put it on the way it was. He rummaged around under the socks in the top drawer of his bureau until he located his .38 Police Positive revolver. He shoved it into his waistband and buttoned his coat and vest to hide it.

Going over to the bed, he picked up the metal case and put it gently in his coat pocket and then went into the front room again.

"Okay," he said to Carstairs. "I'm ready to go now."

It was a sodden, uncomfortable morning with the clouds massed in darkly somber and menacing rolls in a sky that was a threatening gray from horizon to horizon. The wind came in strong and steady, carrying the fresh tang of winter from the mountains to the west, where the snow caps were beginning to push inquiring white fingers down toward the valleys.

Doan stood on the wide steps of his apartment house breathing deeply, staring down the long sweep of the hill ahead of him. Carstairs rooted through the bushes at the side of the building.

A taxi made a sudden spot of color coming over the crest of the

11

hill and skimming fleetly down the slope past Doan. He put his thumb and forefinger in his mouth and whistled. The taxi's brakes groaned, and then it made a half-circle in the middle of the block and came chugging laboriously back up toward him and stopped at the curb.

Doan grabbed Carstairs by his studded collar and hauled him out of the bushes.

"Hey!" the driver said, startled. "What's that?"

"A dog," said Doan.

"You ain't thinkin' of riding that in this cab, are you?"

"Certainly I am." Doan opened the rear door and shoved Carstairs expertly into the back compartment and climbed in after him. Carstairs sat down on the floor, and his pricked ears just brushed the cab's roof.

The driver turned around to stare with a sort of helpless indignation.

"Now listen here. I ain't got no license to haul livestock through the streets. What you want is a freight car. Get that thing out of my cab."

"You do it," Doan advised.

Carstairs leered complacently at the driver, revealing glistening fangs about two inches long.

The driver shuddered. "All right. All right. I sure have plenty of luck—all bad. Where do you want to go?"

"Out to the end of Third Avenue."

The driver turned around again. "Listen, there ain't anything at the end of Third Avenue but three abandoned warehouses and a lot of gullies and weeds."

"Third Avenue," said Doan. "The very end."

CHAPTER II.
EXPLODING CIGAR

THE THREE WAREHOUSES—like three blocked points of a triangle—looked as desolate as the buildings in a war-deserted city. They stared with blank, empty eyes that were broken windows out over the green, waist-high weeds that surrounded them. The city had been designed to grow in this direction, but it hadn't. It had withdrawn instead, leaving only these three battered and deserted reminders of things that might have been.

"Well," said the taxi driver, "are you satisfied now?"

Doan got out and slammed the door before Carstairs could follow him. "Just wait here," he instructed.

"Hey!" the driver said, alarmed. "You mean you're gonna leave this—this giraffe..."

"I'll only be gone a minute."

"Oh no, you don't! You come back and take this—"

Doan walked away. He went around in back of the nearest warehouse and slid down a steep gravel-scarred bank into a gully that snaked its way down toward the flat from the higher ground to the north. He followed along the bottom of the gully, around one sharply angling turn and then another.

The gully ended here in a deep gash against the side of a weed-matted hill. Doan stopped, looking around and listening. There was no one in sight, and he could hear nothing.

He cupped his hands over his mouth and shouted: "Hey! Hey! Is there anyone around here?"

His voice made a flat flutter of echoes, and there was no answer. After waiting a moment he nodded to himself in a satisfied way and took the metal case out of his pocket. Going to the very end of the gully, he placed the case carefully in the center of a deep gash.

Turning around then, he stepped off about fifty paces back down the gully. He drew the Police Positive from his waistband, cocked

13

it and dropped down on one knee. He aimed carefully, using his left forearm for a rest.

The metal case made a bright, glistening spot over the sights, and Doan's forefinger took up the slack in the trigger carefully and expertly. The gun jumped a little against the palm of his hand, but he never heard the report.

It was lost completely in the round, hollow whoom of sound that seemed to travel like a solid ball down the gully and hit his eardrums with a ringing impact. Bits of dirt spattered around his feet, and where the case had been there was a deep round hole gouged in the hillside, with the earth showing yellow and raw around it.

"Well," said Doan. His voice sounded whispery thin in his own ears. He took out his handkerchief and dabbed at the perspiration that was coldly moist on his forehead. He still stared, fascinated, at the raw hole in the hillside where the case had rested.

After a moment he drew a deep, relieved breath. He put the Police Positive back in his waistband, turned around and walked back along the gully to the back of the warehouse. He climbed up the steep bank and plowed through the waist-high weeds to the street and the waiting taxi.

The driver stared with round, scared eyes. "Say, did—did you hear a—a noise a minute ago?"

"Noise?" said Doan, getting in the back of the cab and shoving Carstairs over to give himself room to sit down. "Noise? Oh, yes. A small one. It might have been an exploding cigar."

"Cigar," the driver echoed incredulously. "Cigar. Well, maybe I'm crazy. Where do you want to go now?"

"To a dining car on Turk Street called the Glasgow Limited. Know where it is?"

"I can find it," the driver said gloomily. "That'll be as far as you're ridin' with me, ain't it—I hope?"

The Glasgow Limited was battered and dilapidated, and it sagged forlornly in the middle. Even the tin stack-vent from its cooking range was tilted drunkenly forward. It was fitted in tightly slantwise on the very corner of a lot, and as if to emphasize its down-at-the-heels appearance an enormous, shining office building towered austere and dignified beside it, putting the Glasgow Limited always in the shadow of its imposing presence.

The taxi stopped at the curb in front of it. This was the city's financial district, and on Sunday it was deserted. A lone street car, clanging its way emptily along looked like a visitor from some other age. The meter on the taxi showed a dollar and fifty cents, and Doan asked the driver:

"Can you trip that meter up to show two dollars?"

"No," said the driver. "You think the company's crazy?"

"You've got some change-over slips, haven't you?"

"Say!" said the driver indignantly.

"Are you accusing me of gypping—"

"No," said Doan. "But you aren't going to get a tip, so you might as well pull it off a charge slip. Have you got one that shows two dollars?"

The driver scowled at him for a moment. He tripped the meter and pocketed the slip. Then he took a pad of the same kind of slips from his vest pocket and thumbed through them. He handed Doan one that showed a charge of a dollar and ninety cents.

"Now blow your horn," Doan instructed. "Lots of times."

The driver tooted his horn repeatedly. After he had done it about ten times, the door of the Glasgow Limited opened and a man came out and glared at them.

"Come, come, MacTavish," said Doan. "Bail me out."

MacTavish came down the steps and across the sidewalk. He was a tall gaunt man with bony stooped shoulders. He was bald, and he had a long draggling red mustache and eyes that were a tired, blood-shot blue.

He wore a white jacket that had sleeves too short for him and a stained white apron.

Doan handed him the meter charge slip.

"There's my ransom, MacTavish. Pay the man and put it on my account."

MacTavish looked sourly at the slip. "I have no doubt that there's collusion and fraud hidden somewhere hereabouts. No doubt at all."

"Why, no," said Doan. "You can see the charge printed right on the slip. This driver is an honest and upright citizen, and he's been very considerate. I think you ought to give him a big tip."

"That I will not!" said MacTavish emphatically. "He'll get his fee and no more—not a penny!" He put a ragged dollar bill in the driver's hand and carefully counted out nine dimes on top of it. "There! And it's bare-faced robbery!"

He glared at the driver, but the driver looked blandly innocent. Doan got out and dragged Carstairs after him.

"And that ugly beastie!" said MacTavish. "I'll feed him no more, you hear? Account or no account, I'll not have him gobbling my good meat down his ugly gullet!"

Doan dragged Carstairs across the sidewalk and pushed him up the stairs and into the dining car. MacTavish came in after them, went behind the counter and slammed the flap down emphatically.

Doan sat down on a stool and said cheerfully: "Good morning, MacTavish, my friend. It's a fine bonny morning full of the smell of heather and mountain dew, isn't it? Fix up a pound of round for Carstairs, and be sure it's none of that watery gruel you feed your unsuspecting customers. Carstairs is particular, and he has a delicate stomach. I'll take ham and eggs and toast and coffee—a double order."

MacTavish leaned on the counter. "And what'll you pay for it with, may I ask?"

"Well, it's true that I find myself temporarily short on ready cash, but I have a fine Swiss watch—"

"No, you haven't," said MacTavish, "because I've got it in the cash register right now."

"Good," said Doan. "That watch is worth at least fifty—"

"You lie in your teeth," said MacTavish. "You paid five dollars for it in a pawn shop. I'll have no more to do with such a loafer and a no-good. I've no doubt that if you had your just deserts you'd be in prison this moment. I'll feed you this morning, but this is the last time. The very last time, you hear?"

"I'm desolated," said Doan. "Hurry up with the ham and eggs, will you, MacTavish? And don't forget

Carstairs' ground round."

MacTavish went to the gas range, grumbling under his breath balefully, and meat made a pleasantly sizzling spatter. Carstairs put his head over the counter and drooled in eager anticipation.

"MacTavish," said Doan, raising his voice to speak over the sizzle of the meat, "am I correct in assuming I visited your establishment last night?"

"You are."

"Was I—ah—slightly intoxicated?"

"You were blind, stinking, pig-drunk."

"You have such a pleasant way of putting things," Doan observed. "I was alone, no doubt, bearing up bravely in solitary sadness?"

"You were not. You had one of your drunken, bawdy, criminal companions with you."

MacTavish set a platter of meat on the counter, and Doan put it on top of one of the stools so that Carstairs could get at it more handily. Carstairs gobbled politely, making little grunting sounds of appreciation.

Doan said casually: "This—ah—friend I had with me. Did you know him?"

"I never saw him before, and if my luck lasts I'll never see him again. I liked his looks even less than I do yours."

"You're in rare form this morning, MacTavish. Did you hear me mention my friend's name?"

"It was Smith," said MacTavish, coming up with a platter of ham and eggs and a cup of coffee.

"Smith," said Doan, chewing reflectively. "Well, it's a nice name. Don't happen to know where I picked him up, do you?"

"I know where you said you picked him up. You said he was a stray soul lost in the wilderness of this great metropolis and that you had rescued him. You said you'd found him in front of your apartment building wasting away in the last stages of starvation, so I knew you were blind drunk, because the man had a belly like

17

a balloon."

"In front of my apartment," Doan repeated thoughtfully. "This is all news to me. Could you give me a short and colorful description of this gentleman by the name of Smith?"

"He was tall and pot-bellied, and he had black eyebrows that looked like caterpillars and a mustache the rats had been nesting in, and he wore dark glasses and kept his hat on and his overcoat collar turned up. I mind particularly the mustache, because you kept asking him if you could tweak it."

"Ah," said Doan quietly. He knew now where he had gotten the instinctive warning about the metal case. Drunk as Doan had been, he had retained enough powers of observation to realize that the mysterious Smith's mustache had been false—that the man was disguised.

Doan nodded to himself. That disposed of some of the mystery of the metal case, but there still remained the puzzle of Smith's identity and what his grudge against Doan was.

CHAPTER III.
THE TEMPESTUOUS TOGGERY

A T THAT MOMENT the front door slammed violently open, and J. S. Toggery came in with his head down and his arms swinging belligerently. He was short and stocky and bandy-legged. He had an apoplectically red face and fiercely glistening false teeth.

"A fine thing," he said savagely. "A fine thing, I say! Doan, you bum! Where have you been for the last three days?"

Doan pushed his empty coffee cup toward MacTavish. "Another cup, my friend. I wish you'd tell the more ill-bred of your customers to keep their voices down. It disturbs my digestion. How are you, Mr. Toggery? I have a serious question to ask you."

"What?" Toggery asked suspiciously.

"Do you know a man whose name isn't Smith and who doesn't wear dark glasses and doesn't have black eyebrows or a black mustache or a pot-belly and who isn't a friend of mine?"

Toggery sat down weakly on one of the stools. "Doan, now be reasonable. Haven't you any regard for my health and well-being? Do you want to turn me into a nervous wreck? I have a very important job for you, and I've been hunting you high and low for three days, and when I find you I'm greeted with insolence, evasion and double-talk. Do you know how to ski?"

"Pardon me," said Doan. "I thought you asked me if I knew how to ski."

"I did. Can you use skis or snow-shoes or ice skates?"

"No," said Doan.

"Then you have a half-hour to learn. Here's your railroad ticket. Your train leaves from the Union Station at two-thirty. Get your heavy underwear and your woolen socks and be on it."

"Why?" Doan asked.

"Because I told you to, you fool!" Toggery roared. "And I'm the man who's crazy enough to be paying you a salary! Now, will you listen to me without interposing those crack-pot comments of yours?"

"I'll try," Doan promised.

Toggery drew a deep breath. "All right. A girl by the name of Sheila Alden is spending the first of the mountain winter season at a place in the Desolation Lake country. You're going up there to see that nothing happens to her for the next three or four weeks."

"Why?" Doan said.

"Because she hired the agency to do it! Or rather, the bank that is her guardian did. Now listen carefully. Sheila Alden's mother died when she was born. Her father died five years ago, and he left a trust fund for her that amounts to almost fifty million dollars. She turns twenty-one in two days, and she gets the whole works when she does.

"There's been a lot of comment in the papers about a young girl getting handed all that money, and she's gotten a lot of threats from crack-pots of all varieties. That Desolation Lake country is as deserted as a tomb this time of year. The season don't start up there for another month. The bank wants her to have some protection until the publicity incident to her receiving that enormous amount of money dies down."

Doan nodded. "Fair enough. Where did her old man get all this dough to leave her?"

"He invented things."

"What kind of things?"

"Powder and explosives."

"Oh," said Doan, thinking of the deep yellow gouge the metal case had left in the hillside. "What kind of explosives?"

"All kinds. He specialized in the highly concentrated variety like they use in hand grenades and bombs. That's why the trust he left increased so rapidly. It's all in munitions stock of one kind and another."

"Ummm," said Doan. "Did you tell anyone you were planning on sending me up to look after her?"

"Of course. Everybody I could find who would listen to me. Have you forgotten that I've been looking high and low for you for three days, you numb-wit?"

"I see," said Doan vaguely. "What's the girl doing up there in the mountains?"

"She's a shy kid, and she's been bedeviled persistently by cranks and fortune hunters and every other kind of chiseler." J. S. Toggery sighed and looked dreamily sentimental. "It's a shame when you think of it. That poor lonely kid—she hasn't a relative in the world—all alone up there in that damned barren mountain country. Hurt and bewildered because of the unthinking attitude of the public. No one to love her and protect her and sympathize with her. If I weren't so busy I'd go up there with you. She needs someone older—some steadying influence."

"And fifty million dollars ain't hay," said Doan.

J. S. Toggery nodded, still dreamy. "No, and if I could just get hold of—" He snapped out of it. "Damn you, Doan, must you reduce every higher human emotion to a basis of crass commercialism?"

"Yes, as long as I work for you."

"Huh! Well, anyway she's hiding up there to get away from it all. Her companion-secretary is with her.

They're staying at a lodge her old man owned. Brill, the attorney who handles the income from the trust, is staying with them until you get there. There's a caretaker at the lodge too."

"I see," said Doan, nodding. "It sounds interesting. It's too bad I can't go."

Toggery said numbly: "Too bad you... What! What! Are you crazy? Why can't you go?"

Doan pointed to the floor. "Carstairs. He disapproves of mountains."

Toggery choked. "You mean that damned dog—"

Doan snapped his fingers. "I've got it. I'll leave him in your care."

"That splay-footed monstrosity! I—I'll—"

Doan reached down and tapped Carstairs on the top of his head. "Carstairs, my friend. Pay attention. You are going to visit Mr. Toggery for a few days. Treat him with consideration because he means well."

Carstairs blinked balefully at Toggery, and Toggery shivered.

"And now," said Doan cheerfully. "The money."

"Money!" Toggery shouted. "What did you do with the hundred I advanced you on your next month's salary?"

"I don't remember exactly, but another hundred will do nicely."

Toggery moaned. He counted out bills on the counter with trembling hands. Doan wadded them up and thrust them carelessly into his coat pocket.

"Aren't you forgetting something, Mr. Doan?" MacTavish asked.

"Oh, yes," said Doan. "Toggery, pay MacTavish what I owe him on account. Cheerio, all. Goodbye, Carstairs. I'll give you a ring soon." He went out the door whistling.

Toggery collapsed limply against the counter, shaking his head. "I think I'm going mad now," he said. "My brain is simmering like a teakettle."

"He gets me that way too," said MacTavish. "Why do you put up with him?"

"Hah!" said Toggery. "Listen! If he wasn't the best—the very best—private detective west of the Mississippi, and if this branch of the agency didn't depend entirely on him for its good record, I would personally murder him!"

"I doubt if you could," said MacTavish.

"I know it," Toggery admitted glumly. "He could take on you and me together with Carstairs thrown in and massacre all three of us without mussing his hair. He's the most dangerous little devil I've ever seen, and he's all the worse because of that half-witted manner of his. You never suspect what he's up to until it's too late."

CHAPTER IV.
WELCOME TO DESOLATION

DOAN ROLLED HIS head back and forth on the hard plush cushion, opened his eyes and blinked politely. "You were saying something?"

The conductor's face was red with exertion. "Yes, I was sayin' something! I been sayin' something for the last ten minutes steady! I thought you was in a trance! This here is where you get off!"

Doan yawned and straightened up. He had a crick in his neck, and he winced, poking his finger at the spot.

The roadbed was rough here, and the old-fashioned tubular brass lamps that hung from the arched car top jittered in short nervous arcs. The whaff-whaff-whaff of the engine exhaust sounded laboriously from ahead.

The car was thick and murky with the smell of cinders. Aside from the conductor, Doan was the only occupant.

Doan asked: "Do you stop while I get off, or am I supposed to hop off like a hobo?"

"We'll stop," said the conductor.

He might have been in telepathic communication with the engineer, because that's just what they did right then. The engine brakes screeched, and the car hopped up against the bumpers and dropped back again with a breath-taking jar, groaning in every joint.

"Is he mad at somebody?" Doan asked, referring to the engineer.

"Listen, you," said the conductor indignantly. "This here grade is so steep that a fly couldn't walk up it without his feet were dipped in molasses first."

Doan took a look at the empty seats. "You didn't make this trip especially on my account, did you?"

"No!" The conductor was even more indignant at the injustice of it. "We got to run a train from Palos Junction through here and back every twenty-four hours in the off season to keep our

23

franchise. Otherwise you'd have walked up. Come on! We ain't got all night to sit around here."

Doan hauled his grip from the rack, pausing to peer out the steamed window. "Is it still raining?"

The conductor snorted. "Raining! It's rainin' down on the coast maybe, but not here. You're eight thousand feet up in the Rocky Mountains, son, and it's snowin' like somebody dumped it out of a chute."

Doan was no outdoorsman, and he hadn't taken what J. S. Toggery had said about skis and snow-shoes at all seriously.

"Snowing?" he said incredulously. "Why, it's still summer!"

"Not up here," said the conductor. "She'll make three feet on the level, and it's driftin'. Get goin'."

Still incredulous, Doan hauled his bag down the aisle and through the end door of the car. This was the last car, the only passenger coach, and when he stepped out on the darkness of the platform the snow and the wind slapped across his face like a giant icy hand. Doan sputtered indignantly and went staggering off balance down the iron steps and plumped into powdery wet coldness that congealed above the level of his thighs.

The engine whistle gave a triumphant, echoing scream.

The conductor was a dim, huddled form with one gaunt arm stretched out like a semaphore. His voice drifted thinly with the wind.

"That way! Through snow-sheds... along spur..."

The engine screamed again, impatiently, and bucked the train ahead.

Doan had dropped his bag, and he scrambled around in the snow trying to find it. "Wait! Wait! I've changed my mind."

The red and green lights on the back of the car blinked mockingly at him, and the conductor's howl came blurred and faint through the white swirling darkness.

"Station... quarter-mile... snow-sheds..."

The engine wailed like a banshee, and the snow and the darkness swallowed the sound of it up in one gulp.

"Well, hell," said Doan.

He spat snow out of his mouth and wiped the cold wetness of it off his face. He located his bag and hauled it out into the middle of the tracks. He had a topcoat strapped on the side of the grip, and he unfastened it now and struggled into it. He was thinking darkly bitter thoughts about J. S. Toggery. With the collar pulled up tight around his throat and his hat pulled down as far it would go over his ears, he stood huddled in the middle of the tracks and looked slowly and unbelievingly around him. He had a range of vision of about ten feet in any given direction; beyond that there was nothing but snow and blackness. There was no sign of any other human, and, aside from the railroad tracks, no sign that there ever had been one here.

"Hey!" Doan shouted.

His voice traveled away and came back after a while in a low, thoughtful echo.

"This is very nice, Doan," said Doan. "You're a detective. Make a brilliant deduction."

He couldn't think of an appropriate one, so he shrugged his shoulders casually, picked up his bag and started walking along the track in the direction the conductor had pointed. The wind slapped and tugged at him angrily, hauling him first one way and then the other, and the frozen gravel of the roadbed ground under his shoes.

He kept his head down and continued walking until he tripped over a switch rail. He looked up and stared into what seemed to be the mouth of an immense square cave. He headed for it, kicking through the drifts in front, and then suddenly he was inside and out of the reach of the wind and the persistent, swirling snow.

It began to make sense now. This high square cave was a wooden snow-shed built to keep the drifts off the spur track on which he was standing. If the rest of the conductor's shouted information could be relied on, the station was a quarter mile further along the spur track.

Doan nodded once to himself, satisfied, took a new grip on the handles of his bag and started trudging along the track. It had been dark outside, but the darkness inside the shed was black swimming ink with no slightest glimmer to relieve it. It was a darkness that enclosed Doan like an envelope and seemed to travel along ahead of him, piling up thicker and thicker with each step he took.

He lost his sense of direction, tripped over the rails and banged against the side of the shed, starting up echoes that clattered deafeningly.

Swearing to himself in a whisper, Doan put his bag down on the ground and fumbled around in his pockets until he found a match. He snapped it alight on his thumbnail and held it up in front of him, cupping his hands protectively around the wavering yellow of the flame.

There was a man standing not a yard away from him—standing stiff and rigid against the rough boards of the shed wall, one arm out-thrust awkwardly as though he were mutely offering to shake hands. His eyes reflected the match flame glassily.

"Uh!" said Doan, startled.

The man didn't say anything, didn't move. He was a short, thick man, and his face looked roughened and bluish in the dim light.

"Well... hello," Doan said uncertainly. He felt a queer chill horror.

The man stayed there, unmoving, his right hand outthrust. Very slowly Doan reached out and touched the hand. It was ice-cold, and the fingers were as rigid as steel hooks.

Doan went backward one stumbling step and then another while the shadows jiggled weirdly around him. Then the match burned his fingers and he dropped it, and the darkness slapped down like a giant soft hand. It was then that he heard a noise behind him—a stealthy skitter in the gravel, faint through the swish of the snow against the shed walls.

Doan turned his head a little at a time until he could see over his shoulder. He stood there rigid while the darkness seemed to pulsate with the beat of his heart.

There were eyes watching him. Luminous and yellow and close to the ground, slanted obliquely at their corners. There were three pairs of them.

Doan stood there until the breath ached in his throat. The paired eyes didn't move. Doan exhaled very slowly and softly. He slid his hand inside the bulk of his topcoat, under his suit coat, and closed his fingers on the butt of the Police Positive.

Just as slowly he drew the revolver from under his coat. The hammer made a small cold click. Doan fired straight up in the air.

The report raised a deafening thunder of echoes. The eyes blinked and were gone, and a voice bellowed hollowly at Doan out of the blackness:

"Don't you shoot them dogs! Damn you, don't you shoot them dogs!"

The voice came from somewhere in back of where the yellow eyes had been. Doan dropped on one knee, leveling the revolver in that direction.

"Show a light," he ordered. "Right now."

Light splayed out from an electric lantern and revealed long legs in baggy blue denim pants and high snow-smeared boots with bulging rawhide laces. The yellow eyes were back of the legs, just out of the throw of light from the lantern, staring in savage watchfulness.

"Higher," said Doan. "Higher with the lantern."

The light went up by jerks like a sticky curtain on a stage, showing in turn a clumsy-looking sheepskin coat, a red hatchet-like face with fiercely glaring eyes, and a stained duck-hunter's cap with the ear flaps pulled down. The man stood as tall and stiff as some weird statue with his shadow stretched jagged and menacing beside him.

"I'm the station master. This here's company property. What you doin' on it?"

"Trying to get off it," said Doan.

"Where'd you come from?"

"The train, stupid. You think I'm a parachute trooper?"

"Oh," said the tall man. "Oh. Was you a passenger?"

"Well, certainly."

"Oh. I thought you were a bum or something. Nobody ever comes up here this time of year."

"I'll remember that. Come closer with the light. Keep the dogs back."

The tall man came slowly closer. Doan saw now that he had only one arm—the left—the one that was holding the lantern. His right sleeve was empty.

"Who's our friend here?" Doan asked, indicating the stiff frozen figure against the wall.

The tall man said casually: "Him? Oh, that's Boley, the regular station master. I'm his relief."

"He looks a little on the dead side to me."

The tall man had a lean gash of a mouth, and the thin lips moved now to show jagged yellow teeth. "Dead as a smoked herring."

"What happened to him?"

"Got drunk and lay out in the snow all night and froze stiff as a board."

"Planning on just leaving him here permanently?"

"I can't move him alone, mister." The tall man indicated his empty right sleeve with a jerk of his head. "I told 'em to stop and pick him up tonight, but they musta forgot to do it. I'll call 'em again. It ain't gonna hurt him to stay here. He won't spoil in this weather."

"That's a comforting thought."

"Dead ones don't hurt nobody, mister. I've piled 'em on trench parapets and shot over 'em. They're as good as sandbags for stoppin' bullets."

"That's a nice thought too. Where's this station you're master of?"

"Right ahead a piece."

"Start heading for it. Keep the dogs away. I don't like the way they look at me."

The light lowered. The tall man sidled past Doan, and his thin legs moved shadowy and stick-like in the lantern gleam, going away.

Doan followed cautiously, carrying the grip in one hand and the cocked revolver in the other. He looked back every third step, but the yellow eyes were gone now.

The shed ended abruptly, and the station was around the curve from it, a yellow box-like structure squashed in against the bare rock of the canyon face with light coming very dimly through small, snow-smeared windows. The tall man opened the door, and Doan followed him into a small square room lighted with one unshaded bulb hanging behind the shining grillwork of the oval ticket window. Yellow varnished benches ran along two walls, and a stove gleamed dully red in the corner between them.

Doan kicked the door shut behind him and dropped his grip on the floor. He still held his revolver casually in his right hand.

"What's your name?" he asked. "Jannen," said the tall man. He had taken off his duck-hunter's cap. He was bald, and his head was long and queerly narrow. He stood still, watching Doan, his eyes gleaming with slyly malevolent humor. "You come up here for somethin' special? There ain't no place to stay. There's a couple of hotels down-canyon, but they ain't open except for the snow sports."

Doan jerked his head to indicate the storm outside. "Isn't that snow?"

"This here is just an early storm. It'll melt off mostly on the flats. In the winter season she gets eight-ten feet deep here on the level, and they bring excursion trains up—sometimes four-five hundred people to once—and park 'em on the sidings over weekends."

There was a whine and then a scratching sound on the door behind Doan.

The tall man jerked his head. "Can I let my dogs inside, mister?"

Doan moved over and sat down on the bench. "Go ahead."

Jannen opened the door, and three shadowy gray forms slunk through it. They were enormous beasts, thick-furred, with blunt wedge-shaped heads. They circled the room and sat down in a silent motionless row against the far wall, watching Doan unblinkingly with eyes that were like yellow, cruel jewels.

"Nice friendly pets," Doan observed.

"Them's sled dogs, mister."

"What dogs?" Doan asked.

"Sled dogs—huskies. See, sometimes them tourists that come

up here, they get tired of skiin' and snow-shoein' and then I pick me up a little side money haulin' 'em around on a dog sled with the dogs. Lot of 'em ain't never rid behind dogs before, and they get a big kick out of it. Them are good dogs, mister."

"You can have them. Do you know where the Alden lodge is from here?"

Jannen's lips moved back from the jagged teeth. "You a friend of that girl's?" His voice was low and tight.

"Not yet. Are you?"

Jannen's eyes were gleaming, reddish slits. "Oh, yeah. Oh, sure I am. I got a good reason to be." With his left hand he reached over and tapped his empty right sleeve. "That's a present from her old man."

Doan was watching him speculatively. "So? How did it happen?"

"Grenade. I was fightin' over in China. It blew up in my hand. Tore my arm off. Old man Alden's factory sold the Chinks that grenade. It had a defective fuse."

"That's not the girl's fault."

Jannen's lips curled. "Oh, sure not. Nobody's fault. An accident. Didn't amount to nothin'—just a man's right arm tore off, that's all. Just made me a cripple and stuck me up in this hell-hole at this lousy job. Yeah. I love that Alden girl. Every time I hear that name I laugh fit to bust with joy."

His voice cracked, and his face twisted into a fiendish grimace. The dogs stirred against the wall uneasily, and one of them whimpered a little.

"Yeah," Jannen said hoarsely. "Sure. I like her. Her old man skimped on that grenade job, and skimped on it so he could leave that girl another million. You'd like her too, mister, if an Alden grenade blew your right arm off, wouldn't you? You'd like her every time you fumbled around one-handed like a crippled bug, wouldn't you?

"You'd like her every time the pain started to bite in that arm stump so you couldn't sleep at night, wouldn't you? You'd feel real kind toward her while you was sleepin' in flop houses and she was spendin' the blood money her old man left her, wouldn't you, mister?"

The man was not sane. He stood there swaying, and then he laughed a little in a choking rasp that shook his thin body.

"You want me to show you the way to the lodge? Sure, mister. Glad to. Glad to do a favor for an Alden any old time."

Doan stood up. "Let's start," he said soberly.

CHAPTER V.
MISS MILLION-BUCKS

DOAN SMELLED THE smoke first, coming thin and pungent down-wind, and then Jannen stopped short in front of him and said:

"There it is."

The wind whipped the snow away for a second, and Doan saw the house at the mouth of a ravine that widened out into a flat below them. The walls were black against the white drifts, and the windows stared with dull yellow eyes.

"Thanks," said Doan. "I can make it from here. If I could offer some slight compensation for your time and trouble..."

Jannen was hunched up against the wind like some gaunt beast of prey, staring down at the house, wrapped up in darkly bitter thoughts of his own. His voice came thickly.

"I don't want none of your money."

"So long," said Doan.

"Eh?" said Jannen, looking around.

Doan pointed back the way they had come. "Goodbye, now."

Jannen turned clumsily. "Oh, I'm goin'. But I ain't forgettin' nothin', mister." His mittened left hand touched his empty right sleeve. "Nothin' at all. You tell her that for me."

"I'll try to remember," said Doan.

He stood with his head tilted against the wind, watching Jannen until he disappeared back along the trail, his three huskies slinking along like stunted shadows at his heels. Then he shrugged uneasily and went down the steep slant of the ridge to the flat below. The wind had blown the snow clear of the ground in places, and he followed the faint marks of a path across the stretch of frozen rocky ground.

Close to it, the house looked larger—dark and ugly with the smoke from the chimney drifting in a jaunty plume across the white-plastered roof. The path ended at a small half-enclosed porch, and Doan climbed the log steps up to it and banged hard with his fist against the heavy door.

He waited, shivering. The cold had gotten through his light clothes. His feet tingled numbly, and the skin on his face felt drawn and stiff.

The door swung open, and a man stared out at him unbelievingly. "What—who're you? Where'd you come from?"

"Doan—Severn Agency."

"The detective! But man alive! Come in, come in!"

Doan stepped into a narrow shadowed hall, and the warmth swept over him like a soft grateful wave.

"Good Lord!" said the other man. "I didn't expect you'd come tonight—in this storm!"

"That's Severn service," Doan told him. "When duty calls, we answer. And besides, I'm overdrawn on my salary."

"But you're not dressed for—Why, you must be frozen stiff!"

He was a tall man, very thin, with a sharp dramatically haggard face. His hair was jet-black with a peculiarly distinctive swathe of pure white running back slantwise from his high forehead. He talked in nervous spurts, and he had a way of making quick little half-gestures that had no meaning, as though he were impatiently jittery.

"A trifle rigid in spots," Doan admitted. "Have you got some concentrated heat around the premises?"

"Yes! Yes, surely! Come in here! My name is Brill, by the way. I'm in charge of Miss Alden's account with the National Trust. Taking care of the legal end. But of course you know all about that. In here."

It was a long living room with a high ceiling that matched the peak of the roof. At the far end there was an immense natural stone fireplace with the flame hooking eager little blue fingers around the log that almost filled it.

"But you should have telephoned from the station," Brill was saying. "No need to come out tonight in this."

"Have you a telephone here?" Doan asked.

"Certainly, certainly. Telephone, electricity, central heating, all that.... Miss Alden, this is Mr. Doan, the detective from the Severn

Agency. You know, I told you——"

"Yes, of course," said Sheila Alden. She was sitting on the long, low divan in front of the fire. She was a small, thin girl with prim features, and she looked disapprovingly at Doan and then down at the snow he had tracked across the floor. She had lusterless stringy brown hair and teeth that protruded a little bit, and she wore thick horn-rimmed glasses.

"Hello," said Doan. He didn't think he was going to like her very well.

"This seems all very melodramatic and very unnecessary," said Sheila Alden. "A detective to guard me! It's so absurd."

"Now, not at all, not at all," said Brill in a harassed tone. "It's the thing to do—the only thing. I'm responsible, you know. The National people hold me directly responsible for your well-being. We must take every reasonable precaution. We really must. I'm doing the best I know how."

"I know," said Sheila Alden, faintly contemptuous. "Pull up that chair, Mr. Doan, and get close to the fire. By the way, this is Mr. Crowley."

"Hello, there," said Crowley cheerfully. "You're hardly dressed for the weather, old chap. If you plan to stay around here I'll have to lend you some of my togs."

"Mr. Crowley," said Brill, "has a place over at the other side of Flint Flat."

"A little hide-out, you know," said Crowley. "Just a little shack where a man can hole in and soak up some solitude now and then."

He had a very British-British accent and a hairline black mustache and a smile full of white teeth. He was every bit as handsome as those incredible young men who are always driving the latest sport motor cars in magazine advertisements. He knew it. He had brown eyes with a personality twinkle in them and wavy black hair and an expensive tan.

"Mr. Crowley," said Brill, "got lost in the storm this afternoon and just happened—just happened to stumble in here this afternoon."

"Right-o," said Crowley. "Lucky for me, eh?"

"Very," said Brill sourly.

Crowley was sitting on the divan beside Sheila Alden, and he turned around and gave her the full benefit of his smile. "Yes, indeed! My lucky day!"

Sheila Alden simpered. There was no other word for it. She wiggled on the cushions and poked at her stringy hair and blinked shyly at Crowley through the thick glasses.

"You must stay the night here, Mr. Crowley."

"Must he?" Brill inquired, still more sourly.

Sheila Alden looked up, instantly antagonistic. "Of course! He can't possibly get home tonight, and we have plenty of room, and I've invited him!"

"A little blow like this," said Crowley. "Nothing. Nothing at all. You should see it scream up in the Himalayas. That's something!" He leaned closer to Sheila. "But of course there's no chance to stumble on to such delightful company when you're in the Himalayas, is there? I'll be delighted to stay overnight, Miss Alden, if it won't inconvenience you too much. It's so kind of you to ask me."

"Not at all," said Sheila Alden.

Doan was standing in front of the fire with his arms out-spread, gradually thawing out, and now someone tugged uncertainly at his sleeve.

"You're—the detective?"

Doan turned to look at another girl. She was small too, smaller even than Sheila Alden, and she had a soft round face and full lips that pouted a little. She had blond hair, and her eyes were very wide and very blue and they didn't quite focus.

"This is Miss Alden's secretary," Brill said stiffly. "Miss Joan Greg."

"You're cute," Joan Greg said, swaying just slightly. "You're a cute little detective."

"Cute as a bug's ear," Doan agreed.

"Joan!" Sheila Alden said sharply. "Please behave yourself!"

Joan Greg turned slowly, still keeping her hold on Doan's arm.

"Talking—to me?"

"You're drunk!" Sheila Alden said.

Joan Greg made the words carefully with her soft lips. "Shall I tell you just what you are—you and that thing sitting beside you?"

The tension in the room was like a wire stretched to a breaking point, with them all standing and staring at Joan incredulously. She was swaying, and her lips were twisting to form new words, while her eyes stared at Sheila Alden with glassy, unblinking hate.

"I'll—kill—her," said Joan Greg distinctly.

CHAPTER VI.
DANGEROUS LADY

"**M**ISS GREG!" BRILL gasped, horrified. But he did not make a move. He just stood, gaping.

"Wait until I get warm first, will you?" Doan asked casually.

Joan Greg forgot all about Sheila Alden for the moment. She swayed against Doan and said: "You're just the cutest little fella I've ever seen. Lemme help you out of your coat."

Brill stepped forward. "I'll do—"

"No! No! Lemme!"

Fumblingly, she helped Doan take off his topcoat and staggered back several steps holding it in front of her.

"Gonna—hang it up. Gonna hang the nice cute little detective's coat up for him."

She went at a diagonal across the room, missed the door by ten feet, carefully walked backward until she got a new line on it, and made it through. They could hear her in the hall, stumbling a little.

"I could use some of that," Doan said.

Brill stared at him. "Eh?"

Doan made a motion as though he were lifting a glass.

"Oh!" Brill said. "A drink! Yes, yes. Of course. Kokomo! Kokomo!"

A swinging door squeaked, and light showed through the archway opposite the entrance to the hall. Feet scraped lumberingly on the floor, and a man came in through the archway and said in a surly voice:

"Well, what?"

He had shoulders as wide as a door and long thick arms that were corded with muscle. He was wearing a white apron over blue denim trousers and a checked shirt, and he had a tall chefs hat perched jauntily over the bulging shapeless lump that had once been his left ear. He carried a toothpick in one corner of his pulpy lips, and his eyes were dully expressionless under thick, scarred eyebrows.

"Ah, yes," Brill said nervously. "Bring the whisky, Kokomo, and—and a siphon of soda."

"You want ice?"

"I've had mine tonight already," Doan said.

"No," Brill said. "No ice."

Kokomo lumbered back through the archway and appeared immediately again carrying a decanter and a siphon on a tray with a stacked pile of glasses.

Brill took the tray. "Mr. Doan, this is Kokomo—the cook and caretaker. This is the detective, Kokomo."

"This little squirt?" said Kokomo. "A detective? Hah!"

Brill said: "Kokomo! That's all!"

"Hah!" said Kokomo, staring down at Doan. He moved his big shoulders in a casual shrug and padded back through the archway. The swinging door squeaked shut behind him.

"Really, Mr. Brill," Sheila Alden said severely. "It seems to me that I have grounds for complaint about your choice of employees."

Brill threw his hands wide helplessly. "Miss Alden, I've told you again and again that our Mr. Dibben had been handling all your affairs and that he was injured when an auto ran over him and that his duties were suddenly delegated to me without the slightest warning and that he hadn't made any note of the fact that you intended to come up here.

"When you called me I had to find a man at once who would act as caretaker and cook and open this place up for you. This man Kokomo had excellent references—a great deal of experience—all that. You must admit, Miss Alden, that in spite of his uncouth appearance, he is a very good cook, and it's very difficult to get servants to come clear up here..."

Sheila Alden wasn't through. "And I don't think much of your choice of a secretary, either."

Brill lifted his hands. "Miss Greg had the very finest references. There was nothing in them whatsoever that indicated she was—

ah—inclined to drink too much."

"Lonely country," Crowley said. "Brings it on. Seen it happen to a lot of chaps in Upper Burma. Probably be all right as soon as she gets back to civilization, eh? By the way, Mr. Doan, how on earth did you find this place? I mean, I got jolly well lost myself, and I can't see how a stranger could find his way here."

Doan had filled a glass half with whisky and half with soda and was sipping at it appreciatively. "The station master brought me around—not because he wanted to. He seemed a bit sour on the Alden name."

"And that's another thing!" Brill said worriedly. "The man's a crank—dangerous. He shouldn't be allowed at large. He holds some insane grudge against Miss Alden, and he might—might... I mean, I'm responsible. I tried to talk to him, but all he did was threaten me. And those damned dogs. Mr. Doan, you had better investigate him thoroughly."

"Oh, sure," said Doan.

Brill ran thin nervous fingers through his hair, mussing up the blazed streak of white that centered it. "I don't like you coming up here in this wilderness, Miss Alden. It's a great responsibility to put on my shoulders." He fumbled in his coat pocket and brought out a shiny metal case.

Doan stiffened, his glass half-raised to his lips. "What's that you've got there?"

"This?" said Brill. "A cigar case."

The case was an exact duplicate of the one Doan had found in his pocket—his deadly present from the mysterious Mr. Smith.

Brill snapped the catch with his thumb, and the case opened on his palm, revealing the six cigars fitted into it snugly.

Doan released his breath in a long sigh. "Where," he said, clearing his throat. "Where did you get it?"

Brill was admiring the case. "Nice, isn't it? Just the right size. Eh? Oh, it was a present from a client."

"What was his name?"

"Smith," said Brill. "As a matter of fact, that's a strange thing. We have several clients whose name is Smith, and I don't know which one of them gave me this. Whoever it was just left it on my secretary's desk with a little note saying in appreciation of services rendered and all that and signed, 'Smith'—"

"What was in it?" Doan asked.

Brill looked surprise. "Why, cigars."

"Did you smoke them?"

"Well, no. You see, I smoke a specially mild brand on account of my throat. I gave the ones in the case to the janitor, poor chap."

"Poor chap?" Doan repeated.

"Yes. He was killed that very night. He had a shack on the outskirts of the city, and he was running a still of some sort there—at least that's what the police think—and the thing blew up and blasted him to bits. Terrific explosion."

"Oh," said Doan. He watched thoughtfully while Brill selected a cigar and put the case back in his coat pocket.

"Well," said Brill, making an effort to be more sociable. "Let's think of something pleasant..." His voice trailed off into a startled gulp.

Joan Greg had come quietly in from the hall. She was holding Doan's revolver carefully in her right hand. She was walking straighter now, and she came directly across the floor to the front of the divan. She stopped there and pointed the revolver at Sheila Alden.

"Here!" Crowley shouted in alarm.

Doan flipped the contents of his glass into Joan Greg's face. Her head jerked back when the stinging liquid hit her. She took one uncertain step backward, and then Doan vaulted over the couch and expertly kicked her feet from under her.

She fell on her back, coming down so hard that her blond head bounced forward loosely with the impact.

Doan stepped on her right wrist and twisted the revolver from her lax fingers.

Joan Greg turned over on her stomach and hid her face in her arms. She began to cry in racked, gasping sobs.

The others stared at her, and at Doan with a sort of frozen, dazed horror.

"More fun," said Doan, slipping the revolver into his waistband. "Does she do things like this very often?"

"Gah!" Brill gasped. "She—she would have... Why—why, she's crazy! Crazy drunk! Where—where'd she get that gun?"

"It was in my topcoat pocket," Doan said. "Careless of me, but I didn't think there were any homicidal maniacs wandering around the house."

Sheila Alden's face was paper white. "Get her out of here! She's fired! Take her away!"

"Yes, yes," said Brill. "At once. Terrible. Terrible thing, really. And I'll be blamed—"

"Take her away!" Shield Alden screamed at him.

Doan leaned over and picked Joan Greg up. She had stopped crying and she was utterly relaxed. Her arms flopped laxly. Her eyes were closed, and the tears had made wet jagged streaks down her soft cheeks.

"She's passed out, I think," Doan said. "I'll take her up and lock her in her bedroom."

"Yes, yes," Brill said. "Only thing. This way."

Crowley was bending anxiously over Sheila Alden. "Now, now. It's all over. Gives a person a nasty feeling, I know. Saw a chap run amok in Malay once. Ghastly thing. But you're a brave girl. Just a little sip of this."

Brill led the way across the living room and down the hall to a steep stairway with a rustic natural-wood railing. Brill went on up it and stopped at the first door in the upper hallway. He was still shaky, and he edged away from the limp form of Joan Greg as a man would avoid contact with something poisonous.

"Here," he said, pushing the door open and reaching around to snap on the light. "This—this is awful. Miss Alden is sure to complain to the office. What do you suppose ailed her?"

Doan put Joan Greg down on the narrow bed under the windows. The room was stiflingly hot. He looked at the windows and then down at Joan Greg's flushed face and decided against opening one. While he was looking down at her, she opened her eyes and stared up at him. All the life had drained out of her round face and left it empty and bitter and disillusioned.

"What's the trouble?" Doan asked. "Want to tell me about it?"

She turned her head slowly away from him and closed her eyes again. Doan waited a moment and then said:

"Better get undressed and into bed and sleep it off."

He turned off the light and went out of the room, transferring the key from the inside of the lock to the outside and turning it carefully. He tried the door to make sure and then put the key in his pocket.

Brill was wringing his hands in a distracted way. "I—I can hardly bear to face Miss Alden. She will blame me. Everybody blames me! I didn't want this responsibility.... I've got to go down and out-wait that scoundrel

Crowley."

"Why?" Doan asked.

Brill came closer. "He's a fortune hunter! He didn't get lost today! He came over here on purpose because he's heard that Miss Alden was here! She's an impressionable girl, and I can't let him stay alone with her down there. The office would hold me accountable if he—if she..."

"I get it," Doan said.

"I don't know what to do," said Brill. "I mean, I know Miss Alden will be sure to resent—But I can't let him—"

"That's your problem," said Doan. "But I'm not supposed to protect her from people who want to make love to her—only the ones that don't. So I'm not out-waiting our friend Crowley. I'm tired. Which is my bedroom?"

"Right there. You'll leave your door open, Mr. Doan, in case—in case..."

"In case," Doan agreed. "Just whistle, and I'll pop up like any jack-in-the-box."

"I'm so worried," said Brill. "But I must go down and see that the scoundrel doesn't..."

He went trotting down the steep stairs. Doan went along the hall back to the bedroom Brill had indicated. It was small and as neatly arranged as a model room in a display window, furnished with imitation rustic bed, chairs and bureau.

It, too, was stiflingly hot. Doan spotted the radiator bulking in the corner. He went over and touched it experimentally and jerked his fingers away with a whispered curse. It was so hot the water in it was burbling. Doan looked for the valve to turn it off, but there was none.

He stood looking at the radiator for some time, frowning in a puzzled way. There was something wrong about the whole setup at the lodge. It was like a picture slightly out of focus, and yet he couldn't put his finger on any one thing that was wrong. It bothered Doan, and he didn't like to be bothered. But it was still there. An air of intangible menace.

He discovered now that he had left his grip downstairs. He didn't feel like going and getting it at the moment. He wanted to think about the people in the house, and he had always been able to think better lying down. He shrugged and headed for the bed. Fully dressed, he lay down on top of it and went to sleep.

CHAPTER VII.
NICE NIGHT FOR MURDER

WHEN DOAN AWOKE, he awoke all at once. He was instantly alert, but he didn't make any other motion than opening his eyes. The heat int he bedroom was like a thick oppressive blanket—fantastic and unreal against the shuffling whie of the storm outside.

Doan stayed still and wondered what had awakened him. His bedroom door was still open, and there was a dim light in the hall. A timber creaked eerily somewhere in the house. The seconds ticked off slowly and leadenly, and then a shadow moved and made a rounded silhouette in the hall in front of the bedroom door.

Doan moved his hand and closed his fingers on the slick coolness of his revolver. The shadow thickened, swaying a little, and then Joan Greg came into sight. She was moving along the hall with mincing, elaborately cautious steps. She had evidently taken Doan's advice about going to bed. She was dressed in a green silk nightgown that contrasted with her blond hair. She stopped opposite Doan's doorway and looked that way.

Her soft lips were open, twisted awry, and there was a dribble of saliva on her chin. Her eyes were widened in mesmerized horror. She was holding a short broad-bladed hunting knife in her right hand.

"That's fine," said Doan quietly. "Just stand right where you are."

The knife made a ringing thud falling on the floor. Joan Greg drew a long shuddering breath that pulled the thin green silk taut across her breasts. The cords in her soft throat stood out rigidly.

Then she crumpled like a puppet that has been dropped. She was an awkwardly twisted heap of green silk and white flesh, with the gold of her hair glinting metallically in the light.

Doan swung cat-like off the bed and reached the doorway in two long steps. He didn't look down at Joan Greg, but both ways along the hall. One of the doors on the opposite side moved just a trifle.

"Come out of there," said Doan. "Quick!"

The door opened in hesitant jerks, and Crowley peered out at hi. He was wearing nothihng but a pair of blue shorts, and his wedge-shaped torso was oily with perspiration. His face was a queer yellowish green under its tan.

"So beastly hot. Couldn't get the windows open. I thought—I heard—"

"Come here."

Crowley moistened his lips with a nervous flick of his tongue. He came forward one step at a time. "What—what's the matter with her?"

"Stand right there and stand still."

Crowley's breath whistleed between his teeth. "Blood! Look! All over her hands—"

Doan knelt down beside Joan Greg. Her hands were spread out awkwardly beside her, as though she had tried to hold them away from herself even while she fell. There was blood smeared on her fingers and streaked gruesomely across both her soft palms. Doan poked at the knife she had dropped with the barrel of his revolver.

There was blood clotted ont hem, too. On the handle and on the broad blad. Doan raised his head.

"Brill!" he called sharply.

Bed springs creaked somewhere, and Brill's nervous voice said: "Eh? What? What?"

The springs creaked again protestingly. Brill, looking tall and lath-like in white pajamas, appeared in the open door of the bedroom next to Doan's. His slick hair was rumpeld now, and he held one hand up to shield his eyes from the light.

"What? What is it?" His thin face began to lengthen, then, as though it had been drawn in some enormous vise. "Oh, my God," he said in a whisper.

He came forward with the stiff, jerky steps of a sleep-walker. "Did she commit suicide?"

"I'm afraid not," said Doan. "She's fainted. Which is Miss Alden's room?"

Brill stared at him in pure frozen horror. "You don't think she—" He made a strangled noise in his throat. He turned and ran down the hall, his white pajamas flapping grotesqely. "Miss Alden! Miss Alden!"

The door at the end of the hall was hers, and Brill pounded on the panels with both fists. "Miss Alden!" His voice was raw with panic now, and he tried the knob. The door opened immediately.

"Miss—Miss Alden," Brill said uncertainly.

"The light," said Doan, behind him.

Brill reached inside the door and snapped the switch. There was no sound for a long time, and then Brill moaned a little.

Doan said: "Come here, Crowley. I want you where I can watch you."

Crowley spoke in a jerky voice. "Well, Joan—I mean, Miss Greg. You can't leave her lying—"

"Come here."

Crowley edged inside Sheila Alden's bedroom and backed against the wall in response to a guiding flick of Doan's revolver barrel. Brill was standing in the center of the room with his hands up over his face.

"This will ruin me," he said in a sick mumble. "I was going to get a partnership in the firm. They gave me full responsibility for watching out for her. Account was worth tens of thousands a year. They'll hound me out of the state—can never practice again." His voice trailed off into indistinguishable syllables. This bedroom was as stiflingly hot as Doan's had been. Sheila Alden had only a sheet over her. She was stiffly rigid on her back in the bed. Her throat had been cut from ear to ear, and the pillows under her head were soaked and sticky with blood. Her bony face looked pinched and small and empty, with her nearsighted eyes staring glassily up at the light.

Doan pointed the gun at Crowley. "You talk."

Crowley made an effort to get back his air of British lightheartedness. "But, old chap, you can't imagine I—"

"Yes, I can," said Doan.

Crowley's mouth opened and shut soundlessly.

"It comes a little clearer," said Doan. "You were so scared you got a little rattled for a moment. Just how well do you know Joan Greg?"

Crowley's smile was an agonized grimace. "Well, my dear chap, hardly at all. I just met the young lady today." "We can't use that one." Doan said. "You know her very well. That was what was the trouble with her. She was jealous. You've been living off her, haven't you?"

"That's not a nice thing to accuse a chap—"

"Murder's not nice, either. You've been living off Joan Greg. You haven't any more got a place on Flint Flat than I have. Have you?"

"Well..."

"No, you haven't. Joan Greg told you that she had gotten a job as secretary to Sheila Alden and was coming up here. You knew who Sheila Alden was, and you thought that was a swell chance for you to chisel in and charm the young lady with your entrancing personality.

"You must have let Joan Greg in on it—told her you'd make a killing and split with her probably. But when it came right down to seeing you make passes at Sheila Alden, Joan Greg couldn't take it."

"Fantastic," Crowley said in a stiff unnatural voice. "Utter—rot."

"You!" said Brill, and the blood made a thick red flush in his shallow cheeks. "You rat! I'll see you hung! I'll—I'll—Doan! Hold him until I get my gun!" He blundered wildly out of the room, and his feet made a wild pattering rush down the hall. Crowley had recovered his poise now. His eyes were cold and alert and hard, watching Doan. Brill's bedroom door slammed, and then his voice shrilled out fiercely.

"Get up! Get up, damn you! I know you're faking! I saw your eyes open!"

There was a scuffling sound from the hall, and Joan Greg cried out breathlessly. Crowley moved against the wall.

"No," said Doan.

Confused footsteps came closer, and Brill pushed Joan Greg roughly into the bedroom.

"There!" Brill raged. "Look at her! Look at your handiwork, damn you, you shameless little tramp!"

Joan Greg gave a stifled cry of terror. She held her shaking, blood-smeared hands out in front of her helplessly, and then she turned and ran to Crowley and hid her face against his chest.

"There they are!" Brill shouted. He was holding a .45 Colt automatic in his hand and he waved it wildly in the air. "Look at them! A fine pair of crooks and murderers! But they'll pay! You hear me, do you? You'll pay!"

Doan was looking at the radiator in the corner. He was frowning a little bit and whistling softly and soundlessly to himself.

"Why is it so hot?" he asked.

"Eh?" Brill said. "What?"

"Why is it so hot in the bedrooms?"

"The windows have storm shutters on them," Brill said impatiently. "They can't be opened in a wind like this."

"But why are the radiators so hot? The water in that one is boiling. You can hear it."

"What damned nonsense!" Brill yelled. "Are you going to stand there and ask silly questions about radiators when Sheila Alden has been murdered and these two stand here caught in the very act—"

"No," said Doan. "I'm going to find out about the matter of the temperature around here. You watch these two."

"Doan, you fool!" Brill shouted. "Come back here! You're in my employ and I demand—"

"Watch them," said Doan. "I'll be back in a minute or so."

CHAPTER VIII.
HI, KOKOMO

H E WENT DOWN the hall, down the steep stairs, and across the living room. The log fireplace was dull, glowing red embers now. The wind had blown some of the smoke back down the chimney, and it made a thick murky blue haze. Doan went on across the room through the archway on the other side. Ahead of him light showed dimly around the edge of the swinging door that led into the kitchen. The hinges squeaked as Doan pushed it back.

Kokomo was sitting in the corner beside the gleaming white and chromium of an electric range. He was still wearing his big apron, and the tall chefs hat was tilted down rakishly over his left eye. He had what looked like the same toothpick in one corner of his mouth, and it moved up and down jerkily as he said:

"What can I do for you, sonny?"

"Don't you ever go to bed at night?" Doan asked.

"Naw. I'm an owl."

"It's awfully hot upstairs," said Doan.

"Too bad."

"I notice you have a central hot water heating system here. What does the furnace burn—coal or oil?"

"Coal."

"Who takes care of it?"

"Me."

"Where is it?"

Kokomo jerked a thick thumb at a door in the back wall of the kitchen. "Down cellar."

"I think I'll take a look at it."

Kokomo took the toothpick out of his mouth and snapped it into the far corner of the room. "Run along and roll your hoop, sonny, before I lose my patience and lay you out like a rug. This here end of the premises is my bailiwick and I don't go for any mush-faced snoopers prowlin' around in it. I told the rest that. Now I'm tellin' it to you."

"On the other hand," said Doan cheerfully, "I think I'll have a look at the furnace."

Kokomo got up out of his chair. "Sonny, you're gettin' me irritated. Put that popgun away before I shove it down you throat."

Doan dropped the gun in his coat pocket, smiling. "Aw, you wouldn't do a mean thing like that, would you?"

Kokomo came for him with quick little shuffling steps, his head lowered and tucked between the hunched bulk of his thick shoulders.

Doan was still smiling. He made a fork out of the first two fingers of his left hand and poked them at Kokomo's eyes. Kokomo knew that trick and, instead of ducking, he merely tilted his head back and let Doan's stiffened fingers slide off his low forehead. But when he put his head back, he exposed his thickly muscular throat.

Doan hit him squarely on the adam's apple with a short right jab. It was a wickedly effective blow, and Kokomo made a queer strangling noise and grasped his throat with both hands, rolling his head back and forth in agony. His mouth was wide open, and his eyes bulged horribly.

Doan hit him again, a full roundhouse swing with all his compact weight behind it. His fist smacked on the hinge of Kokomo's jaw. Kokomo went back one step and then another, shaking his head helplessly, still trying to draw a breath.

"I should break my hands on you, cement-head," Doan said casually. He took the revolver out of his coat pocket and slammed Kokomo on the top of the head with the butt of it.

The blow smashed the tall chefs hat into a weirdly lopsided pancake. Kokomo dropped to his knees, sagging loosely. With cold-blooded efficiency Doan hit him again in the same place. Kokomo flopped forward on his face and lay there on the shiny linoleum without moving.

It had happened very fast, and Doan was standing there now, looking down at Kokomo, still smiling in his casually amused way.

He wasn't even breathing hard.

"These tough guys," he said, shrugging.

He dropped the revolver in his coat pocket again and stepped over Kokomo. The cellar door was fastened with a patent bolt. Doan unlatched it and peered down a flight of steep wooden stairs that were lighted dimly from the kitchen behind him. He felt around the door and found a light switch and clicked it. Nothing happened. The light down in the cellar, if there was one, didn't work.

Doan went down the steps, feeling his way cautiously as he got beyond the path of the light from the kitchen door. The cellar was a warm, dark cavern thick with the smell of coal dust. Feeling overhead, Doan located the warmth of a fat asbestos-wrapped pipe and judged from the direction it ran that the furnace was over in the far corner.

He started that way, sliding his feet cautiously along the cement floor. He was somewhere in the middle of it, out of reach of either wall, when something made a quick silent breath going past in front of his face.

He stopped with a jerk, reaching for his revolver. The thing that had gone past his face hit the wall behind him with a dull ominous thud and dropped to the floor. Doan stayed rigidly still, his revolver poised. He was afraid to move for fear of stumbling over something. He listened tensely, his head tilted.

A voice whispered out of the darkness ahead of him. "Don't— don't you dare come any closer. I've got a shovel here. I'll—hit you with it."

Doan was a hard man to surprise, but he was as startled now as he ever had been in his life. He stared in the direction of the voice, his mouth open.

The voice said shakily: "You get out."

"Whoa," Doan said. "Wait a minute. I'm not coming any closer. Just listen to me before you heave any more of that coal."

"Who—who are you?"

"Name's Doan."

"The detective! Oh!"

"That's what I say. And who're you?"

"Sheila Alden."

"Ah," said Doan blankly. He drew a deep breath. "Well, I know I'm not drunk, so this must be happening. If you're Sheila Alden down here in the cellar, who's the Sheila Alden up in the bedroom?"

"That's my secretary, Leila Adams. She's been impersonating me."

"Oh. Sort of a game, huh?"

"No!"

"Well, I was just asking. What's the matter with the light down here?"

"I screwed the bulb out of the socket."

"Well, where is it? I'll screw it back in again. I need some light on the subject."

"Oh, no! No! Don't!"

"Why not?"

"I—I haven't any clothes on."

"You haven't any clothes on," Doan repeated. He shook his head violently. "Maybe I'm a little sleepy or something. I don't seem to be getting this. Suppose you just start and tell me all about it."

"Well, Leila and I came up here alone. Kokomo had come ahead to open up the place. Kokomo and Leila are in this together. When we got here they held me up and locked me in the cellar—in the back room beyond this one. Leila told me she was going to pretend she was me."

"Is Brill crazy? Didn't he know Leila Adams wasn't you?"

"No. Mr. Dibben in the law firm always handled all my business. I don't know Mr. Brill. He's never seen me."

"Well, well," said Doan. "Then what?"

"They just locked me in that cellar room. There's one window, and they didn't want to put bars over it, so they took all my clothes away from me. They knew I wouldn't get out the window then. If I did I'd freeze. "It's two miles to the station and I didn't know which way. And Kokomo said if I screamed he'd..." Her voice trailed off into a little gasping sob. "He told me what he'd do."

"Yeah," said Doan. "I can imagine."

"Where is he now?"

"Kokomo? He's slightly indisposed at the moment. Go on. Tell me the rest."

"I broke a little piece of metal off the window, and I picked the lock on the door and got out here. I know how the heating system works. The valves are down here. I turned off the ones that controlled the downstairs radiators and opened the ones that control the upstairs radiators wide.

"Then I kept putting coal in the furnace with the drafts wide open. I thought if I made it hot enough in the upstairs bedrooms someone besides Kokomo would come down and look."

"Sure," said Doan. "Smart stuff. If I'd had any brains I'd have been down here hours ago. You stay right here and I'll bring you something to wear. Don't be afraid any more."

"I haven't been afraid—not very much. Only—only of Kokomo coming down here and—"

"He won't be coming down. Stay right here. I'll be right back." Doan ran back up the steps. All his cheerful casual air was gone now. His lips were thinned across his teeth, and he moved with a cat-like, lithe efficiency.

Kokomo was still lying flat on his face in the center of the kitchen floor. Doan, moving with the same quiet quickness, opened the cupboard door and located an aluminum kettle.

He filled it with water at the sink. Carrying it carefully, he walked over to Kokomo and, using the toe of one shoe, expertly flipped the big man over on his back.

He dumped the kettle of water in Kokomo's blankly upturned face. For a second there was no reaction, then Kokomo's pulpy lips moved, and he sputtered wetly. His eyes opened and he saw Doan looking thoughtfully down at him.

"Hi, Kokomo," Doan said softly. "Hi, baby."

Kokomo made noises in his throat and heaved himself up on his elbows. Doan took one short step forward and kicked him under the jaw so hard that Kokomo's whole lolling body lifted clear of the floor and rolled half under the stove. He didn't move any more.

"I'll have another present for you later," Doan said.

CHAPTER IX.
BLACK SNOW

HE WENT IN through the living room to the front hall. He had opened the door of the closet and located his snow-damp topcoat when he heard a little shuffling noise at the top of the stairs. He turned around to look.

It was Brill. The light behind him made him look grotesquely thin, sagging in the middle like a broken pencil.

"Doan!" he gasped.

He got hold of the railing with both hands, and then he came down the stairs in a crazily shuffling dance, his skinny legs wavering and twisting weirdly. He tripped and fell headlong down the last ten steps before Doan could catch him.

The skin on his face was yellowish, the cheekbones bulging out in ugly lumps. Blood was streaked in a long smear across his forehead. Doan straightened him out on the steps.

"Doan!" he said desperately. "That damned scoundrel, Crowley. Tricked me. Hit me—hit me—chair." He heaved himself up on his elbows, eyes glaring. "Doan! I'll hold you responsible! Got away! Your fault!"

"They didn't hit me with a chair," Doan pointed out.

"You!" Brill gasped. "Leaving me with them. While you wander off... They'll get away! They'll get to the station! Jannen will help them! Flat-car there—go down the grade..."

"We'll telephone ahead and stop them."

Brill rolled his head back and forth helplessly. "No telephone. Tried it upstairs. Line cut. You've got to go after them! They've got only a few minutes start! You can catch them! That girl—she can't go fast."

Doan said: "You mean you want me to go out in that storm again?"

"Oh, damn you!" Brill swore. "Don't you understand that my whole career is at stake? I hired your agency, and you failed me! I'll have you black-listed. I'll sue!"

"All right, all right," Doan said. "I'll go bring them back. Take another coat and give it to the girl you find down in the cellar."

He went to the front door and opened it. The wind whooped in triumphantly, driving a fine mist of snow ahead of it.

"Light," said Brill weakly. "They've got an electric lantern. You can see—"

Doan slammed the door shut. The wind came whipping down out of the black mouth of the ravine with a fierce howling intensity. Doan was struggling to get into his topcoat, and the wind billowed the coat out like a clumsy sail and blew Doan with it down the steps and across the black, rock-strewn ground.

He stumbled into a drift waist-deep before he caught himself. He stood still for a moment, one arm crooked up to shield his eyes from the cutting whip of the snow. The wind blasted at him, and then he caught the flicker of a light on the path that led up out of the flat.

Doan began to run. He was half-blinded with the snow, and the wind pulled and tugged at him, pushed him in staggering crazy spurts. He stumbled and half-fell, and then the gravel on the steep path grated under his shoes.

The light was high above him, much closer now, and as he watched, it flicked over the edge of the ravine and disappeared.

Doan fumbled under his coat and found the revolver. He went up the path at a lurching run. His breath burned icily in his throat. The air was thin and fine, with no weight to it, and his heart began to drum in a sickening cadence.

He was breathing in sobbing gasps when he hit the top of the ravine, sweat crawling in cold rivulets under his clothes. He paused there swaying, looking for the light, and found it off to his left.

He turned and plowed stubbornly in that direction, and there was no path here, nothing but thick drifts of snow piled against stunted brush that tore at his clothes with myriad clutching fingers.

The light tossed up high ahead of him, very close now, and showed stunted trees lined up in a ghostly gallery, leaning forward in the push of the wind as they watched.

Doan tripped over a snow-hidden log and went down flat on his face in powdery whiteness. He heaved himself stubbornly up on hands and knees, dabbed at his smeared face with his coatsleeve—and he stayed that way, half kneeling, rigid, staring into savagely cruel greenish yellow eyes on a level with his own and not a yard away.

"Hah!" Doan said, grunting with the exhalation of his breath.

The eyes came for him with the sudden slashing gleam of teeth under them. Doan poked the revolver straight out and fired, wondering as he pulled the trigger whether his fall had packed snow in the barrel and whether the gun would blow back at him.

The shot made a bright orange flare, and the eyes were gone. A heavy body kicked and squirmed in the snow. Doan struggled up to his feet, and another dark low form slipped sideways in the whirling darkness, circling him.

Doan leveled the revolver and fired instantly. A shrill ki-yi-ing yip echoed the smash of the shot, and the second dark form went tumbling over and over in the snow, contorting itself into desperate struggling knots.

The third one came in a black streak out of the darkness, up out of the snow in a long lunge, straight at Doan's throat. He fired going over backward. The flat-nosed .38 hit the animal in the chest and turned it clear over in the air. It fell back rigid and still beside the first.

Doan struggled in the snow, heaving himself up, and then Jannen loomed above him, yelling something the wind garbled into an unintelligible, frenzied scream. He had an ax in his hand, and he swung it back up over his shoulder and down at Doan in a full sweep that made its head glitter in a bright, deadly line.

Doan whirled himself sideways, rolling.

"Jannen!" he yelled frantically. "Don't! Don't! I'll shoot—"

The ax-head hissed past is ear, and Jannen caught it on the upswing and chopped back down again with it.

Doan couldn't dodge this time. He didn't try. He shot Jannen just above the grassy gleam of the buckle on the wide web belt around his coat.

Jannen made a queer, choked sound. The ax stopped in midair.

Jannen took one step back and then another, trying to get the ax up over his shoulder again.

"Drop it," said Doan.

The ax was going up inch by desperate inch. Jannen's breath made a high whistling sound. He made a clumsy step forward.

"All right, baby," said Doan.

He pulled the trigger of the revolver again. There was a dull, small click—nothing else. Before Doan even had time to grasp what that meant, Jannen reeled queerly sideways and went down full length on his face, as rigid as a log.

"Good God," said Doan in a whisper.

He got up slowly. The thing had happened in split-seconds, and the echos of the gunfire were still rolling lustily ahead of the wind.

Doan stared at his gun. It was bright and deadly in his hand, with the snow moisture gleaming on its thick cylinder, and he remembered now that he hadn't reloaded it. He had fired once at the metal case and once in the snow-shed. There had been four cartridges left in the gun. He had used them all. If he had missed just one of those four shots...

The wind whistled shrilly through bare branches, chuckling in its high, cruel glee.

Doan stumbled forward, leaned down over Jannen. The man was dead, and the snow already was laying a white cold blanket thinly across his distorted face.

Doan plowed back through the drifts and brush, found the hard surface of the path. He felt weak and numb with cold that was more than cold. His legs were stiff, unwieldy sticks under him as he went back down the steep path, across the flat toward the warmly welcoming glow of the windows that watched for him through the whirl of snow.

CHAPTER X.
TOO MANY GUNS

DOAN WENT BLUNDERING across the porch with his head down and ran into the front door. He found the knob, fumbled it with numb fingers, finally turned it. The wind swept the door out of his grasp, banged it back thunderously against the wall.

Doan stamped through into the soft luxurious warmth of the hall, fought the door shut again behind him.

Sighing in relief, he wiped snow moisture off his face with the palm of his left hand.

"Drop your gun on the floor."

Doan jerked to attention. Brill was standing in the doorway of the living room. He was wearing a blue dressing gown now over his pajamas. He lounged there, quite at ease, with the big .45 automatic bulking huge and black in his right hand.

"Drop your gun on the floor," he repeated in the same confident, quiet voice.

He looked very theatrical, with the white blaze showing up in his smoothly brushed hair, with his eyes narrowed. He was smiling in a dramatically sinister way.

Doan loosened the stiff fingers of his right hand and the .38 thudded on the carpet.

"It wasn't loaded anyway," he observed.

"Come in here," said Brill.

He backed out of the door, and Doan followed him into the living room. Someone had thrown kindling on the fire, and red flames crackled greedily in it.

"You know Miss Alden, I think," Brill said.

She was sitting on the divan. She was wearing a man's overcoat so big that it almost wrapped around her twice. She had brown hair cut in a long bob, mussed a little now, and the fire found warm glints in it. Her brown eyes were wide and scared, and her soft lower lip trembled. There was a smear of coal dust on the end of

her short straight nose.

"Hello, again," said Doan.

She didn't answer, and Brill said:

"You're becoming a nuisance, Doan. What happened to Jannen? I heard you shooting."

"I was just target practicing," Doan said, "but Jannen, that dope, stepped right in front of my gun just when I happened to be pulling the trigger. I expect he's sort of dead."

Kokomo came in from the kitchen. There was a lopsided swollen lump on one side of his jaw, and his eyes glittered malevolently at Doan.

"You tricky little devil! When I get my hands on you—"

"I can hardly wait," Doan told him.

"Later, Kokomo," Brill said. He was watching Doan with gravely speculative eyes. "I suppose you are beginning to understand this now, aren't you?"

"Oh, sure," said Doan. "I figured it out quite a while ago."

"Did you, now?" said Brill sarcastically.

Doan nodded. "Yes. You were next in line for the management of Sheila Alden's trust fund after this gent Dibben. You had all the time in the world to figure things out and get ready for this little play. You saw that an accident happened to Dibben at the right time. You knew Sheila Alden was coming up here—probably suggested the idea yourself—and you made all your arrangements beforehand.

"First you got Leila Adams, Sheila's secretary, to throw in with you by promising to split part of what you got from Sheila with her. Then you got Kokomo to do the muscle-work, promising him a split too. When you were prowling around up here beforehand you found out that Jannen was a crackpot with a grudge against the Aldens.

"Now, there was an ideal fall-guy for you all ready-made. Anything that happened you could always blame on him. But Jannen talks too much, and this poor guy, Boley, the regular station master, got suspicious of what you were cooking up with him, and either you or Kokomo or Jannen—or all three of you—got Boley drunk and probably doped him and left him out in the storm to freeze.

"Leila Adams wasn't going to impersonate Sheila Alden unless it was necessary on account of someone like me coming around. You definitely didn't want anyone around—not with the real Sheila Alden locked in the cellar.

"And so—" Doan paused, ran a hand over his cheek.

"Jannen knew a lot about explosives, and so you got him to fix up that little cigar case present for me. You knew I was going to be on the job because the trust company hired the agency, and Toggery told you he was going to send me up. So you dressed up in a fancy costume and laid for me with your cigar case bomb."

"How did you know I was the one who gave you that case?"

Doan grinned. "I couldn't miss. You spent so much time trying to cover yourself up that you stuck out like a sore thumb. You wanted to be sure that if anything went wrong no one could prove that you had anything to do with the whole business.

"That was the reason for your little fairy tale about the janitor and the cigar case and why you put on that elaborate, nervous and worried act and why you wanted to make sure that I knew you'd just been assigned to handle Sheila Alden's business. You wanted me to think that you were a jittery sort of a dope who couldn't possibly know the score. As a matter of fact, you are a dope."

Brill's lip lifted. "So? And I suppose you can tell me what happened tonight, too?"

"Easy," Doan agreed. "When you found out you hadn't put me away and that I was coming up here, you had to get a girl to act as secretary to the phoney Sheila Alden because you knew I'd expect to find a secretary.

"You hired the first girl you could find—Joan Greg. She wasn't in on the impersonation business. She thought Leila Adams was actually Sheila Alden—and, more important, so did her boy friend, Crowley.

"Crowley just messed the whole works up for you. He started impressing his personality on Leila Adams. He's a slick worker. She fell for him. She was a scrawny, homely dame, and she'd never

61

had anybody like Crowley tell her how beautiful, breath-taking, marvelous and generally all-around wonderful she was before.

"She liked it fine. She liked it so well she began to get out of hand, and you knew that if Crowley worked much more of his sex appeal, she'd spill something to him. You killed her.

"Joan Greg was crazy jealous of Crowley, and she gave you the idea by trying it herself. You knew, then, that you could put Leila Adams away and blame it on Joan Greg.

"You had a master key. You could get into her bedroom. You cut Leila Adams' throat and then went in and planted the knife on Joan Greg and bloodied up her hands. When she woke up she actually didn't know whether or not she had killed the phoney Sheila Alden. As soon as I left you alone with her and Crowley, you told them to beat it. You planned to lay all the blame on them, knowing they'd keep under cover.

"Jannen was prowling around the place, and you tipped him off and then sent me out, thinking Jannen and his damned wolves would take care of me. You tipped your hand twice then. First by that phoney entrance coming downstairs. Nobody who actually got banged with a chair ever acted so screwy as you did. And then you weren't even interested when I told you there was a girl down cellar. As an actor, you stink. What crackpot notion have you got up your sleeve now?"

Brill said smoothly: "I've had to alter my plans slightly, Doan, but I don't think it will really matter—certainly not to you. You see, at first all I wanted to do was to force Sheila to give me her power of attorney for a week or so after she got control of the trust fund. If I could have done that, as I planned, I would have made a fortune."

"Sure. By selling her a few million shares of phoney stock."

Brill looked contemptuous. "Nothing so crude. Merely by forcing the market up and down by alternately selling and buying the huge blocks of stock she owns in several corporations and being on the right side of the market myself each time.

"There would have been nothing criminal in that, and no way for her to prove afterward that she hadn't given the power of attorney voluntarily, because it would have been her word against myself, Kokomo and Leila Adams. But due to the way things have happened, I've been forced—not very reluctantly, I must admit—to ask Miss Alden to do me the honor of becoming my wife."

Sheila Alden spoke for the first time. "No," she said in a small, clear voice.

Brill paid no attention to her. "You see, Doan? Even if my original plan did go on the rocks, I can still pull things together. I'll have control over Miss Alden's money if she's my wife—you can be sure of that. And more important, she can't testify against me."

Sheila Alden said: "I am not going to marry you—now or any other time."

"I think you will," Brill said. "It's really quite essential. Kokomo, will you take Miss Alden into the other room and see if you can—ah—reason with her?"

CHAPTER XI.
GOOD BYE NOW

SHIELA ALDEN DREW in her breath with a little gasp. Kokomo was grinning at her meaningly out of the side of his mouth that wasn't swollen. He came nearer the divan.

"It's warm in there," Brill said. "She won't need that coat."

Sheila Alden wrapped the coat tighter around her, clutching the lapels with fingers that were white with strain.

"No! You can't—"

"Brill," said Doan.

He hadn't made any noticeable move, but now he was holding a flat metal case on the palm of his right hand, looking down at it thoughtfully.

"That's mine!" Brill exclaimed.

"No," said Doan. "No, Brill. Not yours. It's the one you gave me."

Silence stretched over the room like a thin black veil, with the crackle of the flames in the hearth coming through it faint and distant.

"Foolish," Doan said, still staring at the case thoughtfully. "Foolish trying to alibi yourself by carrying one like it and pretending some mysterious Mr. Smith gave it to you and that the cigars in it subsequently blew the janitor to smithereens. There aren't any cigars—explosive or otherwise—in this case. It's packed with explosive."

"Brill said stiffly: "How—how—"

"You're a dope," Doan told him. "Don't you know that the bomb squad on any city police force has equipment—black light, X-ray, fluoroscope—-so they can look into suspicious packages without opening them? I took this case down to a pal of mine on the Bay City bomb squad. He squinted into it and told me it was a very neat little hand-grenade, so I kept it for a souvenir. Here. Catch it." He tossed the case in a spinning, glittering arc. Brill yelled in a choked, horrified voice. He dropped the automatic and grabbed frantically with both hands at the case.

Doan dived for him in a lunging expert tackle. He smashed against Brill's pipe-stem legs. The case was knocked whirling up in the air, and Brill spun around and fell headlong. His head cracked sickeningly against the edge of the hearth, and he stiffened, his whole body quivering, and then was still.

Doan rolled over and sat up and looked down the thick black barrel of the automatic at Kokomo's scared, sagging face.

"Hi, Kokomo," Doan said softly.

Kokomo held both big hands in front of him, fingers spread wide, as though he were trying to push back the expected bullet.

"Don't," he whispered. "Don't shoot."

"Oh, I think I will," Doan said.

Kokomo believed him. He had already had a demonstration of what Doan could and would do. His thick lips opened and shut soundlessly, little sticky threads of saliva glinting at their corners.

Doan got up. "Turn around, Kokomo."

Kokomo turned slowly and stiffly, like a mechanical doll that had almost run down. Doan stepped close to him and slammed him on the head with the barrel of the automatic.

"I'll bet even your cement knob will ache tomorrow after that," Doan said amiably. He winked at Sheila Alden, who was staring with wide unbelieving brown eyes. "Weren't scared, were you? They never had a chance. They're amateurs. I'm a professional. That case was really Brill's—not the one he gave me. I picked it out of his pocket last night. Wanted to look at it more closely."

She continued to stare.

He went over to the door into the hall and picked up the telephone. It was a French type handset with a long cord attached to it. Stringing out the cord behind him, Doan brought the phone back to the divan and sat down on it beside Sheila Alden. He held the receiver against his ear.

"The dopes," he said to Sheila. "They didn't even cut the line."

She turned her head stiffly, little by little, and looked from Brill to Kokomo. "Are they—are they—"

"Dead?" Doan finished. "Oh, no." He was still listening at the receiver, and now he said:

"Hello. Hello, operator? Get me the J. S. Toggery residence in Bay City. I don't know the number. I'll hold the line."

He waited, smiling at Sheila Alden in a speculative way. She had begun to breathe more evenly now, and there was a little color in her cheeks.

"But—but you did it so easily—so quickly. I mean, it all happened before I knew what—"

"The hand is quicker than the eye," said Doan. "At least mine was quicker than theirs."

"I—I've never met anyone like you before."

"There's only one of us," Doan said.

The receiver crackled against his ear, and then J. S. Toggery's voice said:

"What? What? Who's this?"

"Doan—the forgotten man. How are you, Mr. Toggery? How is Carstairs?"

"You! That damned ghoulish giraffe! He pulled all my wife's new drapes down! He broke a vase that cost me a hundred and fifty dollars! He crawled under the dinner table and then stood up and dumped the dinner on the floor! I've got him chained in the garage, and let me tell you, Doan, if he pulls just one more trick, I'll get an elephant gun and so help me I'll pulverize him! You hear me?"

"He's young and exuberant. He probably misses me. You'll have to excuse him. Goodbye now."

"Wait! Wait, you fool! Are you up at the Alden lodge where you're supposed to be? Is everything all right up there?"

"Oh, yes. Now it is. There was a kidnapping and a couple of murders and some attempted thefts and a few assaults with intent to kill and such, but I straightened it all out. Get off the line, Toggery. I've got to call the sheriff."

"Doan!" Toggery screamed. "Doan! What? What did you say? Murders—kidnapping. Doan! Is Miss Alden all right?"

Doan looked at her. "Yes," he said. "Yes, Toggery. Miss Alden is—quite all right."

He hung up the receiver on Toggery's violent voice and nodded at Sheila Alden.

"You know," he said, "you're so very nice that I think I could like you an awful lot even if you didn't have fifty million dollars "

Sheila Alden's soft lips made a round, pink O of surprise and then moved a little into a faint tremulous smile.

The Mouse in the Mountain

CHAPTER 1

W HEN DOAN AND CARSTAIRS CAME down the wide stairway and walked across the pink-tiled floor that was the pride and joy of the Hotel Azteca, the guests in the lobby stopped whatever they were doing to pass the time away and stared open-mouthed. Doan was not such-a-much, but Carstairs usually had this effect on people, and he left a whispering, wondering wake behind him as he stalked across to the glassed side doors and waited with haughty dignity while Doan opened one of the doors. He ambled through it ahead of Doan into the incredibly bright sunlight on the terrace.

Doan halted and drew in a deep breath of air that felt clean and dry and thinly exhilarating. He stared all around him with frank appreciation. He was short and a little on the plump side, and he had a chubby, pink face and a smile as innocent and appealing as a baby's. He looked like a very nice, pleasant sort of person, and on rare occasions he was.

He was wearing a white suit and a wide-brimmed Panama hat and white crepe-soled shoes.

"Breathe some of this air, Carstairs," he ordered. "It's wonderful. This is ideal Mexican weather."

Carstairs yawned in an elaborately bored way. Carstairs was a fawn-colored Great Dane. Standing on four legs, his back came up to Doan's chest. He never did tricks. He considered them beneath him. But had he ever done one that involved standing on his hind feet, his head would have hit a level far above Doan's. Carstairs was so big he could hardly be called a dog. He was a sort of new species.

A girl came very quickly out of the door behind Doan and said Uh! in a startled gasp when she saw Carstairs looming in front of her.

Carstairs didn't move out of her way. He turned lazily to stare at her. So did Doan.

She was a small girl, and she looked slightly underfed. She had very wide, very clear blue eyes. They were nice eyes. Nothing startling, but adequate. Her hair was brown and smooth under a white turban, and she wore a white sports dress and a white jacket and white openwork sandals. She had a clear, smooth skin, and she blushed easily. She was doing it now.

"I'm sorry," she said breathlessly. "He—he frightened me."

"He frightens me, too, sometimes." said Doan.

"What's your name?"

The girl looked at him uncertainly. "My name? It's Janet Martin."

"Mine's Doan," said Doan. "I'm a detective."

"A—a detective?" Janet Martin repeated, fumbling a little over the word. "You don't look like one."

"Of course not," Doan told her. "I'm in disguise. I'm pretending I'm a tourist."

"Oh," said Janet, still uncertain. "But—do you go around telling everybody about it?"

"Certainly," said Doan. "My disguise is so perfect no one would know I was a detective if I didn't tell them, so naturally I do."

"Oh," said Janet. "I see." She looked at Carstairs. "He's beautiful. I mean, not beautiful but—but magnificent. Does he bite?"

"Quite often," Doan admitted.

"May I pet him?"

Doan looked at Carstairs inquiringly. "May she?"

Carstairs studied Janet for a moment and then came one step closer to her and lowered his head regally. Janet patted his broad brow.

"Don't scratch his ears," Doan warned. "He detests that."

A long brown bus pulled around the curve of the drive and stopped in front of the terrace steps. A little man in a spic-and-span brown uniform popped out, clicked his heels snappily, and said, "The tour of sight-seeing presents itself to those who wish to view the magnificence with educated comments."

"Oh, you're the one I was looking for," Janet said. "I'm going on the tour to Los Altos. This is the bus that takes me there, isn't it?"

The little man bowed. "With comfort and speed and also comments."

"I was afraid I was late. What time do you start?"

"On schedule," said the little man. "Always on the schedule— we start when it says. I am Bartolome—accent on the last syllable, if you please—chauffeur licensed and guide most qualified, with English guaranteed by the advanced correspondence school, conversational and classic. Do me the honor of presenting me your ticket."

Janet gave it to him, and he examined it with suspicious care, even turning it over and reading the fine print on the back.

"In order most perfect," he admitted. "Do me the graciousness of entering and sitting. We will start instantly or when I locate the other passengers."

"Here's two more," said Doan, handing him two tickets.

"Ah, yes," said Bartolome, and examined them as carefully as he had Janet's. "Is most fine. But there are the two tickets and of you only one. Where is the other?"

"There," said Doan, pointing.

Bartolome looked at Carstairs, turned his head away quickly, and then looked again. "It has a resemblance to a dog," he said slowly and cautiously.

"Some," said Doan.

"It is a dog!" Bartolome exclaimed. "A dog of the most incredible monstrousness! A veritable nightmare of a dog!"

"Be careful," Doan warned. "He insults easily."

Bartolome looked at the tickets and then at Carstairs. "One of this is for him?"

"Yes."

"No," said Bartolome.

"Yes," said Doan.

"Of a positively not, senor."

Carstairs sprawled himself out on the warm tiles and closed his eyes sleepily. Arguments offended his sense of the fitness of things, so he ignored them.

Bartolome stared narrowly at Doan. "The ticket of the sight-

seeing magnificence is not sold for dogs."

"This one was."

"Dogs do not ride in the luxury of the bus that precedes itself to Los Altos."

"This one does."

"No!" Bartolome shouted suddenly. "Not, not, not! It is the outrage most emphatic! Wait!" He darted through the glassed door into the lobby.

"I'm sorry," Janet told Doan.

"Why?" he asked, surprised.

"Because you can't take your dog to Los Altos"

"I can," said Doan. "And I'm going to. We always have little difficulties like this when we go places. It's a routine we go through."

A fat man wearing a magnificently tailored white suit and a painful smile came out on the terrace ahead of Bartolome. Bartolome pointed at Carstairs and said dramatically, "There is that which is not to go! Never!"

The fat man said: "I am so sorry. It is not permitted for dogs to ride on the bus."

Doan held up the two tickets and pointed eloquently first to himself and then to Carstairs.

The fat man shook his head. "I'm so sorry, sir, but that ticket does not cover a dog."

"It's made out in his name," said Doan.

The fat man shrugged. "But, you see, when your reservations at the hotel and your tickets for this trip were ordered we did not know that one was for a dog. The dog can stay at the hotel—yes. But he cannot ride on the bus."

Doan nodded casually. "All right. He stays here, then. But you'd better chain him up. He's going to get mad if I go away and leave him."

"Mad?" the fat man repeated doubtfully, looking at Carstairs.

Carstairs didn't open his eyes, but he lifted his upper lip and revealed glistening fangs that were as long as a man's little finger. He growled in a low, deep rumble.

The fat man backed up a step. "Is he dangerous?"

"Definitely," said Doan. "But delicate, too. He will attack anyone who tries to feed him, except me. And if he doesn't eat, he'll die. If he dies, I'll sue you for an enormous sum of money."

The fat man closed his eyes and sighed. "He rides in the bus," he said wearily to Bartolome.

"What?" Bartolome shouted, outraged.

"He rides!" the fat man snarled. "Do you hear me, or shall I repeat myself with a slap in the face?"

"I hear," said Bartolome glumly. He waited until the fat man had strutted back through the door into the lobby and then added: "You obese offspring of incredibly corrupt parents." He turned to Doan and made shooing motions. "Kindly persuade yourselves inside."

A woman opened the glass door and put her head out and shouted deafeningly: "Mortimer!" Instantly she pulled her head in again and slammed the door.

The echoes of her shout hung quivering in the still air, and Carstairs raised his head and waggled his pricked ears uncomfortably.

The door opened and a man put his head out and yelled: "Mortimer!" He waited while the echoes died, eyeing the people on the terrace accusingly. "You seen him?"

"I don't recall it," Doan told him.

The man said: "I'll kill that little devil one of these days. Mortimer! Come here, damn you!" He got no results, and he sighed drearily and came out on the terrace. He was squat and solid-looking, and he had a red, heavy-jowled face. His clothes were new, and his shoes squeaked. "My name is Henshaw—Wilbur M. Henshaw."

"Mine's Doan. This is Miss Janet Martin."

"Pleased," said Henshaw. "You sure you haven't seen Mortimer? He's my kid. He looks something like Charlie McCarthy."

"How will that do?" Doan asked, pointing at a feather duster that was poked up over the balcony railing.

"Mortimer, you little stinker!" Henshaw shouted. "Come out from behind that chicken!"

The feather duster waggled coyly, and a wizened, freckled, incredibly evil face slid up into sight and peered at them gimlet-eyed through a tangle of bright red hair.

"What's the beef, punchy?" Mortimer said to his father.

"Now, damn it, I'm going to wring your neck if you don't stick around," Henshaw promised grimly. "I mean it. We're going on a sightseeing trip to Los Altos, and I'm not going to spend the whole day chasing you."

"Go chase yourself, glue-brain," Mortimer advised, "and forget to come back." He swarmed up over the railing like a pint-sized pirate boarding a ship. He was wearing the feather duster for a hat, and he had on khaki scout shorts and a khaki blouse. "A dog!" he exclaimed gleefully. "Watch me give him the hotfoot!"

He took a kitchen match from his pocket and began to stalk the sleeping Carstairs like a big game hunter. Janet started to protest, but Doan winked at her and shook his head.

When Mortimer was still about a yard away, Carstairs sat up and looked at him. Sitting, Carstairs' face was on a level with Mortimer's. Slowly Carstairs opened his mouth until it was wide enough to take in Mortimer's whole head with room to spare. Mortimer stood paralyzed with shock, staring into the yawning red cavern.

Carstairs leaned forward and closed his jaws with a viciously grinding snap just an inch in front of Mortimer's nose.

"Yeow!" Mortimer shrieked. "Yeow! Maw! *Maw!*" He blew across the terrace and through the door into the lobby in a blurred, rust-tipped streak.

"Mister," said Henshaw enthusiastically, "I'll buy that dog! How much?"

"I couldn't sell him," Doan said. "He wouldn't allow it, and besides he supports me in my off-seasons."

"He does?" Janet asked. "How? Does he work?"

"Well," said Doan. "Yes and no. It's a rather delicate subject. You see, there are certain lady Great Danes who clamor for his attentions..."

Janet blushed again. "Oh!"

"Well, would you rent him to me by the day?" Henshaw requested. "I'll be awfully nice to him."

Doan shook his head. "I'm afraid not. I'll have him scare Mortimer for you whenever you want, though, if we're around."

"Friend," said Henshaw, "you do that, and you've got a lifelong pal, and I mean it. I'm in the plumbing business—'Better Bathrooms for a Better America.' What's your line?"

"Crime," Doan told him.

"You mean you're a public enemy?" Henshaw asked, interested.

"There have been rumors to that effect," Doan said. "But I claim I'm a private detective."

"Oh," said Henshaw indifferently. "One of them, huh? Well, I always say a man's got to make a living some way."

The woman who had previously shouted for Mortimer appeared. Mortimer was close behind her, peering around her, first on one side and then the other, as she advanced.

"Now, Mortimer," she said firmly, "you show me that dog that attacked you and I'll—Oh! Oh! Wilbur, save me!"

"From what?" Henshaw asked sourly.

The woman pointed a plump, quivering finger at Carstairs. "From that—that horrible thing!" She was wearing a peasant smock and a varicolored full skirt, and she would really have looked like a peasant except that she affected pince-nez glasses with thin gold rims. "It's a savage beast!"

"You bet," Henshaw agreed. "Savage and smart. I've promised him Mortimer for dinner."

"Yeow!" said Mortimer. "Maw!"

The woman said severely: "Wilbur, you stop saying things like that! You know you'll give Mortimer nightmares!"

"Why not?" Henshaw said. "He gives me plenty. This is my wife, folks. Miss Janet Martin and Mr. Doan. When do we start this trip to Los Altos, anyway?"

"On schedule," said Bartolome. "Just as it exactly prints. Be so kind as to entering and sitting on the luxurious seats with legroom."

Doan flicked Carstairs' ear with his forefinger and said: "Up-si-daisy."

Carstairs got up and sauntered over to the bus.

"He's not going with us!" Mrs. Henshaw said shrilly. "Not that awful animal!"

"With my permission, positively not," Bartolome told her. "I refer you to the bloated brigand who proprietors this foul establishment and also the trips of sight-seeing magnificence."

"I won't go!" said Mrs. Henshaw. "And neither will Mortimer!"

"Good," said Henshaw. "See you later."

Mrs. Henshaw turned her head slowly and ominously and peered through the pince-nez at Janet Martin. She looked Janet over detail by detail once, and then repeated the survey, nodding her head knowingly.

"So," she said. "We're going."

"Maw!" said Mortimer. "That dog—"

"Shut up," said Mrs. Henshaw. "I know your father and his lascivious instincts—to my sorrow!"

Doan opened the door of the bus and helped Carstairs in by giving him a heave from the rear. Carstairs paused to look the bus's interior over in a leisurely way and then padded along the aisle to the back. He sat down on the floor and sighed and stared gloomily out the window. Doan elbowed him out of the way and sat down in the seat beside him.

Janet said shyly: "May I please sit here with you?"

"Certainly," said Doan. He put his hand on the side of Carstairs' head and shoved. "Move over, you oaf."

Carstairs grunted and shifted his position. When Janet sat down, he stared at her calculatingly, tilting his head first on one side and then the other. Finally he slid his forefeet out a little, lowering himself, and put his head in her lap.

Doan watched, amazed. "Why, he likes you!"

Janet patted Carstairs' head. "Doesn't he usually like people?"

"No. He hates them. He despises me."

"Despises you!" Janet exclaimed. "But why?"

"Well, I won him in a crap game. He resents that. And then my name's not in the social register, and his is."

"What is it? His name?"

"Carstairs. Dougal's Laird Carstairs to be exact."

"Does he have a pedigree?"

Doan nodded. "Ten miles long."

"Do you ever show him? I mean, enter him in dog shows?"

"Sure. It's just a bore, though. He always wins."

"He must be worth a lot of money."

"I was offered seven thousand dollars for him once," Doan said, sighing. "In cash, too. I turned it down. I wish I knew why."

"I think that's wonderful!" Janet said. "I mean that you didn't sell him."

"I wish he thought so. I hoped it would make him appreciate me, but he just sneered. Do you want to see him sneer? He does it beautifully. Watch." Doan leaned close to Carstairs and said in a stickily coy voice: "Who is Doansie-woansie's cutesy-wutesey 'itty puppy doggy?"

Carstairs looked up slowly and ominously. He raised one side of his upper lip. His eyes glowed golden-yellow and savage.

"I was only fooling," Doan said quickly.

Carstairs watched him warningly for a moment and then slowly lowered his head to Janet's lap again.

"He *can* sneer!" she said. "Horribly!"

"That was one of his milder ones," Doan told her.

"Do you ever punish him?"

"I tried it once," Doan said.

"What happened?"

"He knocked me down and sat on me for three hours. He weighs about a ton. I didn't enjoy myself at all, so I gave up the idea. Anyway, he has better manners than I have."

The Henshaws had seated themselves at the front of the bus, and Henshaw turned around wearily now and called:

"Say, when did that bird with the double-talk tell us we were going to start? Or is this trip just a rumor?"

"Here he comes," said Janet.

Bartolome trotted down the terrace steps and leaned in the door. "Starting instantly in a few moments. Have the kindness of patience in waiting for the more important passengers."

"Who are they?" Henshaw demanded, interested.

"The lady of incredible richness with the name of Patricia Van Osdel and her parasites."

"No fooling!" Henshaw exclaimed. "You hear that, Doan? Patricia Van Osdel. She's the flypaper queen. Her old man invented stickum that flies like the taste of, and he made fifty billion dollars out of it"

"Is she married?" Mrs. Henshaw asked suspiciously.

"That is a vulgarness to which she would not stoop," said Bartolome. "She has a gigolo. They come! Prepare yourselves!"

A short, elderly lady as thin as a pencil, dressed all in black that wrinkled and rustled and glistened in the sun, came out on the terrace and down the steps. She had a long, sallow face with a black wart on one cheek and teeth that popped out of ambush when she opened her mouth.

Henshaw had his hands cupped against the window, peering eagerly. "She sure has aged a lot, or else her pictures flatter her."

The elderly lady poked Bartolome in the chest with a stiff, bony forefinger. "One side!" She swished through the door into the bus, sniffed twice calculatingly, and then took a perfume atomizer from somewhere in her capacious skirt and squirted it in all directions vigorously. She selected a seat and dusted it with quick, irritated flicks of a silk dustcloth.

"Hey," said Henshaw. "Are you Patricia Van Osdel?"

"I am not," said the elderly lady. "I am Maria, her personal maid. Kindly turn around and mind your own business."

"Okay," said Henshaw amiably. He cupped his hands and peered through the window. "Hey! Here she comes! Get a load of this, Doan. Whee!"

The manager appeared, bowing and nodding and waving his hands gracefully in front of a girl who was as fair and fragile looking as a Dresden china doll. She was wearing a long white cloak, and her hair floated like spun gold above it. Her mouth was pink and petulant, but instead of being blue her eyes were a deep, calculating green. Her bearing and her manner and her features were all rigidly aristocratic.

A young man lounged along sullenly a step behind her. He was as magnificently dark as she was fair. He had black curly hair and an incredibly regular profile. He wore white slacks and a white pullover sweater with a blue silk scarf at his throat. He had a pencil-line mustache and long, slanted sideburns.

He stopped on the steps and pointed a forefinger at the bus. "Are we going in that thing?"

"Yes, Greg," said Patricia Van Osdel gently.

"I won't like it," Greg warned. "You know that, don't you?"

"Now, Greg," Patricia Van Osdel chided. "This is the democratic way, you see. This is the way we do things in America. We don't have any rigid class distinctions."

"It stinks," said Greg. "I mean the bus and Mexico and the United States and your democracy. I tell you that quite frankly because it's true."

"Get in the bus, Greg," said Patricia Van Osdel. "Don't be difficult."

"I don't approve of this," Greg said, getting in. "I'm warning you."

The manager and Bartolome handed Patricia Van Osdel gently through the door.

"You will enjoy yourself most exquisitely," the manager promised. "Bartolome, you cretin, point all the most beautiful views and do not hit any bumps. Not one bump, do you understand?"

Greg had seated himself and was glowering out a window. Maria ushered Patricia Van Osdel carefully to the seat she had selected and dusted.

The stir of movement floated some of the perfume to the back of the bus, and Carstairs sneezed and then sneezed again, more emphatically.

Maria jumped and glared. "That!" she said imperiously. "Out!"

"It is only a dog," the manager said quickly.

81

"A dog of the most intelligent marvelousness," Bartolome added.

"Please!" said Maria.

"Oh, no!" the manager denied, horrified.

"Emphatically never!" Bartolome seconded. "It is a dog of the most delicate and refined nature."

"It's quite all right," Patricia Van Osdel told her. She smiled at Doan and Janet. "I like dogs. They have so much character. Don't they, Greg?"

"No," said Greg.

Henshaw cleared his throat. "My name is Henshaw—"

"Who cares?" Greg inquired coldly.

"Greg," said Patricia Van Osdel, "now please be pleasant. Mr. Henshaw, I'm very glad to know you. And this is your wife and little boy? What a nice family group you make! I'm sure you all know who I am. This lady is my maid, Maria. And this is my refugee friend, Gregor Dvanisnos." She turned graciously toward the back of the bus. "And your names?"

"Doan," said Doan. "And this is Miss Janet Martin. On the floor, here, is Carstairs."

"Carstairs!" Patricia Van Osdel repeated, smiling. "What an amusing name for a dog!"

Carstairs opened one eye and looked at her and mumbled malignantly under his breath.

"Now!" said Patricia Van Osdel brightly. "We all know each other, don't we? We can all be friends having a pleasant day's excursion together, and that's the way it should be. That's the American tradition of equality. Although, in a way you are really all my guests."

"In what way?" Doan asked.

Patricia Van Osdel moved her shoulders gracefully. "It's really nothing. There was some silly hitch, some petty regulation—The hotel was going to cancel this trip to Los Altos until I persuaded them not to."

"How did you persuade them?" Doan inquired.

"Well, Mr. Doan, to be frank I bribed them. Money is a bore, but it's useful sometimes, isn't it?"

"So they tell me," said Doan. "Why did you bribe them?"

"Because I was determined to see Los Altos, of course. You've surely read about it, or you wouldn't be going there. A peaceful, picturesque village of stalwart peasants isolated deep in the mountains—happy in their primitive and peaceful way—unspoiled by the brutalizing forces of civilization. Why, until just recently, since the new military highroad was opened, there was no way to get there except by mule back. The village is famous for its peaceful, archaic atmosphere."

"Is that the only reason you bribed them to put on the trip?" Doan asked. "Just because you wanted to see the peaceful, peaceful peasants at play?"

"You're awfully curious, Mr. Doan, aren't you?"

"He's a detective," said Henshaw. "All them guys do is make trouble and ask questions."

Patricia Van Osdel's voice was sharp suddenly. "A detective? Are you a customs spy?"

"No," said Doan. "Why? Are you going to smuggle some jewelry into the United States?"

Patricia Van Osdel was still smiling, but her eyes narrowed just slightly. "Mr. Doan, I know you're joking, but you shouldn't suggest such a thing even in fun. You know that the very existence of our great country depends on all of us—rich and poor, wellborn and humble—obeying the exact letter of every law. Naturally I wouldn't dream of defrauding the government by not declaring any small jewels I may purchase."

"Oh," said Doan. "Well, I just asked."

"Yeah," said Henshaw. "And I'm just asking when we start this grand tour, if ever?"

"On schedule with preciseness," said Bartolome. "Instantly as printed. As soon as I consult with the tires, oil and gasoline."

"Species of a mumbling moron!" the manager snarled. "In! Start! Now!"

CHAPTER 2

I N LOS ALTOS, THERE HAD BEEN A RUMOR GOING
THE rounds that some rich tourists from the United States
who were staying at the Hotel Azteca outside Mazalar were
going to make the bus trip up to Los Altos. It was obvious, of
course, that this rumor wasn't entirely to be trusted. Anyone with
any brains or a radio knew that the people from the United States
were too busy raising hell up and down the world to have any time
to look at scenery except through a bombsight.

But tourists of any brand had been so remarkably scarce of
late that the mere hint of their impending arrival was enough to
touch off a sort of impromptu fiesta. The inhabitants of Los Altos
shook the mothballs out of their serapes, mantillas, rebozas and
similar bric-a-brac and prepared to look colorful at the drop of a
sombrero. They gathered in the marketplace with their pigs and
chickens and burros and dogs and children, and slept, argued,
bellowed, squealed, cackled or urinated on the age-old pavement
according to their various natural urges.

All this was very boring to a man who, for the time being,
was named Garcia. He sat and drank beer the general color
and consistency of warm vinegar, and glowered. He had a thin,
yellowish face and a straggling black mustache, and he was cross-
eyed. He should really have been more interested in the tourists
coming from the Hotel Azteca, because in a short time one of
them was going to shoot him dead. However, he didn't know that,
and had you told him he would have laughed or spat in your eye
or perhaps both. He was a bad man.

He was sitting now in the Dos Hermanos, which was according
to its brotherly proprietors, a cafe very high class. It was one door
off the marketplace on the street running north. Since it was early
and no one yet had any money to get drunk on and Garcia looked
mean, he was the only customer. One of the proprietors was
sleeping with his head on the bar while flies explored gingerly in
the dark and gusty cavern of his mouth. Garcia could look out the

open front of the cafe and see kitty-corner across the marketplace, but it was hard for anyone outside to see him.

Private Serez of the Mexican Army had found that out some time ago. He was in the abandoned building directly across the street from the cafe. He was lying on his stomach on some very rough boards peering out and down through a high, glassless window. His rifle, bayonet attached, lay beside him. He was very tired, and his eyes ached, and his elbows were sore. He wanted a cigarette, a beer, and a siesta in that order, but he didn't really think he was going to get any of them for a long time to come.

The reason for this pessimism was a sergeant by the name of Obrian, also of the Mexican Army. Sergeant Obrian had inherited a red mustache and a violent temper from his Irish grandfather, and he was very sticky about having his commands obeyed literally. He had ordered Private Serez to lie right where he was and keep out of sight and watch Garcia with all due vigilance. Private Serez knew he had better do just that and keep on doing it until he got some further orders.

Even as he was thinking drearily about the prospect, he heard a board creak in the hall outside the closed door of his watch-room. That would be Sergeant Obrian with his bad disposition and worse vocabulary coming around to check up. Private Serez wiggled himself higher on his sore elbows and looked out the window in as soldierly and alert a manner as possible.

The heavy, wrought-iron door hinges creaked just slightly, and then something hit the floorboards beside Private Serez with a heavy thud. He looked back over his shoulder. The door was closing again very gently, but Private Serez didn't even notice it.

He was staring in paralyzed horror at what had made the thud. That was a diamondback rattlesnake five feet long and thicker around the middle than a man's doubled biceps.

The snake had had its rattles clipped off and had been submitted to other indignities that hadn't improved its temper. It whipped back into a coil—all lithely sinister muscle—and struck. It missed Private Serez's leg by half an inch.

He yelled—loudly. He could no more have helped that than

he could have helped breathing. He scrambled frantically on the floor, grabbing for his rifle, trying to get back out of range of the next strike. There was no furniture in the room. The snake was between Private Serez and the door. He jumped for the only other place that promised temporary refuge. He climbed right up into the window.

Garcia heard the yell. He looked up, and he saw Private Serez in the window. His yellowish face showed neither shock nor fear, but his lips peeled back thinly from his teeth, and he drew a thick, nickel-plated revolver from his coat pocket. He got up from his table, watching the proprietor. The proprietor mumbled and rolled his head on the bar, faintly disturbed by the yell, but luckily for him he didn't wake up. Garcia went quietly to the back of the room, opened the door there and went down a short passageway past a kitchen that smelled abominably. At the end of the passageway he opened another door and stepped out into a small, high-walled patio paved with garbage and less mentionable refuse.

He was halfway across the patio, heading for the side door, when a soldier stood up behind the back wall. Garcia and the soldier stared at each other, rigid with surprise, for the space of two heartbeats, and then Garcia whipped up his revolver and fired.

The report was a flat, ragged crash, and the bullet hit the soldier just under his chin. He clapped both hands to his throat and flopped backwards out of sight. Garcia opened the side door and looked at the butcher who owned the shop next to the cafe .

The butcher had been interrupted in the process of carving up a skinny cow with the aid of three cats and one million flies. He opened his mouth to yell, but he didn't, because Garcia hit him on top of the head with the revolver and knocked him flat. The cats went in three directions, and the flies droned up in an angry swarm and then settled back on the beef and the butcher indiscriminately.

Garcia didn't hurry. He went cautiously along the alley in the direction of the marketplace, sliding along one wall with the revolver thrust out ahead of him. He reached the alley-mouth and peered out. The people in the marketplace were beginning to stir and wonder uneasily.

Sergeant Obrian stood up on the roof of a building two doors away and leaned over the parapet, peering down to see what was happening. Garcia raised his revolver and aimed carefully at him. He was shooting up at an angle and against the sun. He missed by six inches. The bullet slapped a silvery blob of lead against the adobe. Instantly Sergeant Obrian dropped back out of sight behind the parapet.

In the same split second, Private Serez managed to spear the rattlesnake with his bayonet. He didn't know exactly what to do with it now that he had it, so he pitched it out the window into the marketplace. The snake, still writhing, fell across the nose of a burro below. The burro kicked out backward with both heels and hit its master squarely in the stomach. He fell down and screamed and flailed the ground with his arms.

The burro stamped on the snake and then ran away, and the butcher woke up and yelled, and the whole marketplace went off like a time bomb. All the people decided they would go somewhere else right away and, if possible, take their various dependents, human and animal, along with them. The confusion was something terrific, and Garcia stepped right into the middle of it and disappeared.

CHAPTER 3

THE ROLLED GRAVEL ROAD WAS LIKE A CLEAN white ribbon laid in graceful loops along the side of the mountain that towered red and enormous up into the thin, clear blue of the sky. Heat waves shimmered and wiggled above bare rock, and the dust from the bus's passage drifted back in a lazy plume. The engine burbled and muttered to itself in quiet protest over the steepness of the grade.

"This is a pretty sizeable rock pile," Henshaw volunteered, trying to look out the window and up toward the summit.

"Kindly do not waste the astonishment," Bartolome ordered. "This is not yet the magnificence. This is called 'La Cabeza,' the head, because that is its name. The scenery here is only ordinarily wonderful." Janet Martin's eyes were shining. "It's the beginning of the middle range," she said in a low voice to Doan. "One of Cortez's lieutenants discovered it. He thought the whole length of the range looked like a sleeping woman. He saw it first from the other side of Azela Valley—a hundred and ten miles from here"

"What was the guy's name?" Doan asked.

"Lieutenant Emile Perona. He was a soldier of fortune—an adventurer. He was the younger son of a very noble Spanish family, and he was one of the first men to come to America. He loved this country—its beauty and its ruggedness. It just suited his own nature."

"Was he handsome?" Doan asked, watching her.

"Oh, yes," said Janet softly. "Very. He was tall and hawk-faced and dark, with piercing eyes and a smile that seemed like a light in a darkened room. He was ruthless and cruel, too, as all brave men could be cruel in those old days, but he had integrity and honesty—" Her voice trailed away dreamily.

"You seem to know him pretty well," Doan observed, "seeing he's been dead for four hundred years or so."

"I read about him," Janet said.

"I can read, too," said Doan, "and often *do*. But I never ran across Lieutenant Perona. Where'd you find him?"

"He was mentioned in Cortez's reports."

"Did Cortez say he was handsome?"

"No," Janet said stiffly.

"Tell me some more," Doan invited.

Janet shook her head. "No. You're laughing at me."

"I'm not," Doan denied. "Neither is Carstairs. We like you."

"Do you—do you think I look sexy?"

"What?" Doan said, startled.

Janet was blushing furiously. "You don't! You weren't thinking of anything like that!"

"I was, too," Doan contradicted. "I was just working up to it in a roundabout way."

"Now you are laughing at me!" Janet bit down hard on her lower lip. "I don't care! It's not true, and it's wicked to make girls think it is!"

"What's not true?" Doan inquired.

"What they say in novels and movies about how you can go to beauty parlors and fix yourself all over and men will be—will be attracted to you."

"In a nice way, of course," Doan added.

"No!" said Janet angrily. "I don't want them to be attracted in a nice way!"

"I can work up a pretty fair leer if you give me time," Doan offered. "Will that help?"

"You stop making fun of me!"

Greg turned around in his seat and looked back at them. "Miss Martin, is that detective fellow annoying you?"

"What?" Janet said blankly.

"He looks like that sort," Greg said. "Wouldn't you like to sit up here with me?"

"Greg," said Patricia Van Osdel. "If you want someone to sit with you, Maria will."

Greg ignored her. He was smiling, and his teeth were white and glistening under the pencil-line mustache. He had quite a personality when he wanted to exert it. It hung around him like an aura.

Maria got up, and Greg turned to look at her with the slow, dangerous movement of a snake picking out the place it is going to bite.

"Stay where you are, you hag," Greg said evenly. Maria sat down again quickly.

"I'll sit next to you, then, Greg," Patricia Van Osdel said sweetly.

"When I ask you to—not before," Greg told her. "Won't you join me, Miss Martin?"

"Thank you," Janet said uncertainly. "But—I'm quite comfortable here."

"Later, then," Greg said, and he made the two words a promise and an insinuation.

Janet sat still, her face stiff and surprised looking. Patricia Van Osdel watched her with greenish, calculating eyes.

Henshaw cleared his throat.

"The scenery we came to see," said Mrs. Henshaw, "is outside the bus."

"Yeah," Henshaw agreed absently. "Pretty, huh?"

"How do you know?" Mrs. Henshaw asked.

"Huh?" said Henshaw. "Oh." He peered industriously out through the window.

"Feel better now?" Doan murmured to Janet. "Oh!" said Janet. "Why, then, it must be true about beauty parlors!"

"Undoubtedly," Doan agreed.

"I know it makes me sound awfully stupid," said Janet, "but you see I did spend seventy-five dollars in them before I started, and I was beginning to be very disappointed in the results. No men seemed to—to look at me. I mean—"

"I know what you mean," Doan told her.

Janet stretched out her legs. Carstairs grunted in sleepy protest as his headrest was shifted, but he didn't open his eyes. Janet looked at her legs thoughtfully.

"Are they the kind of legs men like?" she asked.

Doan studied them judicially. "Yes."

"I'm not wearing any stockings."

"I noticed."

"My toenails are tinted."

"Very prettily, too," Doan commented.

Janet relaxed again and sighed contentedly. "I can't believe I'm here and that this is really happening. It's much more wonderful even than I'd dreamed it would be. I've just got to talk to somebody. Can I tell you about it?"

"On one condition," said Doan. "And that is that you don't confess any crimes. Just because I'm a detective people are always taking advantage of me and confessing. You can't imagine how boring that is."

Janet looked at him. "Why, I should think you'd want people to confess to you. It would save so much time."

"That's the point," Doan told her. "I don't want to save time. I get paid by the week. The longer a job takes, the more I make. I always try to stretch them out, but it's pretty hard to do. Take the last one I was on, for instance. A clerk embezzled fifty grand or so from a loan company. No sooner did I walk in the joint and ask him his name than he started to confess."

"What did you do, then?" Janet asked, fascinated.

"Shut him up, of course, and went around making like I was looking for clues. But the guy wouldn't drop it. He haunted me. Every time I sat down to rest my feet, he started confessing all over again. It got so obvious I had to arrest him."

"Well, is that—ethical? I mean to—to stall around like you did?"

"Is it what?" Doan said.

"Ethical."

"I'm a detective," said Doan. "A private detective."

"Don't private detectives have ethics?"

"I don't know," Doan answered, frowning. "I never thought about it. I'll have to look the matter up sometime. But what was it you were going to tell me?"

"You won't laugh or make fun?"

"I promise."

"I'm a schoolteacher," Janet whispered.

Doan looked shocked. "No!"

"You promised!"

"I'm sober as a judge," Doan said.

Janet said: "I'm a schoolteacher in the Wisteria Young Ladies' Seminary."

"Now, after all," said Doan.

"It's true! There is such a place, and I teach in it. I'm on a leave of absence to visit my sick aunt. I haven't any aunt, of course. I haven't any relatives at all. I was raised in an orphanage—until I was eighteen. It was horrible there. We had to wear *uniforms!* With cotton stockings that were all prickly and lumpy."

"That's bad," Doan agreed.

"The orphanage got me a job at the seminary. I'm really very clever at studies and books. But little girls are horrible people, specially rich ones—and I was just a frump and—and a drab. I never saw any men, and if I did they didn't see me. And the seminary is in a small town and terribly strict and conservative, and I was just turning right into an old maid!"

"Until you discovered Mexico and Cortez—and Lieutenant Perona."

"Yes. I was studying Spanish because the seminary is going to give courses in it. They never did before, because it wasn't refined enough. But now, with all the horrible things that are happening in Europe—"

"Lots of people are rediscovering America," Doan commented. "Including our flypaper queen up ahead. She never got closer to the United States than the south of France or Bali until Hitler and Hirohito started on the prowl. Now she's suddenly discovered she's wild about democracy. But go on—you were studying Spanish."

"It's such a beautiful language! And then I got interested in the countries where it is spoken, and their histories. I read just thousands of books. Even dusty old manuscripts that had never been printed. The seminary has a marvelous historical library that no one ever uses. I read all about Cortez and his men, and then I came across the diary of a man called Gil De Lico. He was a scribe—a sort of a secretary and historian for Cortez. He kept all the official records, and he wrote this diary just for his family back in Spain. He traveled around with Lieutenant Perona, and he wrote lots about him. They were good friends. I—I feel as though I knew them both—personally, I mean."

"I understand," said Doan.

"And then I started reading about modern Mexico—the way the country they traveled through looks and is now. It—it's perfectly fascinating!"

"I know," said Doan.

Janet's eyes were shining. "I had to come and see it! I *had* to! I've never had a real vacation in all my life, and I saved and saved, and I came. I'm here! I'm really and truly here in Mexico!"

"That's right," Doan told her.

"Oh, you don't know how I've dreamed about it. All the glamour, and color and—and romance! I ached for it until I could hardly stand it, and there I was teaching horrid, stupid, rich girls how to parse French verbs!"

"Hunting for romance is much more fun," Doan said.

Janet nodded seriously. "It is, and that's just what I'm doing. I know it's foolish and crazy, but I've done sensible things all my life. I was getting—getting moldy! A girl has a *right* to romance and glamour and—and other things, hasn't she? There's nothing wrong with that, is there?"

"Not a thing," Doan said. "I hope you find romance by the carload. If I see any, I'll run it down and hogtie it for you."

Janet sighed again. "I feel better now that I've told somebody." She said suddenly and seriously, "What are you looking for?"

"A cop."

"A policeman?" Janet inquired blankly.

"Yeah. From the United States."

"Well, what's he doing in Mexico?"

"Hiding."

"Why? Did he commit some crime?"

"Oh, I suppose so," Doan said indifferently.

"Well, are you going to find him and bring him back to justice?"

"What?" said Doan, startled. "Me? No! I'm going to persuade him to keep on hiding."

"But why?"

"Because I'm hired to," Doan answered patiently.

"I don't understand," said Janet. "Why were you hired to persuade him to keep hiding?"

"He's not like you. He doesn't like Mexico. He can't speak Spanish, and the food gives him indigestion, and he doesn't think the people are friendly. He says he would rather be in the United States—even if he's in jail—than to have to stay here any longer."

"You mean he wants to come back and give himself up and answer for his crimes?"

"Yeah."

"And you're going to try to persuade him not to?"

"Not try," Doan corrected. "I am going to persuade him."

"But that's wrong! That's against the law!"

"It probably will be before I'm through," Doan admitted casually.

Janet stared at him. "Well then, you shouldn't do it, Mr. Doan. Why don't you let this man surrender like he wants to?"

Doan sighed. "The guy—Eldridge is his name—was a police captain in Bay City. They had a big graft scandal and a grand jury investigation there. Everybody in the city administration was involved. So the rest of them persuaded Eldridge to beat it to Mexico. Then they said he was to blame for everything that had happened since the city was founded. If he came back, he would pop off about some of his old pals. They're still holding their jobs, and they want to keep them. They won't if Eldridge starts telling secrets."

Janet studied over it for a moment. "It doesn't sound quite— quite *honest* to me, some way. Are you sure you have your facts right, Mr. Doan?"

"Reasonably sure," said Doan.

"Oh," said Janet, still studying. "Well, perhaps these other city officials are afraid Eldridge would tell *lies* about them if he came back?"

"He'd certainly do that," Doan agreed. "He couldn't tell the truth if he tried."

"That's it, then!" said Janet triumphantly. "I understand it all now."

"That's good," said Doan.

"Of course, I knew all the time that you wouldn't do anything that was *really* dishonest."

"Oh, no," said Doan. "Not me."

The road dipped into a little swale and slid through the deep shadow between two needle-like rock pinnacles. A black and white striped board, like a railroad crossing guard, swung out slowly and blocked the way. Bartolome yelped angrily and hit the brake so hard that everything movable in the bus slid forward six inches.

The bus stopped with its radiator a foot from the board. Bartolome leaned out the window and screeched fiercely, "Do not delay this bus under extreme penalties. It contains tourists of the most vital!"

There were two soldiers standing beside the braced white pivot from which the warning gate swung. They were small men with dark and impassive faces. They stared gravely at the bus. Neither of them said anything.

"What's all this?" Henshaw demanded.

"Is a military outpost," Bartolome explained, "full of soldiers of the most incredible stupidity. Kindly ignore the unforgivable insolence of this delay." He yelled out at the soldiers again: "Donkeys! Elevate the gate instantly!"

The soldiers stared, unmoving and unmoved. There was a little white building, so small it reminded Doan of the cupola of an old-fashioned roof, pushed in against the steep rock face. A man came out of it now.

"You!" Bartolome shouted belligerently. "There will be punishments of unbelievable severity—" He caught a glimpse of the man's face. His mouth stayed open, but he didn't say anything more.

The man walked up to the bus. He was wearing a field uniform, and there were no rank markings on it. He was short and thickset,

and there was a broad white scar on his right cheek. His eyes were as cold as greenish glass. He spoke English in a flat, toneless voice without any accent.

"Yes?" he said, looking up at Bartolome. "You wanted something?"

Bartolome swallowed. "This is the bus of sight-seeing from the Hotel Azteca," he said meekly. "Is of the utmost harmlessness and innocence."

The thickset man said: "You were asked not to schedule this trip to Los Altos."

"Not I!" Bartolome protested. "I am only a humble employee of that flesh-laden criminal who owns the Hotel Azteca."

Patricia Van Osdel opened the window beside her. "What is it, please? Why can't we go to Los Altos?"

"It is not advisable."

"Why not?"

"There is trouble in Los Altos."

"What trouble?" Patricia Van Osdel demanded

"It is a military matter and not a concern of civilians."

"Nonsense!" said Patricia Van Osdel. "I've paid a great deal to take this trip, and I intend to finish it."

"Why?" the thickset man asked casually.

"What? Well—well, to see the scenery and buy some native handicrafts—"

"The scenery," said the thickset man, "and the handicrafts will be there after the trouble is gone. I would wait, if I were you."

"Are you proposing to stop us by force?" Patricia Van Osdel demanded.

"Not I, senorita. I never stand between fools and their follies. I have warned you. That is the end of my responsibility. Now you may do as you please."

"We will!" Patricia Van Osdel snapped. "Bartolome, drive on! Drive on!"

The soldiers swung the warning board aside, and the bus rumbled slowly past it and picked up speed. Patricia Van Osdel's thin face was flushed, and she was breathing rapidly.

Henshaw cleared his throat. "Say, who was that tough-looking monkey?"

"Major Nacio," Bartolome answered soberly. "A very great bandit chaser. A supremely superb fighter."

"Well, that don't give him any right to try to scare us. Where does he get that trouble talk? He's just tryin' to show off his authority, that's all."

"Soldiers are always fools," said Greg.

"What army do you belong to?" Doan asked.

"Greg is going to join the United States Army just as soon as we return from this trip!" Patricia Van Osdel snapped. "Aren't you, Greg?"

"No," said Greg.

"And besides," said Patricia Van Osdel, ignoring the answer, "just why aren't you in service, Mr. Doan?"

"Aw, they wouldn't let him in the army," Henshaw said. "They got rules against admitting detectives and immoral characters like that."

"It's not true!" Janet protested.

"It certainly is," Mrs. Henshaw informed her. "They wouldn't let our boys be submitted to any influences like that."

Janet poked Doan in the ribs. "Why don't you answer them?"

"I wouldn't lower myself," said Doan disdainfully. "Anyway, Carstairs is in the army."

"What?" Janet said, amazed.

"Yes, he is," Doan assured her. "He trains dogs to help defend airfields and things. He's on furlough now."

"How does he train them?" Janet asked curiously.

"I'm his assistant and interpreter and orderly. I tell him what the other dogs are supposed to do, and he does it a few times while they watch. Then I tell them to do it, and if they don't, Carstairs reasons with them."

"How?" Janet inquired.

"Show her," Doan ordered.

Carstairs mumbled sleepily.

"We didn't like that," Doan told him. "Again."

Carstairs didn't open his eyes, but he made a noise like a buzz saw hitting a nail in a log. Janet jumped and jerked her hands away from his head.

"That was better," Doan said. "Go to sleep again, but no snoring." Carstairs yawned stickily and wiggled his head into a more comfortable position on Janet's lap.

I T WAS JUST AFTER NOON NOW, AND THE sun was a hot, brassy disc in the thin blue bowl of the sky. The bus rumbled laboriously around a hairpin turn at the summit of a straight,' mile-long climb and paused there, puffing.

"Now," said Bartolome. "This is the scenery nearly supreme. Have the goodness to admire it."

Azela Valley spread out below them—an incredibly enormous raw-red gash with nothing green in it to hide the jagged rock formations, with nothing alive anywhere, nothing moving except the tireless heat waves. It stretched endlessly down, down and away from them, like the landscape of a new world that was as yet only half-formed. As their eyes traveled over it, trying to comprehend its immensity, the red shaded slowly into bluish rust and then into dull, flat brown in the distance. On beyond, still further away, mountains rose steep and serrated and savage against the horizon.

"Wow!" said Henshaw softly.

Doan said to Janet: "Your lieutenant—Perona—came across that?"

She nodded, her eyes wide. "Yes. He walked most of the way. His horse was lame."

"Was he wearing armor, too?"

"Yes."

"What a man," said Doan.

"It looks like a city dump," said Henshaw. "Multiplied by seven hundred million. What lives there, Barty?"

"Rattlesnakes," said Bartolome.

"They can have it," said Henshaw.

"It is one hundred and fifty miles with no road and no water," said Bartolome, "to Santa Lucia on the other side of those mountains."

"I don't want to go there," Henshaw told him. "Where's Los Altos?"

"It approaches," said Bartolome, releasing the brake. The road wove in and out along the mountain top, and the valley followed it, unending and unchanging, stalking them with sinister patience, until suddenly they turned inward between narrow, massive rock walls. Shadows folded down over them darkly.

The road straightened and tilted down like a long, smooth chute. Bartolome kept dabbing at the foot brake, but the bus gathered speed until the wind whistled breathlessly past the windows and Doan could hear a queer, light singing in his ears. "Hey, Barty!" Henshaw said, alarmed.

"Quiet, please," said Bartolome.

The moan of the tires grew higher and higher, and then abruptly the cut opened away from them, bringing the sun in a bright flood, and the road stretched as straight and clean as a tight-wire with nothing on either side of it.

"Yeow!" Mortimer yelled suddenly.

The brakes groaned dismally, and the thick, hot smell of the linings came up into the bus. The tires caught and slid, screaming like souls in torment, and the bus rocked and slewed and suddenly stopped.

"Now observe," said Bartolome.

There was a choked silence for a long time.

Henshaw coughed finally. "What's holdin' this road up here where it is?"

"Is not a road," said Bartolome. "Is a bridge. Kindly get out and exclaim in appreciation."

They got out slowly and stiffly, reluctant to leave the island of comparative safety that was the bus. Carstairs sat down and looked bored and put upon. Mortimer went crawling to the edge of the road and peered over.

"Hey!" he said in a strangled voice. "There ain't nothin' under us but air!"

"That's just what I was afraid of," said Henshaw. "Let's get the hell out of here."

"Observe," Bartolome repeated. "One long span unsupported except at either end."

They could see it more in perspective now, and it was still like a tight-wire strung across space that was a canyon so deep that the sunlight could not penetrate it and the shadows grew darker and darker in its depths until they blended into a thick, formless haze that had no bottom. The steel supports underneath the anchoring pillars were intertwined like spiderwebs and looked as delicately fragile. The wind was a hot, smooth rush in their faces.

"The Canyon of Black Shadow," said Bartolome proudly. "By the bridge, two minutes across. Before the bridge, by mule trail, three days to get down, one day to rest, three days to get up the other side—total one week."

"Did Perona cross this, too?" Doan asked.

Janet nodded, staring down into the shadows. "Yes. The first time he saw it he didn't believe his guides when they said it could be crossed, and he didn't want to risk his men; so he went down and up the other side alone and then came back to get the others."

"I'd like to have met him," said Doan.

He found a big white rock that someone had left as a marker and heaved it over the side. It glistened in the sunlight and slid down smoothly into the shadow and was gone. Everyone waited, listening.

There was no sound.

"That stone," said Bartolome severely, "was a possession of the government."

"I'll go right down and bring it back," Doan promised. "Lend me your parachute."

"I wanna go home!" Mortimer wailed.

"Where's Los Altos, Barty?" Henshaw demanded.

"There," said Bartolome.

They could see it high above them on the other side of the canyon, red roofs and white walls, neat and dainty in the clear air, clinging to what looked like the barren side of a cliff.

"Let's go," said Henshaw.

They climbed back into the bus, and it rumbled on across the threadlike span and commenced to climb on a road that was much narrower and more twisting than the new highway. Bartolome blew his horn at each curve.

"Burros," he explained. "They are often walking in the road and violating the traffic."

The road slanted up a rock ledge, followed its crooked, steeple-like summit for a while, dipped down and turned again, and they were in Los Altos.

The street was narrow and paved raggedly with dark rock. It was like one tread of a steep stairway, with houses going on above it and on down below. The walls of the houses were not quite so white and neat, seen more closely. They were blank, aged faces with cracks like jagged wrinkles in them and narrow, iron-barred windows for eyes and iron-studded doors for mouths.

There was no one in sight. The bus rolled along, rumbling vacantly, to the point where the street widened into the market square. It was empty.

"Is this a ghost town?" Henshaw asked.

Bartolome's mouth was open. He stopped the bus at the curb and got out and looked around. He put his hands over his eyes, took them away, and looked again. The marketplace was still empty. He got in the car and blew the horn loudly and repeatedly. It made noise, but nothing else happened. He got out of the bus again.

"There is no one here," he said in a small, unbelieving voice. "It is unreasonable."

The passengers climbed out of the bus one by one and stood in the street close together, staring uneasily.

"What do you suppose it is?" Janet whispered to Doan.

"I don't know," Doan said. "But I've got a feeling it's something we won't like."

There was a ragged, blunt report that echoed dully. Instantly afterwards a man spun out of a narrow alleyway across the square. It was Garcia approaching his destination. He still had his shiny revolver in his hand, but he wasn't so well in control of the situation any more. He was breathing in great, sobbing gasps, and he stopped and tried to steady himself and fired twice back into the alleyway.

"Revolution!" Henshaw said shakily.

"Revolutions are forbidden," Bartolome said in a numb,

incredulous voice.

Garcia turned and ran toward them. His mouth was wide open with the agony of breathing, and his eyes were glazed blearily. He didn't see the bus or its passengers until he was no more than thirty paces from them.

He half tripped, then, and staggered sideways, but the shiny revolver flipped up in his hand and roared again. The bullet popped metallically against the side of the bus. There was a sudden chorus of yells and a thin, bubbling scream from Mrs. Henshaw.

Doan put his left hand against Janet's shoulder and pushed hard. With his right hand he drew a short, stubby-barreled revolver from under his coat. He produced it as casually as a man would take out a cigarette lighter. He kneed Carstairs out of the way and walked steadily toward Garcia.

"Drop that gun," he said conversationally. "Now."

Garcia fired at him. The bullet went over Doan's head and hit a wall somewhere and bounced off in a whooping ricochet. Doan shot at him, and Garcia sat down suddenly on the pavement, looking blandly incredulous. He stared at Doan, his teeth white and jagged under his stringy mustache, and then he raised his right hand slowly.

Doan's second bullet hit him in the mouth. Garcia fell backwards, and his head made a wet, thick sound as it hit the ground. He didn't move again. Carstairs growled softly from behind Doan.

"I know," Doan said. He was leaning forward tensely, watching the alley from which Garcia had appeared.

A second man jumped out into sight and dropped instantly on one knee. He was carrying a Luger automatic with a long, thin barrel.

"*Alto ahi!*" he called sharply. "*Manos arriba!*"

"Same to you," said Doan.

They stared at each other for long dragging seconds. The kneeling man turned his head a little at last, taking in the huddled passengers, the parked bus. He smiled suddenly and nodded once. He spoke in smooth, unaccented English

"You may put away your gun now."

"So may you," said Doan.

The man laughed and slid the Luger inside his coat. He was dressed in a tan gabardine suit that was rumpled and smeared with dust. He was young and very tall, and he had a quick, sure way of moving. His features were thin and even, and his eyes were a deep blue-gray with a hard little twinkle of amusement in them. He got up and walked over to Garcia and prodded him casually with the toe of one brown oxford. Garcia's head rolled loosely. Blood spilled slickly from the corner of his mouth.

"Dead," said the tall man. "That is unfortunate."

"For him," Doan agreed.

The tall man studied Doan thoughtfully. "Ah, yes. A little, mild, fat man with an enormous dog. We were expecting you, but not quite so soon. What is the name? I have it! Doan! The detective who looks so harmlessly stupid."

"I know how you look, too," said Doan. "But what's your name?"

"I am Captain Emile Perona."

"Oh!" Janet exclaimed.

Perona looked at her. "Yes, senorita?"

"Oh," said Janet, staring with eyes that were enormously dilated.

"What is it, senorita?" Captain Perona asked politely. "Are you ill?"

"No," said Doan. "She's a little surprised, and so am I. You've been promoted since the last time we heard of you, although I suppose anyone could work up from lieutenant to captain in four hundred years."

"What?" said Captain Perona.

"How is Cortez getting along these days?"

Captain Perona frowned. "Perhaps I do not understand your language as well as I thought. The only Cortez I know of is the great explorer and conqueror of this country."

"That's the boy. Didn't you serve under him?"

"Please do not be ridiculous. It is quite useless for you to try to disarm my suspicions with silly remarks. My ancestor—the first Emile Perona—was one of Cortez's lieutenants, but that is none of your business and has nothing whatsoever to do with your presence here—which, I may add, we consider not only unfortunate but undesirable."

"Well, thanks," said Doan.

Captain Perona pointed to Garcia. "We were warned that things like this happen when you are in the vicinity."

"Somebody's been kidding you," said Doan.

"You shot this man."

"Well, certainly," said Doan. "But he shot at me first. Ask anybody. He shot at me twice, in fact, and was all set to go again. What was I supposed to do—stand here and make noises like a target?"

"He saved our lives!" Janet said indignantly.

Captain Perona looked at her, and his eyes sharpened suddenly. "Why were you so startled when you heard my name?"

"B-because we were just talking about the other Emile Perona on the way here."

"Why?"

"I'd read about him—"

"Where?"

"In—in Cortez's reports—"

"In that diary, too," Doan reminded.

"Diary!" Captain Perona snapped. "What diary?"

Janet said uncertainly: "Well... Well..."

Captain Perona came a long, pouncing step closer to her. "What diary?"

Janet swallowed. "Gil De Lico's diary."

"Hah!" said Captain Perona, expelling his breath triumphantly. "I thought so!"

A soldier trotted wearily out of the alley across the square. He came to a sudden halt, half raising his rifle, when he saw the bus and passengers. He stood there peering uncertainly for a moment and then turned and yelled back into the alley

"*Aqui! Aqui esta el capitan!*"

He trudged toward them, bayonet glittering dangerously. Three other soldiers came out of the alley and trailed along behind him.

"Hey, pop," said Mortimer. "This fella ain't got no back to his head, and his mouth is all full of pieces of teeth and blood and stuff."

"Mortimer!" Mrs. Henshaw warned. "You come right here! Don't you look!"

"Why not?" Mortimer asked reasonably. "He ain't near as sliced up as them two guys I saw in that auto wreck last summer."

"Police!" Mrs. Henshaw screamed. "Police!"

Captain Perona looked at her impatiently. "Senora, please be quiet. I am the police."

"What police?" Doan asked.

"The Military Secret Police."

It seemed that this was true enough because the first soldier—Sergeant Obrian of the red mustache and the evil temper—came up and saluted Perona and stood waiting for orders.

Captain Perona pointed absently to Garcia. "Take that away somewhere."

"Yes, sir," said Sergeant Obrian.

"What army is this, anyway?" Doan inquired.

"The Mexican Army, dumbness," said Sergeant Obrian. "I can speak your lingo on account I used to be a waiter in double New York."

"Where?" Doan said.

"New York, New York. It ain't New York City—didn't you know that? It's New York. Just like Mexico City is Mexico."

"Take that body away," said Captain Perona.

"*Si. Capitan!*" said Sergeant Obrian.

He snarled at his three soldiers. One of them—Private Serez—had a black eye and a limp. They slung their rifles and picked Garcia up and carried him down the street. One of his skinny legs swung loose, and his heel dragged on the pavement with a sly, grating sound.

Captain Perona hadn't taken his eyes from Janet. "Where is that diary, senorita?"

"What?"

"You have it, eh? Give it to me."

"Why, I—I don't—"

"I think you lie."

"I bet this is that old-time Mexican courtesy," Doan observed.

Captain Perona said shortly, "Be quiet. This is important to me. That diary belongs to my family. It is a very precious heirloom. I want it."

"Inquire at the Wisteria Young Ladies' Seminary," Doan advised.

"At what?" Captain Perona asked blankly.

"I didn't believe there could be such a joint, either, but there is, and she teaches in it. That's where she read the diary. It belongs to the school."

"It does not. It belongs to me. Is it true that you found the diary at the school, senorita?"

Janet nodded. "Yes."

"Where is the school?"

"Valley View, Ohio."

"I will go there at once," said Captain Perona.

"Wait a minute," Doan said. "Before you go, suppose you sort of explain this and that."

"Eh?" said Captain Perona.

Doan made a wide gesture. "The shooting and the soldiers and the dead man and where all the people are hiding—"

There was no longer any need to ask about the people. They appeared as suddenly and as thickly as a mob on the stage. Every door and most windows on the street disgorged a few, and they scurried around breathlessly, slamming up wood shutters, hauling counters of goods out on the pavement. Someone clanged a gong, and a little girl shrieked shrilly.

"Is American speaken in this store very nice! Is prices guaranteed cheapest on anything! Here, here, here! Beautiful, beautiful! Cheap, cheap!"

"Feelthy pictures?" a sly little man whispered in Doan's ear. He saw Captain Perona looking his way and disappeared in the crowd like a puff of smoke.

A fat, thick-shouldered woman tackled Mrs. Henshaw. "Serape! See? Hand wove most pretty! Cheap!"

Three mongrel dogs came up and barked at Carstairs. Carstairs closed his eyes and looked bored. Doan rapped him sharply on top of the head with his knuckles and said:

"None of that, now."

"What did he do?" Janet demanded.

"Nothing, yet. He hates mongrels—especially ones that bark at him. He was just getting ready to tear a leg off the nearest one. Carstairs. Relax."

Carstairs opened his eyes and leered malignantly at the three mongrels. They went away quickly.

"Come this way, please," said Captain Perona. He took Janet's arm and led her through the crowd, fending off storekeepers and souvenir salesmen by merely scowling at them. Doan trailed right behind.

Clear of the crowd, Captain Perona said to Janet: "Please pardon the way I spoke to you. I am very anxious to recover that diary. For many years we have been trying to trace it."

"I hate to interrupt," said Doan, "but how about that bird I killed?"

Captain Perona shrugged. "You should not have done that, really. It is annoying."

"No doubt," said Doan. "But who was he?"

Captain Perona shrugged again. "He called himself Garcia most of the time, I believe. He was of no importance in himself. He was allowed to escape from the Islas Tres Marias."

"The what?" Doan asked.

"You heard me," Janet said: "It's a Mexican prison. It's on an island like Alcatraz. It's for the most dangerous confirmed criminals."

Captain Perona nodded. "Correct."

"You say he was allowed to escape?" Doan inquired.

"Yes. At my orders. I wanted to follow him in order to find a confederate of his. I followed him here successfully, but then his confederate threw a rattlesnake at one of my men and frightened him so badly that he shouted and thus let Garcia know that he was being watched."

"A rattlesnake?" Doan repeated. "Threw it?"

"Yes."

"That confederate must be sort of a tough bimbo," Doan observed. "No wonder you wanted to find him. Did you?"

"Did we find him? No. But now we are positive he is here somewhere in Los Altos, so we will soon. I had hoped that if we kept chasing Garcia back and forth through the town long enough his confederate would try to help him, but of course you spoiled that possibility."

"Who is this confederate, anyway?"

"It is a military matter," Captain Perona said, politely but definitely.

"Oh," said Doan. "Well, what should I do now? Go and lock myself in jail?"

"No. I will make the proper reports to the authorities. This is a military district. You may go and see the Senor Eldridge. He lives on the Avenida Revolution—three streets up and south one block. I will talk to the senorita."

"Okay with you?" Doan asked Janet.

She nodded, a little uncertain. "I wanted to look at a little church—"

"I know the one you mean," Captain Perona said. "It is no longer a church, but it is kept as a museum. I will take you there."

"So long, then," said Doan.

Captain Perona said: "One moment, please. As I told you, we have been expecting you. You may go and see Senor Eldridge, but you are not to strike him or beat him or torture him in any other manner to persuade him not to return to the United States as he wishes to do. If you harm him, you will be held very strictly to account."

"Me?" said Doan. "Torture him?"

"We have heard of your methods of detection," said Captain Perona stiffly. "They are not allowed in Mexico. You are warned."

"I am warned," Doan admitted. "Come on, Carstairs."

THE AVENIDA REVOLUCION WAS narrow and straggling and dusty, built on a slope so steep that even the road itself had a tilt to it. The houses were older and more decrepit than those on the main street, with tiles on their roofs missing and plaster crumbling at the corners of the walls.

The people here evidently weren't sure the shooting was over. Faces peered through barred windows at Doan and Carstairs, but there was no one on the street. Several dogs came out of hiding to investigate Carstairs, and he began to dawdle along pretending to sniff at the walls while he watched them out of the corners of his eyes.

Doan bunted him in the rear with his knee. "Go on. Keep moving."

Carstairs swung his head toward the sightseers and lifted his upper lip. The dogs went away yipping in incredulous terror. Carstairs ambled arrogantly on ahead of Doan. He stopped at the corner and looked around it, ears pricked inquiringly, and Doan stopped beside him to look, too.

There was nothing in the little jog in the street except an easel, looking like a foreshortened skeleton of an Indian tepee, with a big canvas fastened on it. There was no sign of the artist.

Doan walked up to the easel and examined the canvas. It was a half-finished painting, and he turned his head first one way and then the other, trying to figure out what it was meant to represent.

"Hey, you!"

Doan turned and after a moment spotted the source of the voice. It was coming out of the barred porthole of the front door of a house across the street.

"Yes?" he said.

"Have they nailed that gun-crazy screwball?"

"Yes," said Doan.

"You're sure?"

"Sort of," said Doan.

The door opened and a woman came out. She was short and squat and broad without being a bit fat. She had an upstanding mane of gray hair that frizzed wildly around a face as lined and weather-beaten as an old boot. She wore an orange painter's smock and a floppy pair of moccasins.

"A hell of a note," she said. "Shooting in the streets. How can you paint with stuff like that going on? What's your name, and where'd you come from?"

"Doan. United States."

"I'm Amanda Tracy. Ever heard of me? Don't lie."

"No," said Doan.

"Good. Know anything about art?"

"No."

"Fine. What do you think of that picture?"

Doan studied it again. "Well—"

"It's lousy, isn't it? It looks like a cold fried egg in a pan of congealed grease, doesn't it?"

"Yes," Doan admitted.

Amanda Tracy whacked him on the back so hard his neck snapped. "That's the old pepper, fatso! Now I know it'll sell! If they stink, they sell. Always. Remember that when you start painting pictures."

"Okay," said Doan, feeling the back of his neck tenderly.

Amanda Tracy pointed at Carstairs. "Where'd you get that stilt-legged abortion?"

"I won him in a crap game," said Doan. "And he's not an abortion. He's a very fine dog."

"The only good dog is a dead dog, Doan. No one but morons and perverts keep pets. Are you a pervert?"

"No," said Doan. "Just a moron."

"Good," said Amanda Tracy. "I like morons. Did you come on the bus with that burbling little twerp of a Bartolome?"

"Yes."

"Any more morons come with you?"

"A couple," Doan admitted.

"Any dough in the crowd?"

"Plenty."

Amanda Tracy picked up the easel, painting and all. "Then I'll go down and paint in the marketplace and act artistic as all hell and probably I can take some sucker for a dime or two. See you later."

"Wait a minute," Doan requested. "Do you know which of these houses Eldridge lives in?"

"Don't tell me you're a friend of that mealy-mouthed rum-dumb."

"No friend," said Doan. "But which house?"

"Second one around the jog. See you later, fatso. Keep your nose clean."

"All right," said Doan.

He watched her stride solidly around the corner and out of sight down the slope, easel trailing behind her.

"That's quite a character," he said absently to Carstairs. "Let's go."

They went on around the jog. The second house was set a little apart from its neighbors. The bars on the front windows were newer and thicker and not so ornamental, and it was walled up high with no windows at all on either side.

There was a knocker in the shape of a stirrup on the wide, arched front door, and Doan hammered it loudly. He could hear the echoes inside the house, sodden and dull, but there was no answer.

Doan waited awhile and banged the knocker again, even more emphatically. There was still no answer, and he tried the long, wrought-iron latch. It clicked, and the big door swung silently and slowly inward. Carstairs growled in a low rumble.

"Shut up," said Doan.

He stepped into a narrow hallway. The air felt still and moist and cool against his face. He blinked his eyes, trying to accustom them to the deep shadow. The hall was floored with stone, and its walls were dimly white.

Doan jerked his head at Carstairs. "Come in, lame-brain."

Carstairs' growl raised a little in tone. He stood with his feet braced in the doorway, head lowered. His eyes glistened dully. Doan caught him by his spiked collar and hauled him inside. "Don't get temperamental with me."

Carstairs' claws scraped on the floor, and then a voice—a little sad and a little thick—said. "I guess he smells the blood."

The man who had spoken was standing in the shadow of a draped doorway back a little along the hall. His face was invisible, but he was short and thick-bodied, and he was holding a revolver in his right hand.

Doan let go of Carstairs and straightened up slowly. "Eldridge?" he asked.

"Yes."

"Are you planning on using that gun in the near future, or are you just carrying it around to scare small children?"

"Oh," said Eldridge. "This? Well, I guess I'm kinda scared, to tell the truth. You're Doan, huh? I mean, I know you on account of the dog. I'm glad you got here so quick. You wanna drink?"

"Sure."

Eldridge led the way along the hall and out into the bright-walled enclosure of a tiled patio. There were palms and ferns, green and lacy, around the borders, and a fountain burbled softly in the center.

Carstairs strolled over and lapped at the water and then turned his head to watch Doan, drops drooling from his broad muzzle. When Doan glanced at him, he ambled over to a green trash box half hidden behind a fern against the back wall. He snorted once at it and then came back and sat down beside the fountain and began to pant comfortably.

"What's in the box?" Doan asked.

"That was what he smelled, all right," Eldridge said. "Go look."

Doan walked over and lifted the hinged lid. The box was half filled with empty cans and bottles. A small dog that looked like a dusty, black mop lay on top of them. The dog's eyes were rolled back, and its tongue protruded purple-red between its teeth. Its throat had been cut.

"Nice," said Doan, dropping the lid. "Are you saving it for supper?"

"That there was a nice dog," said Eldridge. "It wasn't no fancy number like you got, but it was a friendly little guy, and I think it maybe liked me."

"So you killed it."

"Now, Doan," said Eldridge. "You know I wouldn't do a dirty thing like that."

"Who did, then?"

"A fella," said Eldridge vaguely. "A fella that don't like me, I guess." He had very light blue eyes shot with reddened veins, and even when he was relaxed, as he was now, his hands shook slightly. His thick body had a weakened, self-pitying sag. "Sit down, Doan."

Doan sat down in one of the rawhide easy chairs. Eldridge walked slowly over to another one that was pushed flush against the back wall of the house. He lowered himself into it laboriously, breathing hard.

"Want a drink, Doan?"

"I haven't changed my mind," Doan answered.

"Concha!" Eldridge called. "Whiskey!"

A girl came through the rear door of the patio. She was carrying a bottle and two glasses on a tray. She was young and slim and lithe, and her hair gleamed blue-black in the sunlight. Her eyes were lowered modestly, and the front of her dress was just lowered.

"Pour him one," Eldridge said. "It's Johnny Walker Black, Doan. You want a chaser or a mix?"

"No," said Doan, watching Concha. "Where'd you find this little gadget?"

Concha presented the tray to Eldridge, and he poured himself an eight-fingered dollop.

"This here is that fella Doan I told you about, Concha," he said. "Concha's my wife, Doan."

"Another?" Doan asked. "What did you do with the one you left in the States?"

"Oh, I divorced her."

"Does she know it?"

"I guess not," Eldridge admitted. "I just never did get around to telling her about it."

Doan raised his glass to take a sip and looked at Concha over the top of it. Her eyes weren't lowered now. They were staring at Doan with such pure venom in them that he could feel it plainly at a distance of ten feet. He lowered his glass very carefully.

"Come here, honey," he said softly. "You take a sip of this before I drink it."

Concha stepped closer and jerked the glass out of his fingers. She didn't drink out of it. She threw it at the patio wall. It made a crunch and an ugly little splatter against the clean white plaster.

"Now Concha, lovey," said Eldridge mildly.

Concha went back through the rear door and slammed it violently behind her.

"She's shy with strangers," said Eldridge.

"I never would have guessed it," Doan told him.

"But don't think she'd poison your drink. Why, she don't know any more about poison than I do."

"That's what I was afraid of."

"Well, have a drink out of the bottle, then."

"I'll sit this one out," Doan said. "You go ahead and get drunk for both of us."

"Okay." Eldridge took a big gulp of whiskey and sighed contentedly. "Well, Doan, how much are they offering?"

"How much is who offering of what?" Doan asked.

"Dough. How much are the boys willing to pay?"

"Oh, that. They said the best they could do was dollar sign decimal zero zero."

"Dollar sign decimal—" Eldridge sat up straight with a jerk. "What? You mean, nothing?"

"Correct," said Doan.

"Why, they can't do this to me! I'm gonna go right back to the States and raise hell!"

"Oh, no."

"Why ain't I?"

115

"Look real closely," Doan invited.

"At you?" Eldridge said. "You mean you think you could stop me?"

"Yes," said Doan.

"Hah!" said Eldridge, taking another drink. "Well, you couldn't. And even if you could—for a little while—there's nothing to prevent me from going back as soon as you leave."

"I know one thing that would."

"What?" Eldridge asked skeptically.

"A funeral," Doan said. "Yours."

"Well, of course, if I was dead I couldn't—Hey! Just what do you mean by that?"

"Just what you think I mean."

Eldridge had laid his revolver down in his lap. He picked the gun up now and looked warily from it to Doan. Doan didn't move a muscle. Eldridge put the revolver down again and took another drink.

"You wouldn't dare pull anything like that in Mexico," he said defensively. "You ain't got no drag down here, and I have."

Doan shrugged. "Do you remember the guy who was district attorney when you pulled out of Bay City?"

"You mean Bumpy? Sure, I remember that oily little rat."

"He's going to be elected governor any minute now."

"Bumpy?" Eldridge said incredulously. "Governor?"

"Yes. If somebody got in trouble down here, Bumpy could fix it for the guy to be charged with treason or murder or something and then request the Mexican government to extradite him. As soon as the guy got out of Mexico, Bumpy could kill the charge against him."

Eldridge stared. "Bumpy never thought that one up—he's too dumb!"

"I thought it up," said Doan. "Before I came down here."

"What a twister you are!" said Eldridge admiringly. He sat still for a moment, thinking. "How much are you making out of this, Doan?"

"Just my salary—a hundred and fifty a week. I figured the

job would take four weeks, and if it does I can jump my expense account for another four hundred."

"A thousand bucks," Eldridge said. "Not bad—not good. How would you like to make another thousand in a hurry?"

"Just dandy."

"Ummm," said Eldridge. "Bumpy... Governor... That sort of throws a new light on the situation. Now I wasn't kidding the boys, Doan, about not being so fond of this dump. The people ain't friendly. They don't seem to like me."

"I can't imagine why not," Doan observed.

"Neither can I. It bothers me. It ain't as if I wasn't legitimate. If I was a crook on the lam or something, it'd be different. But just because there was a little misunderstanding about some presents I took—Why, all cops take honest graft! You know that yourself, Doan."

"Oh, sure," said Doan.

"But, of course, I was kiddin' about wantin' to go to jail. Nobody with good sense wants to go to jail. I was just tryin' to shake the boys up a little bit."

"Sure," Doan repeated. "I thought I heard you say something about a thousand dollars."

"I'm coming to that. I wouldn't go to jail if Bumpy was governor. I know enough about him to hang him six times. He wouldn't dare even sneeze at me. Why, I could damned near own that state, Doan! Now listen. Supposing you missed fire on this job—supposing I turned up in the States right away—would you lose your job with the agency you're working for?"

"No," said Doan. "They don't dare fire me. I know too much about the outfit."

Eldridge nodded. "I figured you would. All right, Doan. I'll give you a thousand bucks the day I step over the border into the United States. No use tryin' to pump the price up any higher than that, because I ain't got any more."

"It's a deal," said Doan.

"No!" Concha shrieked. She came out of the rear door like a small whirlwind and stood in front of Eldridge's chair and stamped her foot. "No! You big drunker! You big cheat! You do not take the college money! No!"

"What's this?" Doan asked. "Are you going to college, Eldridge?"

"No," Eldridge said. "Concha is. Acting college. In Hollywood. She's going to be a movie star."

"Think of that," Doan remarked.

"Big liar!" Concha said to Eldridge. "You promise to send me! Thief!"

"Now, lovey."

Concha pointed at Doan. "Why do you give him my money? Why, why, why? He is nothing! He is not even a policeman!"

"He's a private detective."

"Pah! Not here! Not in my country! Here he is nothing but what he looks like! Nothing but a little man with too much fats and a big, lazy dog."

"That's right," Doan admitted, looking down at Carstairs, who was sleeping peacefully.

Concha stamped both feet, one after the other. "You do not give him my money! No, no, no!"

"Now, lovey," said Eldridge. "Why don't you be reasonable. A thousand dollars! Chicken-feed! Peanuts! When I get back, Bumpy is gonna give me the key to the state treasury, and I can run in and fill my pockets any old time. I'll buy you a movie studio—just for you!"

"Pah! Big-mouth!"

"Now, now. Be nice, lovey."

"You give me the ditch! You try for run away with this fats and leave me!"

"Aw, Concha," said Eldridge. "Now you know I wouldn't do that. I love you."

"Pah! Pooey! I spit!" She did.

"Lovey," said Eldridge persuasively. "I'm gonna make you famous. You'll be the best actress in the world. I'll give you fur coats and dresses and rings and a house with an inside toilet. I mean it!"

Concha leaned close over him. "Coward!"

"I'm not, neither!"

"Bautiste Bonofile!" Concha hissed at him.

Eldridge cringed slightly and took a quick drink.

"See?" Concha sneered. "You are with the shakes like the jello! You think to give the fats my money to keep away Bautiste Bonofile. Pah! Bautiste Bonofile takes the fats in one bite. Crunch, crunch, crunch! Then he takes the big, dumb dog in another bite. Crunch, crunch, crunch!"

"You've got it all wrong, Concha," said Eldridge. "This is just a business deal. We're gonna make a big profit, and we'll be rich."

"*You—don't—give—the—fats—my—money!*"

"Yes," said Eldridge.

"No! No, no, no! I'm telling Colonel Callao! He fixes you and the fats, too! He shoots you both! Bang, bang, bang! Pah!"

She whirled and ran across the patio and through the door into the hallway. The front door of the house boomed behind her like a sullen gun. Eldridge smiled painfully at Doan and shrugged his shoulders.

"So far," said Doan, "I'm due to be eaten—crunch, crunch, crunch—and then shot for dessert."

"Concha exaggerates," Eldridge told him.

"Yes. But how much? Who is Colonel Callao?"

"This is a military district, and he's supposed to be in charge of it. He's a dope."

"Is he a friend of Concha's?"

"Yeah. Anyway, he was. I sort of acquired her from him."

"How?" Doan asked curiously.

"I married her—or so they tell me. I don't remember much about it. I was drunk at the time."

"How about the other party she mentioned?"

"Him?" Eldridge said vaguely. "Oh, I was gonna mention him to you. It might be that he'd start a little something or other if I was to leave here, and then maybe you'd have to calm him down. He's the gent who cut my dog's throat."

"What's his name?"

"Bautiste Bonofile. At least, that was his name. I don't know what he calls himself now."

"All right," said Doan. "I'll go have a chat with him. Where is he?"

"I don't know."

"Well, what does he look like?"

"I don't know that, either."

"Maybe it would help if you explained a bit," Doan suggested.

Eldridge sighed. "There were two of them at first—brothers. Bautiste and Louis Bonofile. They were Canadian breeds—half some kind of Indian. They were always tough guys. They served a few terms in Canadian jails, and then they sneaked across into the United States. They were arrested in a dozen states for everything in the book, but they only served a couple of short terms. The rest was probation, parole, bailskips, indictment quashed, insufficient evidence—"

"The payoff," Doan finished.

"Yeah. Bautiste was the one who could put in the fixes. He was sharper than a razor, but he finally got caught short on a federal charge and had to beat it. He came to Mexico. Louis stayed in the United States. He was a dumb one. Just a killer. I nailed him for shooting a clerk in a cigar store during a ten dollar holdup."

"And he couldn't fix you?"

"Not for ten dollars. And he didn't have any other dough, so naturally he got hung. I mean, I had to turn somebody up once in awhile, or how could I have kept my job?"

"Sure," said Doan.

"So Bautiste blames me for gettin' Louis hung. He claims I framed Louis."

"Did you?"

"Well, yes. He was guilty, though—I think. Bautiste wrote me some dirty letters at the time, but I didn't worry because I knew he didn't dare come back to the United States, and I figured he'd forget it or get killed pretty quick, but he didn't. He's here in Los Altos and he's still mad. He's been writin' me notes about what he's gonna do to me when he gets to it, and throwin' rocks and knives in the windows and cutting my dog's throat and dirty stuff like that. He's mean. He says he wants to make me suffer before he finishes me off. He wants to scare me."

"Of course he hasn't succeeded."

Eldridge reached for the whiskey. "Naw. I just laugh it off." The neck of the bottle rattled a little against the edge of his glass. "The hell of it is, I don't know who he is now. I've never seen him when he was pullin' his tricks. He might be anybody in the damned town. He's had years to get himself a new name and a new identity, and he did a honey of a job. Even Perona hasn't been able to dig him out."

"Perona?" Doan repeated. "Captain Perona? What's he got to do with it? I thought he was in the Intelligence or something."

"He is. That's why he's looking for Bautiste Bonofile. Did you ever hear of Zapata?"

"No."

"Well, Pancho Villa was to Zapata what Mussolini is to Hitler. I mean, Zapata was big stuff. He controlled all of middle Mexico at one time—even took over Mexico City. He was a revolutionary raider, not a bandit or a holdup man. He was an Indian, and he didn't like white men. Bautiste Bonofile got in with him because Bautiste was part Indian. He was one of Zapata's lieutenants for a long time. That was a long time ago. Bautiste is no spring chicken. He's older than I am—a lot."

"Tell me more," Doan invited.

"Zapata was killed finally, and his army was broken up. Bautiste took over his own particular company and started playing bandit. The government ran him down and killed most of his men and put Bautiste away on the Islas Tres Marias."

"I've heard of it," said Doan.

"Yeah. After a few years Bautiste crushed out. They've never had hold of him since, and that was ten-fifteen years ago. He could be anybody by this time."

"Why does the government want him so badly? They seem to be taking quite a lot of trouble."

"Well, in the old days in Mexico the government was very

121

corrupt at times. An officer of the army would have the right to purchase supplies for his men. Some of them who commanded twenty or thirty soldiers would order supplies—and rifles and ammunition—to equip five hundred. If no one protested the orders, the seller kicked back a percentage on the deal."

"I wondered how so many of those old-time Mexican generals got to be millionaires."

"They had a soft racket," Eldridge said regretfully. "Anyway, all the stuff they couldn't use, they just stored. Zapata, when he raided military outposts and forts and such, picked up thousands of rifles and millions of rounds of ammunition. What he couldn't use, he hid. Bautiste knows where he did the hiding. This is a bad time to have thousands of rifles lying around loose. They're old now, but they're Mausers, and they could be used."

"Yes," said Doan thoughtfully. "Hitler's army uses Mausers. I can see why the government might be a little worried about the matter. Why doesn't Bautiste cough up and make a deal?"

"Naw," said Eldridge. "Not him. He's mean. Anyway, the government wouldn't deal with him. He's a murderer about ninety times over."

"That's nice to know," Doan observed. "So Concha was right. You were going to pay me a thousand dollars to stand in front of you when Bautiste started shooting."

Eldridge dropped his glass, and it made a little tinkling sound. "Doan! You ain't gonna back out! We made a deal! You promised! You got to keep Bautiste off my back until I can get out of here!"

"What's the good of that? He'll just follow you."

"Naw! He couldn't do that—not with Perona after him. Perona is smart, and with the country at war like it is, he's got all kinds of power and the whole army to hunt with. Bautiste will have to stay under cover right where he is now—which is here in Los Altos. Once I get away from here, I'll be free as the air."

"After," Doan said warningly, "you pay me a thousand dollars."

"Sure. That's what I meant."

"If I got you to the border in one piece," Doan said, "and you didn't have the thousand dollars, I wouldn't think it was a bit funny. And you wouldn't, either."

"I've got it. I'll pay you. Why, I wouldn't double-cross you, Doan!"

"Not twice," Doan agreed. "What about Concha?"

"Oh, her. She stays here, of course."

"After all that song and dance about Hollywood and a house with an inside toilet?"

Eldridge shrugged. "You know how a guy talks to a dame. I was only fooling. What would I want with a little stupe like her? Once I contact Bumpy I'll get something really fancy. Colonel Callao can have Concha back."

"I have an idea," Doan said, "that when Colonel Callao finds out he's going to get Concha back, we're going to have more trouble with him than we do with Bautiste Bonofile."

"Callao's a dope, like I said. And besides that, he's ignorant."

"I hope so," said Doan. He stood up. "Well, I'm going to find Perona now and tell him you and I have come to an agreement, and after that we can arrange—"

The tiles moved slightly under his feet. It was just a slight shudder back and forth that made his knees feel queerly stiff and numb. Carstairs got up very quickly.

"That's just an earth tremor," said Eldridge. "We have them all the time here. There's a fault through this range. We never have a serious one—not what you'd call an earthquake or anything like that."

The tiles moved in a quick little jerk. Carstairs barked angrily at Doan.

"Shut up, you fool," Doan told him. "I'm not responsible for this."

The tiles rippled. There was no other word for it. It was as though someone had stirred their hard surface with a spoon, and they cracked and crumbled and split. Doan went staggering, and dust came up hot and acrid into his nostrils. Carstairs sneezed indignantly.

There was a long, ominous rumble that was like thunder but

more terrible and spine-chilling, and the earth began to move back and forth slowly and relentlessly. Doan went headlong. Carstairs scrambled desperately for his balance, slipped and fell hard on tiles that were slick from the water that had been in the fountain.

The dust was a thick veil, and through it things clumped and banged and groaned weirdly. The patio mall moved and hovered over Doan, and before he could get up it moved back again reluctantly, back and back at an impossible angle, and then it crumbled away and hit the ground, and dust rose from it in a yellow, rolling puff like a smoke signal. The noise of its fall was lost in the greater jarring rumble that came from everywhere.

The seconds dragged like hollow centuries. Doan got up, and the ground moved out from under him, and he went down again. Carstairs clawed frantically, breathing in short, hard snarls, trying to get his feet under him. The ground stopped jerking, and quivered like jelly and then quieted.

Doan sat up and looked across the patio. Eldridge was still sitting in his chair against the house wall. His eyes were bulged wide, and he moved his lips stiffly. Everything was suddenly deathly still.

Very slowly, as if it were tired now, the earth moved up and then dropped back again. In the house, timbers screamed like agonized things, and then the roof sagged a little and started to slide.

Doan's throat was tight. "Eldridge! Look out!"

Eldridge tried to move, tried to fight out of his chair, and then a solid waterfall of plaster and tile and broken adobe poured down over him.

Doan got up and scrambled toward the pile of debris. It had knocked Eldridge forward and down. Doan heaved at a broken timber, threw it sideways, pulled out another. He clawed tile and thick chunks of adobe right and left behind him, and then he saw Eldridge's head and shoulders, queerly flattened and deflated, gray with plaster dust.

Doan dug his hands under Eldridge's armpits and hauled back. A tile fell off the roof and tucked into the ground beside him, and the top of the house wall crumbled slightly. Doan heaved again, and then Eldridge was free. Doan dragged him toward the empty space at the side of the patio where the wall had fallen outward.

Eldridge was limp and unmoving, but he was breathing in short, choked gasps. His legs and lower body were twisted grotesquely askew.

Doan took his handkerchief from his coat pocket and dampened it in the water that was left in the fountain. He wiped the layer of plaster dust from Eldridge's face and saw that there was a thin trickle of bright, arterial blood coming out of the corner of Eldridge's mouth.

Eldridge opened his eyes. "Why, Doan," he said in a faint, surprised voice.

"Take it easy," said Doan.

"Why, what're you looking at me that way for, Doan? I ain't hurt. I can't feel—Doan!"

"Take it easy," said Doan. "Don't try to move."

"Doan! My legs won't—Doan! Something's wrong with me! Don't stand there! Get a doctor!"

"A doctor won't do you any good."

"Doan! I'm not—I'm not—"

"Yes," said Doan.

Eldridge's face was purple-red, and his throat bulged with his straining effort to hold up his head.

"No! I won't—I can't—Bumpy... governor whole state... No! Doan! You're lying,, damn you!"

"Your back's broken," said Doan. "And you're all scrambled up inside."

Eldridge's breath bubbled and sputtered in his throat. His lips pulled back and showed the blood on his teeth, and he said thickly but very clearly:

"God damn you to hell."

His head rolled limply to one side. Doan stood up lowly. He looked at the wadded, damp handkerchief in his hand and then dropped it with a little distasteful grimace.

From behind him a voice said: "You will stand still, if you please."

Doan didn't move, but he looked at Carstairs murderously.

Carstairs was involved in a complicated exercise that would enable him to lick one hind paw. His legs were sprawled out eccentrically in all directions, and he stared back at Doan with an expression of sheepish apology.

"You brainless, incompetent giraffe," said Doan.

"Do not blame your dog for not warning you," aid the voice behind him. "I was downwind, and I can move so very quietly sometimes. Please do stand still."

Doan didn't move his arms or legs or body or head, but he flicked his eyes to the left, then looked at Carstairs, and then flicked them to the left again. Carstairs got up instantly and began to sidle to his own right.

"No," said the voice. "I would not like to kill your dog. Stop him."

Doan nodded once. Carstairs sat down, watching him.

"No," said the voice.

Doan nodded again. Carstairs slid his forelegs out slowly and sprawled on the broken tiles.

"That is so much better," said the voice. "Your dog is beautifully trained. It would be a shame if he were hurt. I think you have a gun. Do not try to use it. Keep your hands away from your body and turn around slowly."

Doan turned around. The voice belonged to a thin, elderly man who looked very neat and well-tailored in a gray tweed suit. He had a long nose and a shapeless, bulging mustache, and he wore thick glasses that distorted his watery blue eyes. He had no gun, but he was holding a rolled green umbrella under his right arm, and Doan was not so foolish as to think it was actually only an umbrella.

"What is your name?"

"Doan," said Doan. "What's yours?"

"I am Lepicik. Were you robbing that man?"

"I hadn't gotten around to it yet."

"Did you kill him?"

"No," said Doan. "The earthquake did. We just had one, or didn't you notice?"

"Yes," said Lepicik pleasantly. "It was quite violent, wasn't it? From where did you come here?"

"From the Hotel Azteca in Mazalar."

"You have been staying there?"

"For a couple of days."

"How did you come here to Los Altos? By what means of travel?"

"On a sight-seeing bus."

"Who came with you?"

"Why?" Doan asked.

Lepicik moved the umbrella slightly. "You would really be so much wiser to answer my questions."

"Okay," said Doan. "An heiress by the name of Patricia Van Osdel and her maid, name of Maria, and her gigolo, name of Greg. A man named Henshaw and his wife and kid. A schoolteacher by the name of Janet Martin."

"Thank you," said Lepicik. "Thank you so very much. Good day."

"Good day," said Doan.

Lepicik walked backwards away from him. He didn't hesitate or feel his way. He walked as confidently as though he had eyes in the back of his head. He disappeared around the edge of the broken patio wall.

Doan leaned over and picked up a chunk of adobe and hurled it at Carstairs. Carstairs jumped up nimbly and let the adobe skid harmlessly under him.

"What do you think I drag you around for?" Doan demanded angrily. "Keep your eyes open after this."

Carstairs looked even more apologetic than he had at first. He moved back and forth in tight, uneasy steps, lowering his head.

"All right," said Doan. "Come on, and we'll see if there's anyone else left alive in this town."

WHEN DOAN LEFT THEM AT the corner, Janet and Captain Perona stood still for a moment watching him trudge up the slope toward the Avenida Revolucion with Carstairs wandering along ahead of him.

"Why did you say that to him?" Janet demanded.

"I beg pardon?" said Captain Perona.

"Why did you warn him about torturing and beating Eldridge? That's perfect nonsense."

"I think not," Captain Perona denied.

"Mr. Doan is a very mild, polite, pleasant person. He would no more torture anyone than I would."

"Oh, yes," said Captain Perona. "We have his record, you see. He is what you call a private detective. Very successful. His record is full of violence. He does not care at all what he does to solve a case. But he never quite gets caught breaking the law. He is very clever and very lucky."

"Clever!" Janet echoed incredulously. "Mr. Doan? Why—why, he's the most talkative, open, naive, boyish—"

"Oh, no," said Captain Perona positively. "That is also in his record. He fools people with his innocent manner, but he is not innocent in the slightest. Assuredly not."

"I think you're just making this up."

"Senorita," said Captain Perona, "I do not make things up, if you please."

"Well, you're mistaken, then."

"And I do not make mistakes."

"Not ever?" Janet asked in an awed tone.

"No. I am—" Captain Perona stopped short, staring narrowly at her. "So you are mocking me!"

"Yes," said Janet.

Captain Perona breathed hard. "I will forgive you—this time, senorita. Mocking people and ridiculing them is, I understand, a custom in your detestable country."

"My what?" Janet said, stung.

"The United States. I have heard that its people are very ignorant and uncouth."

"They are not!"

"Especially the women. They have loud, shrill voices, and they shout in public."

"They do not!" Janet cried.

Captain Perano smiled at her blandly. Several passersby turned to look curiously at her. She began to blush, and she put her hand up to her lips. "You see?" asked Captain Perona. "Even you do it. Shouting in public is considered very unmannerly in Mexico."

Janet said in a choked whisper: "You said those things just to make me mad so I'd raise my voice and—and make myself look foolish!"

"That is correct," said Captain Perona. "And you did. Very foolish."

"Please go away and leave me alone."

"No," said Captain Perona.

Janet turned around and started blindly across the marketplace. After three steps she staggered just a little, groping for her balance, and then Captain Perona's hand was under her arm, supporting her.

"You are ill, senorita?" he asked. There was no mockery in his voice now.

Janet said: "If—if I could just sit down..."

"Here, senorita! This way. The bench. One step and now another..."

Janet sank down on the cool stone of the bench in a shaded niche in the thick wall. The wavery black haze in front of her eyes cleared away, and she could see Captain Perona's thin, worried face.

"It's nothing," she said breathlessly. "I'm all right now, really. It—it was just that man. The dead man. I'd never seen a man killed before, and—and I tried to act—to act nonchalant. But the blood and the way his face looked and his leg dragging when they carried him away..."

Captain Perona sat down beside her. "It is understandable, of course. Do not think about him any more. He is not worth it, and besides he killed one of my soldiers when he first discovered we were watching him. I was going to kill him sooner or later, myself."

"Talk about something else, please," Janet begged.

"Surely," said Captain Perona. "We will talk about Gil De Lico's diary, because I wish to know much more about it. What is the name of this place where you found it, again?"

"The Wisteria Young Ladies' Seminary."

"How peculiar," said Captain Perona. "It seems odd to me to name a school such a thing. Who owns it—the state?"

"Oh, no. It's a private school."

"I see. What is the name of the owner?"

"Why—why, I think it's a corporation. I mean, it isn't *owned* by anyone. Different people contributed money to found it."

"Do you know who these people were?"

"Some of them."

"Would one be called Ruggles?"

"Oh, yes! Ebenezer Ruggles. He was the main founder. He was a very old-fashioned, strict, conservative sort of man, and he thought colleges were teaching girls too much they shouldn't know. Nobody would pay any attention to his ideas, so he started a school of his own. He's been dead for several years now."

"Good," said Captain Perona. "He was a thief."

"Ebenezer Ruggles?"

"Yes."

"Are you sure?"

"Yes. My mother told me so."

"What?" Janet said blankly.

"My mother told me so. My family did not realize they had been robbed by this Ruggles criminal until she told them. But she knows. She knows everything about people from the United States because she came from there herself."

"You mean, your mother is an American?"

Captain Perona looked at her. "That is a very disgusting habit your countrymen have. Calling themselves Americans as though they were the only ones. I will have you know that Mexicans are Americans. We are more Americans than people from the United States are, because we came to America before they did."

"I'm sorry," Janet said meekly.

"You should be. Kindly be more careful of your language in the future. My ancestor, Emile Perona, was one of the first men to come to this continent. That is why we wish Gil De Lico's diary. It was presented to our family by the family of Gil De Lico three hundred-odd years ago. I can show you the presentation letter if you wish to see it, although you could not read it, of course."

"Yes, I could."

"No," said Captain Perona patronizingly. "It is in old-fashioned Spanish and written in script."

"I could still read it. How do you think I read Gil De Lico's diary?"

Captain Perona stared at her. "You *read* the diary? Really read it? All of it?"

"Why, yes."

"It is incredible," said Captain Perona, respectfully though. "No one in our family ever read it. It was so very difficult. Only professors can read such old-fashioned script."

"I'm a professor."

"Oh, no. You are a woman."

"I'm—a—professor!"

"How strange. Well, if you are a professor and really did read the diary, then you must know what it says about the first Emile Perona—where he went and all the things he saw and did."

"Yes, I do."

"Then tell me, please."

"But there's so much of it!" Janet protested. "Why, it would take days and days!"

"Good," said Captain Perona.

"But I haven't time! I'm leaving on the bus!"

"I am, too," said Captain Perona.

"There still wouldn't be enough time. I'm only going to stay at the Hotel Azteca another two days, and then I'm going to Mazatlan."

"I am too," said Captain Perona.

"Why?"

"It is a military matter."

"It is not! You're just going to follow me!"

"Please, senorita," said Captain Perona severely. "Are you accusing me of being a—a—What is that fascinating word? I have it! Masher! Are you accusing me of being a masher?"

"Yes."

"I will have you know, senorita, that I am a gentleman and an officer of the Mexican Army. I have many important and confidential duties. Do you think I would waste my time following a mere woman around—even a very pretty one?"

"What?" said Janet, surprised.

"Oh, yes," said Captain Perona. "You are very pretty, indeed. Has not anyone told you that before? What is the matter with the men in the United States?"

"Why, I—I don't—"

"You blush, too," said Captain Perona. "That is very attractive, I think."

Janet swallowed hard. "Well... Please tell me some more about Ebenezer Ruggles being a thief. That's very hard for me to believe."

"A long time ago he was traveling in Mexico. He was invited to the home of my grandfather and grandmother. He was their guest, you understand? He collected books at that time—old books."

Janet nodded. "I knew he did. He left his collection to the school. It's enormous."

"No doubt. My grandfather and grandmother showed him the heirlooms of my family. We have a great many. They are very precious to us. This Ruggles villain saw the diary of Gil De Lico. He was fascinated. He could not take his hands off it, although he could not read it, of course. He wanted it for his own. He hinted and hinted, and finally he asked my grandfather for the diary."

"Well?" Janet inquired.

"So my grandfather said he could have it. And he took it, the thief!"

"But why?" Janet asked, puzzled. "If your grandfather gave him the diary, how does that make him a thief?"

"Ah!" said Captain Perona. "That is the whole trick! We did not understand until my mother explained. She was very angry when she heard about it. You see, when you are a guest in Mexico everything in the house is yours. That is the custom here. When you enter, the host says: 'This house is yours.' He means it."

"That's a very beautiful custom," Janet said.

"Certainly. Unless dishonest foreigners take advantage of it. Like that thief, Ruggles. He knew he could not buy the book, but he also knew—since he was a guest—that if he asked for it my grandfather could not think of refusing him because that would be a violation of hospitality. My grandfather was very sad, but he thought he could do nothing else but present the diary to Ruggles. He thought Ruggles would do the same thing in the same circumstances. My mother says he would not have."

"She's right," said Janet.

"So that makes Ruggles a thief," said Captain Perona. "A swindler. A trickster. He takes advantage of a custom in which he does not join or believe. He abuses his privilege as a guest to rob my family. But I will fix things. I will go to this school and swindle the book back. I will offer to buy it and then pay in counterfeit money or with a bad check."

Janet stared at him. "You can't do that!"

"Oh, yes. I am very clever at swindling, and I understand the people in the United States are exceedingly stupid about such things."

"You'll be arrested!"

"All right," said Captain Perona. "I have heard there is no justice in the United States, but I will get the diary back for my family, so I will be contented in prison."

Janet cleared her throat. "The—the diary isn't at the school now."

Captain Perona sat up straight. "What? Have you been lying

133

to me?"

"No! I said I found it there and read it there. Mr. Doan was the one who told you it was there now. I didn't."

"Where is it?"

"In my suitcase at the hotel Azteca."

"Good!" Captain Perona chortled triumphantly. "You can give it to me!"

"No, I can't. The school doesn't know I have it. If I didn't bring it back, they'd say I stole it and put me in jail."

Captain Perona shook his head. "I cannot understand this at all. It seems very weird that they put people in prison in the United States for taking things from thieves. A thief does not own what he steals. It should be perfectly all right to take such things away from him and return them to their real owners. It must be that there are so many thieves in the United States that they have gotten laws passed to protect themselves from honest people."

"The school didn't steal your book!" Janet protested.

"If it is Ebenezer Ruggles' school—and you said it was—then it certainly did. He stole it for the school. It is all the same thing."

Janet moved her hands helplessly, giving it up.

Captain Perona said: "And what are you doing with our diary, if you please? Why did you steal it from the school?"

"I didn't steal it!"

Captain Perona shrugged. "All right. But what are you doing with it?"

"I was interested. I wanted to go to the places that were mentioned in it and see what they looked like now. I wanted the diary for reference."

"What places?" Captain Perona asked suspiciously.

"The places that Lieutenant Perona went."

"Why?"

"To see them!"

"Why?"

"Stop saying that! It's none of your business!"

"It is," Captain Perona corrected politely. "It is my ancestor, hence it is my business. Why, please?"

"I won't tell you!"

"Hmmm," said Captain Perona. He sat for a moment watching Janet in thoughtful silence, and then he said: "Did you know that Lieutenant Perona, my ancestor, was a very immoral man? That he forced his attentions on hundreds of poor, innocent, helpless Indian maidens?"

"That's a lie!" Janet snapped indignantly.

"Ha!" said Captain Perona. "I thought so! You are not interested in where my ancestor went. You are interested in him personally."

Janet got up and started to walk away from him. She walked determinedly, holding her head high, clicking her heels hard. After she had gone about fifty yards, Captain Perona said from behind her:

"Senorita."

"Go away. Leave me alone."

"Senorita, it is said that I resemble my ancestor very closely."

"That's a lie, too. He was a gentleman. You stop following me! Go away!"

"Senorita, unless you give me my diary it will be my sad duty to arrest you."

Janet stopped short. "What?"

"Yes," said Captain Perona.

"You wouldn't dare! Why would you arrest me?"

"I do not know," Captain Perona admitted. "But I will think of some reason."

Janet stuttered with fury. "Why, you—you—"

"Want me to poke him one for you, dearie?"

Janet whirled around, startled. The woman who had spoken was watching them, looking grimly amused. She had gray, frizzy hair that floated around her weather-beaten face like a lopsided halo, and she was wearing an orange smock. She had a bundle of sticks that Janet identified as a collapsed easel tucked under one arm.

"So it is you, again," said Captain Perona sourly.

"Yeah, baby. And I'm going to tell Colonel Callao that you're annoying tourists."

"That greasy pig!" said Captain Perona.

"I'll tell him you called him that, too. And mind your manners. Introduce me to the little lady."

Captain Perona said awkwardly: "Senorita, may I present to you Amanda Tracy?"

"Hah!" said Amanda Tracy. "I thought so! You don't even know her name! What is it, dearie?"

"Janet Martin."

"Howdy, Janet," said Amanda Tracy. "Want to come along with me? I'm looking for a sucker to sell one of my smears to. Don't let Perona worry you. If he tries to arrest you, I'll push him in the puss with this easel."

"You are flouting military authority," Captain Perona warned her. "Besides, I am escorting the senorita on a sight-seeing tour."

"Is he?" Amanda Tracy asked Janet.

"Well, he started to."

"I will continue it," said Captain Perona stiffly.

"To the jail?" Janet asked.

Captain Perona cleared his throat. "Not at the moment. To the museum. It is very beautiful, senorita. Full of many ancient treasures."

"I'd like to go," said Janet, "but not if you're going to threaten me and—and accuse me—of things."

"If he does," said Amanda Tracy, "just come and tell me. I'll run him clear out of town."

"Bah!" said Captain Perona. "Good day." He took Janet's arm firmly and started to lead her away.

"Hey, Perona," said Amanda Tracy. "There's another tourist wandering around you'd better keep an eye on. A little fat number called Doan. He's a crook if ever I saw one."

"Mr. Doan's a detective," Janet told her.

Amanda Tracy shrugged husky shoulders. "Maybe so. That wouldn't mean he wasn't a crook. Better watch him, Perona. He's a tough cookie, and that dog of his is a bad dream."

"I am watching him," said Captain Perona. "Kindly attend to your painting and leave my business to me."

"From me to you—phooey." said Amanda Tracy. "So long, dearie. See you later." She walked on into the market square, easel trailing behind her.

"She is an artist," Captain Perona told Janet. "She lives here and paints and paints, and everything she paints is most horrible, but tourists buy it and pay good sums for it. I think tourists are crazy, myself."

"I'm one," Janet reminded.

"Senorita, you are trying to trick me into insulting you, as I understand is the custom of women from the United States. They trick a man into insulting them, and then they threaten to have the man arrested unless he marries them. They are so unattractive they cannot get a husband in any other way. But it is useless for you to try that method on me. I refuse flatly to marry you."

"Why, you—you arrogant, ignorant—"

"Never mind," Captain Perona comforted. "Perhaps you can find someone more stupid and marry him. Shall we proceed?"

Janet was speechless. She tried to drag back, scuffling her heels, but Captain Perona pulled her along with no effort at all. They turned a corner and followed a straggling street down the steep slope of the mountain.

"This is the older part of the town," Captain Perona explained. "Some has been rebuilt, of course. But some is very ancient, indeed."

The buildings here looked lower and thicker, and their windows were mere slits. Their walls were not white, either, but faded to a mottled gray by age and weather.

"There is the museum," Captain Perona said.

It was a long one-story building nudged in sideways against the slope. The front had once been built up high, like the false front of a western store, but it had crumbled away in jagged, cracked crevices. The immense black door was slightly ajar.

It was old, this building. But the word old was not enough to express the aged, tired look of it. There was an air of decay—of ancient-ness beyond expression. It was a thing of another age—something that had been left behind in the march of the centuries and was now forlorn and deserted and alone.

Janet breathed in deeply, staring at it with a sort of awed fascination, forgetting all about her quarrel with Captain Perona.

"It was a church once, as you know," he said softly. "The very first church in this whole state. It was built by a priest, who came with Lieutenant Emile Perona and Gil De Lico, with the help of my ancestor's soldiers and converted Indians. Services were held here for many, many years, and then a hundred and fifty years ago there was an earthquake that shook it badly. You can see the front—how it is broken away. After that it wasn't thought to be safe, and another and larger church was built in the center of town."

Janet didn't answer. Captain Perona was watching her with a sympathetic little smile.

"It takes one's breath away if one imagines all it has seen and endured. The people, when they left it, thought there would be other earthquakes, but there have been no serious ones. Of course, if we ever have another bad one the old church will surely be destroyed. It will collapse. Shall we go inside, senorita?"

"Yes," said Janet.

They went up the steps, and the great iron hinges squealed as Captain Perona pushed the heavy door open wider. The air in the tiny vestibule was thin and dry, and dust motes danced in the narrow shaft of sunlight that filtered through a side window. The shadows were as old and patient as time.

"Yes?" said a soft voice. "Yes? May I help you?"

He was standing in the doorway ahead of them—tall and dressed in black that rustled slightly when he moved. His face had the delicately soft pallor of old ivory, and his eyes were long and slanted at little at the corners, luminously black.

"This is Tio Riquez," Captain Perona said to Janet. "He has been the keeper of this museum for many years. The senorita is a North American, Tio, but not ignorant like most of them. She knows much of our history and is very interested in it."

"You shall see my treasures, senorita," said Tio Riquez, smiling. "They are very beautiful. Come."

Janet followed him through the doorway into a long, narrow room with age-blackened beams across its ceiling. The floor was stone, and through the centuries shuffling feet had worn smooth little pathways in it.

"Oh!" said Janet breathlessly.

The windows were narrow niches, with the sun bright and piercing back of them. Its yellow shafts were like spotlights focused on the displays along the walls. They were not moldering relics, these ancient things. They had been cleaned and restored with infinite care.

"You like this?" asked Tio Riquez.

Janet nodded wordlessly.

The sunlight reflected from burnished conquistador armor, from gold hammered Damascus steel, from the linked plates that had protected the chest of a horse when there were only sixteen horses in all of America. A bell-mouthed harquebus slanted over the red leather of a high-backed saddle, and two pistols as long as a man's arm crossed their clumsy barrels above a thinly wicked lance.

There were native weapons, too, jag-toothed and ugly. And handwoven cloths with the colors in them still brightly defiant. And on beyond the weapons were household goods—drinking cups and plates and even a lopsided spoon beaten out of copper ore. There was the frail shadow of a wooden water canteen and vases made with delicate, sure grace. And then, also, the clumsy tools that had chipped and scraped the rock of Los Altos four hundred-odd years ago.

Janet wandered like a child lost in a candy store, gasping as she saw and comprehended each new wonder. She made the circuit of the room once and then again and then came back and sat down beside Captain Perona on a hand-carved wooden bench.

"They're wonderful," she said, sighing. "Are they all *yours*, Mr. Riquez?"

"No," said Tio Riquez, chuckling. "They belong to the state, senorita. I speak of them as mine because I have been here with them so long. It gives me pleasure to see you admire them, too.

Many people nowadays are bored with the old and beautiful."

"They're just wonderful," Janet repeated. "I'd like to look and look... May I see the cellar, too?"

The sound of her voice echoed a little and fell in the stillness.

"Pardon?" said Tio Riquez. "The what?"

"The cellar," Janet said. "Underneath here"

"There is no cellar," said Tio Riquez.

"But there is," said Janet. She turned to Captain Perona. "It tells all about building this church in Gil De Lico's diary. They dug a cellar in solid rock because they wanted a storage place for supplies and seed they were leaving for the priest in charge."

"It was filled up long ago," said Tio Riquez.

"Why?" Janet asked. "Why would they fill it up? It was very difficult to dig, and they put a concealed door on it—a balanced and pivoted stone."

"The church was built over many times," said Tio Riquez. "They cemented up the doorway."

"Why, no," said Janet. "That's it, there. That oblong stone. You just push at the top. Let me show—"

"Senorita," said Tio Riquez, "it is forbidden to tamper with the property of the museum."

"Of course it is," Captain Perona said. "Naturally. Come along now, senorita. We are not interested in imaginary cellars, and it is boring and close in here." He jerked at her arm urgently.

Janet pulled back. "I'm not going! I want to sit here and look and look and look. Why, I saved for years and came thousands of miles—" She stared at Captain Perona. "What? What is it?"

Captain Perona's face was white. He didn't answer.

Tio Riquez said mockingly. "Captain Perona is surprised. He has been looking for me so industriously, you see, and now he has suddenly found me where I was all the time—right under his nose. Stand still, Captain."

Tio Riquez had a revolver in his hand. It was a big revolver with a pearl handle and a long, elaborately silvered barrel.

Captain Perona had his right hand inside the loose front of his coat.

"No," warned Tio Riquez. "Don't. It is too late for that now, Captain. You didn't think fast enough or act quickly enough. You were too interested in the senorita."

"What—what's the matter?" Janet demanded.

"She knows nothing about this—or you," Captain Perona said. "She is just a harmless tourist."

"No," Tio Riquez denied. "Not harmless any more. The cellar is there, senorita. You will see it now. You and Captain Perona. Push the stone as you suggested. It works very easily."

Janet swallowed. "What's the matter with the cellar? What—what's down there?"

Tio Riquez smiled at her. "Guns, senorita. Rifles. A great many of them. A trifle obsolete, but not as much as you'd think. Many of the troops in your up-to-date country are armed with Springfield rifles of a similar model. Captain Perona has been hunting them and some others I know about. Hunting me, too. Releasing old companions of mine and following them, hoping they knew where to find me. They didn't know, as a matter of fact, Captain. They knew ways they could make themselves known, so I could contact them if I wished. They didn't know my identity or where I was hiding. I contacted Garcia and had him come here. I could have used him in a little project I have in mind."

Janet said: "The rattlesnake! You're the one—"

"Yes," said Tio Riquez. "I thought that was rather clever of me, didn't you? I didn't know just what would happen when I threw the snake in with the soldier, but I imagined the results would have been violent enough to warn Garcia, and in that way I didn't have to risk revealing myself to him or to anyone else."

"Who are you?" Janet asked.

"Hasn't Captain Perona told you? I am Bautiste Bonofile, and I've been convicted of murder, armed rebellion, train robbery, kidnapping and a few other things I can't recall at the moment. Do you know what that means—to you?"

Janet shook her head wordlessly.

"I can't let you go now, senorita. I'm sorry, but it took me many years and much effort to build up this identity, and I like it. Open

141

the cellar door. And you, Captain Perona. Don't move at all. You are going to die anyway, as you know, but it would take you much longer to do it if I shot you in the stomach."

Janet backed slowly and woodenly away from the two of them, back and back, until the stone wall felt cool through her thin dress. She put out one arm and pushed at the pivot stone. The stone moved reluctantly, and as if in protest the earth growled and grumbled deep within itself.

"Don't move," Tio Riquez warned sharply. "It is just an earth tremor. We have many of them here. It is nothing."

The earth rose to make a roaring denial of that. The floor rocked sickeningly, and Janet saw a crack widen and run down the crumbling wall like a quick black snake. Dust swirled in a blinding cloud that thrust stinging fingers into her eyes.

A shot plopped out dully, dwarfed by the greater uproar, and then Captain Perona's voice shouted:

"Janet! Run! Run outside!"

There were more shots, like a string of small firecrackers in the distance, and the stone floor heaved and moaned in its agony. Janet staggered away from the wall, and a rafter swung down slowly in front of her and shattered into ancient shards. She had lost all sense of direction, and she cried out weakly and breathlessly.

Captain Perona' s arm whipped around her waist and dragged her forward. She could hear his short, sharp gasps for breath. He was swearing in Spanish.

The floor stretched like the loose hide of an animal. Janet fell and tripped Captain Perona. Dust smothered them, and a piece of armor rolled and clanged brightly past.

Captain Perona was up again, staggering drunkenly. His fingers dug into Janet's arms. He thrust and pulled and bunted her with his shoulder, and then they were in the tiny vestibule.

The dust was thinner, and Janet stared with burning eyes at the side wall. It was bulging inward slowly and awfully, as though a giant fist was pushing it from the outside. The big front door was closed now, and Captain Perona gripped the collarlike latch in both hands and heaved back.

Janet wondered dully why he didn't just open the door and get them out of here. It was dangerous. The wall was behaving in a way no wall should or could. It was coming inexorably closer. And so were the other walls now.

The cords stood out on the back of Captain Perona's neck, and the shoulder seam of his coat split suddenly. The door moved and threw him backward, and then he had Janet's arm again, and they were outside running down the steps that slid under them like an escalator.

Janet looked back. The old church was wavering, crumbling, slumping slowly down. And then the earth gave one sharp final heave. The church groaned under that death blow, and then it fell majestically in on itself and was no longer a building but merely a heap of rubble with dust rising over it like a pall.

As suddenly as the noise had come, it was gone. The silence was so intense it was a pressure against the eardrums. Sensation returned to Janet like a stinging slap in the face, and she was suddenly more frightened than she had ever been in her life.

Captain Perona seized her by both shoulders and shook her until her teeth rattled. His face was dust-smeared and pallid, staring tensely into hers.

"Are you hurt?" he yelled. "Answer me? Are you hurt?"

"N—no," Janet whimpered, and then she caught her breath and her self-possession and was instantly angry. "You stop that! Let go of me!"

"*Gracias a Dios!*" said Captain Perona reverently. "I was afraid for you. You would not speak. You would only look without seeing anything."

"Was that an earthquake?" Janet asked.

Captain Perona stared at her out of bleary, reddened eyes. "Was that—was that..." He drew a deep breath. "Yes, senorita. That was an earthquake."

"Well, don't be so superior! I've never been in one before!" Janet turned to look at the pile of rubble that had been the church, and then she was suddenly frightened all over again. "Oh! If we hadn't gotten out..." She remembered, then, and looked at the split shoulder-seam of Captain Perona's coat. "If you hadn't gotten us out... Your hand is hurt!"

Captain Perona sucked ruefully at his torn fingers. "I pulled too hard at the door. It was stuck, and I was really in a great hurry."

"You—you saved my life."

"Yes," Captain Perona admitted. "I did. And you are a fool."

"What?" Janet cried. "What?"

"I said you were a fool. Why did you not inform me about the location of that cellar?"

"How did I know you didn't know it was there? It was your ancestor who built the church!"

"So it was," Captain Perona agreed. There was dust even on his eyelashes. "But you should have told me anyway. Then I would have caught that devil."

"Oh," said Janet, remembering more. "That Tio—that Bautiste person! He had a gun!"

"Yes," said Captain Perona. "When the floor moved it threw him off balance, and I hit him with my fist." He looked at the fist distastefully. "We Mexicans do not believe in brawling and mauling at people with our fists as you people do, but I did not have time to draw my gun and shoot him."

"Somebody shot," Janet said.

"Yes. He did. But the dust blinded him."

Janet looked at the church. "Where ..."

"I hope he's under that," Captain Perona answered grimly. "But I am afraid he is not. He is too smart and too quick. He probably has a dozen secret exits. If we could get out, so could he. If you had only told me about that cellar ...

"Why did that give everything away?" Janet demanded.

"We have spent a long time narrowing down possibilities. We suspected Bautiste Bonofile was hidden somewhere near here, and we knew that if he was, there was also a cache near here because he has been selling loot. Not rifles—but other things he had stolen and hidden long ago. When Garcia came here, we were sure we were right. As soon as you mentioned that cellar, I thought that must be the cache. I tried not to show it, but he knew. He had no intention of letting me get away after that."

"But you'd have been missed at once."

"Yes. You, also. But he would have had time to remove some of the most valuable loot and to disappear himself if he thought he would be suspected. I do not think he would have been. He has had his position as Tio Riquez for over ten years. He is a fixture in Los Altos."

Faintly, all around them, like some weird off-scene chorus, cries and shouts began to rise. A woman wept in wailing shrieks. The dust clouds had heightened and thinned, and the sun showed ghastly yellow-red through it.

Captain Perona straightened up. "I forget myself! I must go at once, senorita! There must be a guard put here by this building, and there will be injured people to care for and property to protect. I must find my men. Will you go to the main square and wait? You will be perfectly safe now, I think."

"Yes." said Janet. "Go ahead. Hurry. I'll be all right."

Captain Perona trotted up the steep street toward the marketplace. Janet watched him until he disappeared, and then turned to stare at her surroundings.

She felt a sort of awed disbelief. There was no real change. The squat houses were still there, just as they had been before. There were fresh cracks in the walls, and roofs sagged, and tile lay broken in the street, but there was no vast waste of desolation such as she had expected.

And the people were there, too. Scurrying in and out of their houses like ants on a griddle—afraid to stay where they were, and afraid to go anywhere else. Janet saw a woman in her black, rustling Sunday dress kneeling quite alone in the middle of the street, praying. A man came out of the house across the way carrying a wicker bird cage with a parakeet inside. He stopped and stared cautiously in all directions and then yelled crazily and pelted up the street with the bird cage flopping and the parakeet screeching.

"*Senorita! Senorita Americana!*"

Janet turned around. A ragged little girl with a smear of dirt

145

around her mouth was staring up at her with eyes that were as bright and gleaming as black jewels. She wasn't scared. She was panting with delicious excitement.

"*Senorita, venga usted! La otra senorita—la turista rica! Venga!*"

She seized Janet's hand and pulled at her, and Janet followed. The little girl danced beside her, gesturing with impatience. She turned the first corner into a narrow lane.

"*Aqui! Mira!*"

There was a little group of people, both men and women, standing there in the lane, and they turned at the little girl's cry, separating.

Janet saw the blond, loose swirl of hair first, like spun gold against the dust. Her breath caught in her throat, and she ran forward and stopped suddenly. Patricia Van Osdel was lying crumpled on her side. Her profile was white and austere and aristocratic. Her eyes were closed, and a trickle of blood made a bright, jagged streak across her cheek.

A little man wearing a faded serape knelt beside her. He looked up at Janet with sad, regretful eyes.

"She is—died," he said in careful English. He made a shy, quick gesture with his hands. "All died."

DOAN CAME OUT ON THE AVENIDA REVOLUCION, and it seemed to him now that the street was appropriately named. It looked as though it had just gone through a revolution or one had gone through it. Broken tile lay in windrows, and a stovepipe, canted over a wall, leered like a warped cannon. A house across the way had lost its front wall, and its owners capered around inside like zany actors in a movie set. They were making enough noise for a massacre, but none of them seemed to be injured.

Right in front of Doan a little boy sat in the center of the street with his eyes shut and his fists clenched and his mouth wide open. He was howling mightily, and no one paid him the slightest attention.

Doan walked over to him. "Hey, shorty. Where are you hurt?"

The little boy turned off his howl and opened his eyes cautiously. He looked Doan over and then saw Carstairs. His mouth made a round O of admiration. He looked back at Doan and smiled winningly. He had three front teeth missing.

"Gimme dime."

Doan gave him a dime. The little boy tested it with a couple of his remaining teeth.

"Denk goo," he said.

He put the dime carefully in the pocket of his ragged shirt, shut his eyes and opened his mouth. He started to yell exactly where he had left off.

Doan walked on down the street. The houses, and apparently their inmates, were mostly intact. Roofs sagged, and broken glass glittered dangerously, and open doors leaned like weary drunks. Women hopped and ran and screamed, and children squalled. Men worked feverishly carrying things out of their houses into the street and then back into their houses again.

Doan went down the steep slope to the market square. There was more noise and even less sense here. The quake had jarred the display counters and rolled their goods out into the gutters in jumbled piles. Owners—and evidently some non-owners—fought and scrambled over the piles like carrion crows.

Doan found Bartolome sitting on top of a ten-foot heap of debris. Bartolome was slumped forward, holding his head in his hands.

"Are you hurt?" Doan asked.

"I am dying," said Bartolome.

"You don't look it," Doan told him. "Where'd you park the bus?"

"Under," said Bartolome, pointing down.

Doan stared at the heap of debris. "You mean the bus is underneath all that?"

"Yes," said Bartolome, dignified in his grief. "It is catastrophe beyond reason."

"Where are the passengers?"

"I do not know," said Bartolome. "And I do not care. Of passengers there are a great number too many—of the bus only one too less. It is unendurable."

A thin harassed young man in a smeared khaki uniform hurried across the plaza toward them. He said to Doan

"*Dispenseme, senor, pero donde esta—*"

"I can't speak Spanish," Doan interrupted.

"English?" said the young man. "Good. I am Lieutenant Ortega, the medical officer in charge of this district. Did you come with the party in this bus?"

"Yes," Doan answered. "Was there anyone in it when the quake dumped all this on top of it?"

"No. I was just across the square. All the party had left the bus before that. Will you please find them if you can? Tell them to report here and they will be taken care of. If any are injured, bring them to that white building there, and I will attend them. If they cannot be moved, send for me. Will you do this at once?"

"Sure," said Doan.

"You will pardon me... There are injured..."

He trotted back across the square, pausing to bark angry orders at a pair of soldiers who were standing and gaping around them with the casual air of sightseers at a fair. The soldiers jumped to attention and then followed him at a snappy run.

"Which way did the others go?" Doan asked Bartolome.

"I am in a state of nervous collapse," Bartolome informed him. "I have many things on my mind. The one with the loud mouth and the stupid wife and the hellish child went in that direction. The others I did not notice."

Doan crossed the square, and Carstairs followed, picking his way distastefully through the debris and the yowling throng that was growing in numbers and volume every second. Doan took the first side street and found Mr. and Mrs. Henshaw in the middle of it fifty yards further along.

Mrs. Henshaw was sitting down on the pavement with her peasant skirt draped in a swirl over her chubby legs. One of the lenses in her pince-nez had cracked, and she glared narrow-eyed through the whole one.

"I can't get up," she informed Doan. "I'm paralyzed. Call an ambulance."

"There ain't no ambulance," said Henshaw wearily. "And anyway you ain't paralyzed. You ran out of that store like a rabbit with its pants on fire."

"It's shock," said Mrs. Henshaw. "My nerve centers are shattered. I can feel them."

"Baloney," said Henshaw.

"It's your fault," Mrs. Henshaw accused bitterly.

"What?" Henshaw yelped. "My fault? Did I think up this earthquake?"

"You brought me here."

"Now damn it, I didn't. It was you that brought me. You're the one that heard about Mouser Puddledip at the Ladies' Aid and insisted on seeing this anthill because he once lived here and it was full of artistic history."

"*Monsieur*," Mrs. Henshaw corrected. "*Monsieur Predilip*. This town and its beautiful primitive surroundings were his inspiration."

"They're a pain in the neck to me. Did you feel that earthquake we had, Doan?"

"Faintly," said Doan. "Where's Mortimer?"

"Hi-yo, Silver!" Mortimer screeched. He came sailing across the street carrying a pair of silvered spurs in one fist and a sombrero so big he could have used it for a tent in the other. "Look, Pop! Look what I snitched! Here. Hold 'em while I go back for another load. Boy, I wish the gang was here!"

Henshaw took the spurs and sombrero helplessly. "Now look, you little rat! These belong to somebody!"

"Hi-yo, Silver!" Mortimer yelled. "A-waay!" He pelted back across the street and dived into the broken doorway of a store.

Mrs. Henshaw got up instantly. "Mortimer! You come right out of there! Don't you touch anything! Don't you dare! *Mortimer!*"

"The hell with it," said Henshaw wearily. "I think I'll get paralyzed myself."

Doan said: "When you get around to it, report back in the square where the bus was parked."

"Was?" Henshaw repeated. "What do you mean—*was?*"

"A building fell on it."

"No foolin'," said Henshaw. "Well, how do we get back to the Hotel Azteca? Ride a mule?"

"I won't ride one of those nasty little beasts." Mrs. Henshaw snapped. "They're dirty. Don't you argue with me, either! I won't do it, that's all."

"Have you seen any of the other passengers?" Doan asked.

"That bird, Greg, was ahead of us. I haven't seen him since the big shake."

Doan and Carstairs walked on, and behind them Mrs. Henshaw shrieked:

"Mortimer! Put that down! Don't you dare eat that horrible candy! It's *got germs!*"

Doan and Carstairs detoured around a group of people busily burrowing into what had evidently been a bakery, and then a voice called:

"Doan."

Greg was leaning against a cracked building wall. His handsome face was drawn now, and his lips were pale with agony. He had his scarf wrapped around his right arm above the elbow. He was holding his right forearm cradled across his chest with his left hand.

"Do you know where I can find a doctor?" he asked.

"Back in the square. The big white building on the west side. Want me to help you?"

"No. It's just my arm. It's broken. I fell over that damned horse trough there when the quake came."

"Where is Miss Van Osdel?" Doan asked.

"Who wants to know?"

"I do," said Doan.

"Try and find out," Greg told him, and walked back up the street, leaning over sideways to ease his arm.

"Hey, fatso!"

Amanda Tracy came up at a lumbering run, dragging the easel behind her. Her hair was frizzed more wildly than ever, and her eyes gleamed bright and excited in the leathery toughness of her face.

"Some shimmy, huh? Listen, fat, I'm gonna make my fortune out of it!"

"How?" Doan asked.

Amanda Tracy pulled the canvas out of the easel clamps and thrust it in front of his face. "See that? That's a picture of some buildings, believe it or not. See how squeegeed and cockeyed they look?"

"Yes," Doan admitted.

"Well, they weren't ruins when I painted them, but they are now. Get it? The ruins of Los Altos. I got a lot more pictures just as lousy as this one. I'll sell them for souvenirs of the disaster!"

"If you live in that house where you were when I first saw you—and your pictures are there—you'd better run up and take them in out of the weather."

"Hah?" Amanda Tracy barked.

"You haven't got a roof any more."

151

"Wow!" said Amanda Tracy. She ran up the street, whacking at anyone who was unfortunate enough to get in her way with the legs of the easel. "Gangway! Gangway!"

Somebody poked Doan in the stomach. He looked down into the face of a little girl who had a smear of dirt around her mouth. Her eyes were black beads that goggled at him excitedly.

"Senor! La senorita rica y la otra senorita turista son..."

Doan was shaking his head.

The little girl shook her head, too.

"No habla Mexicano?"

"I guess not," said Doan.

The little girl dug at her ear with one finger, and then her face lighted up. *"Mira!"* She struck herself in the head with her fist. "Bong!" She staggered dramatically and fell down in the street.

Doan got it. "Where? Who? Which way?"

The little girl jumped up. *"Venga usted!"*

They went down a steep side street and through a lane where chickens squawked and scurried frantically to get out of Carstairs' way. They turned to the right and to the left and scattered a family group who were trying to haul a sewing machine out through a shattered window.

"Mil," the little girl shrilled, *"Ahieston las senoritas!"*

The little group was still there in the lane, and they drew back now, murmuring among themselves. Doan saw Janet Martin and the little man in the faded scrape kneeling down in the dust beside the limp form of Patricia Van Osdel.

"What is it?" Doan asked breathlessly. "Is she hurt?"

The little man shook his head sadly.

Janet said in a stifled voice: "She's dead, Mr. Doan. Her head... I think she died instantly."

"Let me see." Doan knelt down. The golden hair was as soft as mist in his fingers, and then he saw the deep-sunken wound in the back of the small head. "Yes."

He stood up and looked around slowly—at the ground, at the walls of the buildings on either side of the lane.

"Was she moved?" he asked. "Did someone carry her in

here?"

"No," said the little man. "No. Was lie here."

"Why?" Janet inquired blankly. "What difference does that make?"

"None right now," said Doan. "You go on up to the main drag and find Captain Perona. He ought to know about this right away. If you can't find him, there's a lieutenant by the name of Ortega in the big white building across from where the bus parked. Tell him. I'll wait here."

"All right," said Janet obediently. She turned and ran out of the lane.

Doan squatted down on his heels.

The little man nodded at him shyly and said, *"Es lastima."*

"Probably it is," Doan agreed.

A voice, far away, shouted an indistinguishable string of words. Other voices, closer, took up the cry. Excitement gathered like an electric charge in the air, and the little man's eyes were wide and shocked staring into Doan's.

"What's the matter?" Doan asked.

The little man struggled for words. *"Puente!"* He braced his forefingers together end-to-end and stared at Doan over the top of them. *"Puente!"*

"Arch," Doan guessed. "Roof." Then he jumped. "Bridge!"

"Si! Si, si! Bridge! Is away!"

"What?"

"Gone. No longer."

"You mean the earthquake shook the bridge down?" Doan demanded.

The little man nodded. "Si. Shook down. Bust."

"That makes everything just dandy," Doan commented.

The small girl with the dirty face burst through the onlookers blubbering words in a stuttering stream. She planted herself in front of Doan and waved both arms at him.

"What's the beef, sister?" Doan inquired.

The girl pointed down at Patricia Van Osdel and then held up one finger.

"One," said Doan, nodding.

The girl pointed back the way she had come and held up two fingers.

"Two," said Doan, and then he leaped to his feet. "What? Another? Who? Where?"

"Venga usted!"

They went down the lane—the girl in front and Doan and Carstairs right behind her, and the little man running along behind with his serape flipping in the breeze of their passage. They went around the corner and up the street and across into another lane.

A muttering, peering crowd of people was huddled close around a fat woman kneeling on the ground. Doan looked over the fat woman's shoulder and saw the long, bony form of Maria, the personal maid, flattened on the dusty ground. Maria's face was pallidly white and empty, and the mole was like a black spider crouched on her cheek.

Doan dropped down beside her and touched one skinny, outstretched arm. "She's not dead! She's—"

The fat woman shoved him angrily. *"No! Cuidado!"*

"What's your trouble?" Doan asked.

"She feex," said the little man.

"Is she a nurse?" Doan demanded.

"Nurse?" said the little man, testing the word. "No." He pointed to the small girl and then held his hands about a foot apart. "Child," said Doan. "Dwarf. Midget. Baby!"

"Si. Baby."

"You mean the old doll is a baby nurse?"

"No. Middle momma."

"Baby," Doan said. "Middle. Momma. Midwife!"

"Si."

"Well, this is a little out of her regular line of business," Doan commented, "but she probably knows more about it than I do."

A pudgy little man with an enormous mustache bustled out of the house next door carrying a steaming kettle of water carefully in front of him. He had clean cloths folded over both his forearms. He put the kettle down on the ground beside the fat woman. She selected one of the cloths, moistened it in the water, and dabbed carefully at Maria's temple.

"*Muy malo,*" she said.

"Hurts bad," the little man translated.

Doan nodded absently. "Yeah. I can see that."

The fat woman snapped her fingers, and the pudgy man instantly presented her with a pair of blunt surgical scissors. She snipped at Maria's lank hair.

"Sister," said the little man, pointing at the man who had brought the water.

"She's his sister?" Doan inquired.

"No. He."

"He's her sister?"

"Si."

"I don't get that," said Doan. "Sister, sister... Assistant! He assists her!"

"Si. Sisted. Also hatband."

"Hatband," Doan repeated. "Husband?"

"Si, si!"

Doan nodded at Carstairs. "I'm catching on, kid. I'll be able to rattle off Spanish in no time at all."

Carstairs looked skeptical.

The small girl shrieked suddenly: "*Soldados!*"

Sergeant Obrian was peering around the corner at them. He turned back now and called:

"Captain! I found him! Here he is!"

Captain Perona and Janet came into the lane. There were two soldiers behind them, one carrying a rolled army stretcher on his shoulder.

"Now what is this?" Captain Perona demanded.

"It's Maria!" Janet exclaimed. "She's Miss Van Osdel's maid! Is she—is she—"

"She's not dead," Doan said. "From the looks of her eyes, I think her skull is fractured. She got a smaller dose of the same thing Van Osdel did. You'd better run her up and let Ortega look her over."

Captain Perona nodded to the soldiers. They unrolled the stretcher and lifted Maria on it with the help of Sergeant Obrian and the fat midwife and her assistant.

"Stay here, Sergeant," Captain Perona said.

The two soldiers carried Maria carefully out of the lane.

Captain Perona was staring at Doan. "Just what did you have to do with this?"

"Not a thing," said Doan. "I was sitting over there by Van Osdel, waiting for you, when this little kid—Where'd she go? She was here a minute ago. Anyway, she came along and said there was another casualty down here. So I came to see if I could help. Ask Ignatz, here. He was with me all the time."

"Es verdad?"

Captain Perona inquired, looking at the little man.

"Si, Capitan."

"That rock over there is what hit Maria," said Doan, pointing to a jagged piece of stone slightly larger than a paving brick. "You'd better save it."

"Why?"

"Because I'm pretty sure it's the same one that hit Patricia Van Osdel."

"What?" said Captain Perona, startled.

Doan nodded. "Yeah. There was nothing near the Van Osdel that could have given her the kind of a bat she got. But that rock *is* just about the right shape. Of course, I could be wrong, but you'd better check up."

"State plainly what you mean!" Captain Perona ordered.

"I don't think either Maria or the Van Osdel was hit by accident. I think they were in that alley where Patricia was found, talking to some third party. When the earthquake let loose, the third party picked up that rock and slammed Patricia with it. Maria ran. The third party chased her and caught her here in this alley and bopped her with the same rock. During the earthquake everyone was yelling and running back and forth like crazy, so no one would pay much attention. Maybe you might find some witnesses, though, if you look."

"What made you think of all this?"

"Patricia Van Osdel was carrying a purse—a big red patent leather affair about the size of a brief case. It's gone."

Captain Perona looked at Janet, and she nodded.

"Miss Van Osdel *did* have a purse like that. I noticed it, and it wasn't in the lane where she was found."

Captain Perona looked back at Doan. "Have you got any more remarks to make at this time?"

"Well, there was one other thing."

"What?"

"About Eldridge. His roof fell on him"

Captain Perona breathed in deeply. "I do not suppose he was hurt? I do not suppose he was injured seriously, by any chance?"

"No," Doan admitted.

"I knew it! He is dead, of course!"

"Yes," said Doan.

"And what were you doing at the time? Something entirely innocent, I have no doubt!"

"I was just picking myself up from where the earthquake dumped me."

"How very convenient that earthquake was!" Captain Perona snarled. "You came here to prevent Eldridge from returning to the United States, and now you have succeeded!"

"Well," said Doan, "if you put it that way—yes."

"Consider yourself under arrest!"

"Hey, now," Doan protested mildly. "I didn't push Eldridge's roof over on him."

"Captain," said Janet, "I'm sure Mr. Doan is telling the truth! You're making a terrible mistake to—"

Captain Perona turned on her. "Do you wish to be arrested also?"

"No," said Janet.

"Then be quiet. Sergeant! Take this man to the barracks and keep him there until I investigate."

"You heard him, pudgy," said Sergeant Obrian. "On your way. And don't try any tricks. I don't carry this bayonet just because it shines so pretty."

"Can I take Carstairs?" Doan asked. "He usually goes to jail with me."

"Yes!"

Doan rapped Carstairs on the forehead with his knuckle. "Up-si-daisy, pal. Off to clink, we go."

"I'm so sorry, Mr. Doan," Janet told him.

"Think nothing of it," Doan said. "We'll get right out again. We always do."

"Do not be too confident," Captain Perona advised dangerously.

DOAN WAS SITTING ON ONE END OF a bench in a very small, very barren room with one narrow window and a rough board floor that was covered with dust which the quake had shaken from the walls and ceiling. Carstairs was sleeping on the rest of the bench. Sergeant Obrian stood just inside the door and watched them both grimly.

Captain Perona and Lieutenant Ortega came in the door.

"Tell us what you learned," Captain Perona ordered. "Speak in English so he may understand."

Lieutenant Ortega said: "I examined the body of Senor Eldridge. There was dust and plaster and bits of mortar in his clothes and in his hair. His spine was broken and severed below his waist, and his left arm was fractured, and he had five fractured ribs, one of which penetrated the lung cavity close to his heart. These wounds resulted in his death."

"Could Doan have given him those wounds?"

Lieutenant Ortega looked at Doan. "Oh, I think not."

"Look again," Captain Perona said. "His appearance is very deceptive."

Lieutenant Ortega shook his head. "There is no evidence of any human agency. I think Senor Eldridge was crushed by the fall of his roof."

"Sure he was," said Doan. "Why, I've even got a witness who saw me try trying to give Eldridge first aid."

"Who?" Captain Perona demanded.

"A fellow by the name of Lepicik."

"I do not know anyone by that name," said Captain Perona. "Was he a Mexican or a foreigner?"

"Foreigner, I guess."

Captain Perona looked at Sergeant Obrian inquiringly.

Sergeant Obrian shook his head. "No. There ain't nobody by that name in this burg—foreigner or otherwise. I checked 'em all."

"Well, I saw the guy," said Doan.

"No," Captain Perona contradicted flatly. "It is impossible for anyone to come into this district without us knowing him and identifying him. You are lying again."

"But, please," said a voice outside the door. "If you will pardon me, I must see the Captain. It is really quite important."

Sergeant Obrian jumped outside the door and came back in again immediately shoving Lepicik ahead of him. Lepicik smiled and nodded in a mildly apologetic way.

"I'm so sorry to bother you, but I was informed that I must report my presence in Los Altos to you."

"What is your name?" Captain Perona demanded.

"I am Leon Lepicik."

"Ahem," said Doan.

Captain Perona bowed ironically. "I apologize. You were not lying—again. Senor Lepicik, how did you come to Los Altos?"

"I came from Santa Lucia."

"He's screwy," said Sergeant Obrian. "That's a gutbuster of a hike. No old droop like this could make it."

"Nevertheless," said Lepicik, "you will observe that I am here."

"Who guided you?" asked Captain Perona.

"A man by the name of Adolfo Morales and a burro named Carmencita. They—or at least Adolfo—are now in the process of getting drunk at the Dos Hermanos, if you wish to verify my story."

"We do wish to," said Captain Perona. "And we will. Are you a North American?"

"No, sir."

"Let me see your passport."

Lepicik produced a worn leather folder, and Captain Perona examined it carefully.

"Albanian, eh?" he said, looking up.

Lepicik nodded. "Yes. But you will note that the passport was issued before the Italian invasion and also bears the stamp of the Albanian government-in-exile."

"Hmmm," said Captain Perona, handing back the passport. "Have you ever seen this man?"

"Yes," said Lepicik. "Once."

"Where?"

"In the patio in back of a house on the Avenida Revolution."

"What was he doing?"

"Attempting to help a man who was fatally injured in the earthquake."

Doan had been holding his breath, and he let it out now in a long, gentle sigh.

"How do you know the man was injured in the earthquake?" Captain Perona asked.

"I saw it happen. I saw the roof of his house fall on him."

"How could you see that? The patio is enclosed by a high wall."

"The earthquake demolished the wall, and besides I was up on the hill above and in back of the house."

"What were you doing up there?"

Lepicik smiled at him. "Exploring. I find that a very interesting and educational pastime."

"Why did you come to Los Altos?"

"To explore."

"I see," said Captain Perona coldly. "Doan, you are released— for the moment. Go to the Hacienda Nueva Inglesa and register— and stay there. Senor Lepicik, you accompany him and do the same."

"I have already registered," said Lepicik, "and met the other charming members of the tourist party."

"Doan," said Captain Perona, "before you leave I wish to tell you certain things we know about your recent actions. You are employed by an agency called the Severn International Detectives, which has headquarters in New York. The agency was employed by a certain group of politicians in a certain state to send you to Mexico to bribe Senor Eldridge to stay here and to stop bothering them. You were given ten thousand dollars for that purpose, but you did not bring the ten thousand dollars to Mexico."

"Didn't I?" Doan asked.

"No. Instead you deposited it in the Commercial Trust Bank in Chicago under the name of D.L. Carstairs."

"It's a fund for his college education," said Doan, indicating Carstairs.

"I find your humor nauseating," Captain Perona told him shortly. "You never had any intention of paying that money to Eldridge. You embezzled it."

"Shame on me," said Doan. "I guess these certain politicians will sue me or put me in jail or something, then, won't they?"

Captain Perona scowled at him in silence.

"What is it?" Lieutenant Ortega asked. "I do not understand."

Captain Perona said: "He knows the politicians do not dare prosecute him because then they would have to explain why they gave him the money which would result in just the scandal they are trying to avoid."

"Hey!" Sergeant Obrian exclaimed. "You mean that pudgy gets to keep the ten grand? And then they try to tell you that crime don't pay!"

"Did you speak?" Captain Perona inquired.

"No, sir," said Sergeant Obrian.

Captain Perona pointed to Carstairs, to Doan, and to Lepicik. "Get out. All of you."

Doan nudged Carstairs with his elbow. "Come on, chum. We beat the rap."

THE HACIENDA NUEVA INGLESA WAS neither a ranch nor new, and English only by adoption, but it had adobe walls six feet thick that had survived the earthquake with only a few exterior cracks. It was a narrow, two-story building on the west side of the plaza. Doan and Carstairs and Lepicik went in through the side entrance into a low, dim, musty-smelling room optimistically labeled a restaurant-bar.

"Mr. Doan!" Janet greeted. She was sitting at one of the round wire-legged tables under a poster which luridly proclaimed the virtues of Guinness Stout. "You were released! Oh, I'm so glad!"

"I told you not to worry about him," said Mrs. Henshaw. She was seated at another of the tables, writing busily in a leather-mounted diary with a tiny gold pencil. "I knew he'd manage to bribe somebody."

"I saved my money this time," Doan said. "Lepicik got me out."

"It was nothing," said Lepicik politely. "If you will excuse me now, I think I will take a nap in my room. I am very weary."

He went up the steep stairway to the second floor.

"Miss Martin," said Mrs. Henshaw, "what was that queer dish we had for lunch?"

"Chiles rellenos," Janet told her.

"How do you spell it?"

Janet spelled it for her.

Greg was sitting by himself in the corner staring darkly at the tall, round bottle of Plymouth gin on the table in front of him. Doan walked over to him.

"Can I have a drink of that?"

"I suppose so," Greg said. "If you pay for it. There are some glasses on the shelf back of the bar. If you want a mix, yell for Timpkins."

"I'll try it straight," Doan said. He found a glass and sat down at the table opposite Greg. "Let's get drunk, shall we?"

"Okay," said Greg.

Doan took off his hat and put it down on the table and unbuttoned his coat. He poured some gin into his glass and tasted it.

"It's good," he said. He finished the drink and poured himself another.

Carstairs walked up to the table and growled at him.

"As for you," said Doan. "You can go straight to hell."

Carstairs growled at him again.

"I'll get drunk if I feel like it," Doan told him. "It's my stomach. Lie down before somebody bops you with a bottle."

Carstairs lowered himself to the floor with a series of loose, bony thuds. He snorted once and then closed his eyes in a resigned way.

"Doesn't he like you to drink?" Janet asked.

"No " said Doan. "I got maudlin once when I was crocked and kissed him. He's never forgotten it. Every time he smells alcohol, he starts acting like he just bit into a lemon. He's intolerant. It's a serious defect in his character."

"Mr. Doan," said Mrs. Henshaw severely, "don't annoy Mr. Greg. He is mourning Miss Van Osdel."

"Are you?" Doan asked him.

"No," said Greg. "I'm trying to think of the name of a girl I met in London last summer. Her father owns a glue factory. Do you know anyone in England who owns a glue factory?"

"Nope," said Doan. "Did Ortega fix your arm for you?"

"Yes. He said he set it. I think personally that he cut it off. It feels like hell."

"Have a drink," Doan invited.

"Okay."

Feet thundered along the hall above them, and then Henshaw shouted down the staircase:

"Hey! Have you seen this bathroom up here?"

"Now, Wilbur," Mrs. Henshaw said absently. "No business on this trip. You promised."

"Business, hell!" Henshaw said. "Why, the thing is a disgrace! I bet it's fifty years old! Where's the guy that owns this dive?

Timpkins! *Timpkins!*"

A man came in through the door beyond the end of the bar. He was scrawny and small and bow-legged, and he was wearing a soiled flour sack for an apron. He looked as though being born had been such a disappointment to him that he had never recovered.

"Well, what?"

"Timpkins," said Henshaw, "that bathroom of yours is a terrible hole."

"It works, don't it?"

"After a fashion. But that isn't the point, Timpkins. It's obsolete. Why, it's an antique."

"If you don't like it, you don't have to use it."

"What would I do if I didn't?" Henshaw asked blankly.

"That's your question," said Timpkins. "You answer it."

"Hey, you," said Doan. "Captain Perona told me to stay here. Trot out your register, and I'll sign up."

Timpkins stared at him sourly. "You the chap that goes around killing people?"

"Now and then," Doan said.

"You ain't to kill nobody in my hotel, just remember that. I'm a British subject, and I know my rights. One murder, and out you go, Captain Perona or no Captain Perona."

"Okay," said Doan amiably.

"The register is under the bar. You sign yourself up—and by your right name, too. If there's a room upstairs that's empty, you can use it.... And just remember I marked the level on that gin bottle and one of you two is gonna pay for what's gone out of it. And I don't want none of you guests hollerin' at me and botherin' me any more because I'm busy."

Henshaw had come very quietly down the stairs. "Timpkins," he said softly. "Timpkins, look." He whipped a shiny, colored folder out of his pocket. "Look at Model 9-A illustrated here. Orchid tile, Timpkins!"

"Arr!" Timpkins snarled. He went back into the kitchen and slammed the door violently behind him.

"He's a tough prospect," Henshaw said in a pleased tone. "But

165

that's the kind I like. I'll work up a little sales talk especially for him. Would you like to see Model 9-A, Doan?"

"No," said Doan.

"Where's Mortimer, Wilbur?" Mrs. Henshaw asked.

"He's takin' a nap. He said he was tired."

"The little sweet," said Mrs. Henshaw. "He's been so brave through it all."

"Brave, hell," said Henshaw. "He loved it. He's got no more sense than a sawhorse."

"Gangway! Gangway!" Amanda Tracy shouted hoarsely. She slapped the side door back against the wall and wiggled her way through, almost hidden under an immense stack of canvases. She dumped them carelessly on the floor and shouted over the racketing clatter:

"Hello, Janet, dearie. Hello, Doan. Hi, everybody else. Where's Timpkins? Timpkins, you dirty little thief! Come here! Front and center!"

Timpkins opened the kitchen door. "Well, what? Oh, it's you now, is it? What you want?"

"I want a room and a good one," said Amanda Tracy. "And no bedbugs, either."

"Ain't got one," said Timpkins.

"You'd better find one, chum," said Amanda Tracy. "Starting now. And I mean a room, not a bedbug."

"Why don't you stay home where you belong?"

"My house has got no roof. Scram, Timpkins! Scat!"

"Arr," said Timpkins sullenly, retiring back into the kitchen.

Amanda Tracy nodded cheerily at Doan. "I got to hand it to you, fatso. You must not be near so dumb as you look. That was very nifty the way you rubbed out Eldridge."

"Mr. Doan didn't do that," Janet protested. "The earthquake killed Mr. Eldridge."

"Ha-ha," said Amanda Tracy. "Don't you believe it, dearie. Doan did it. He's snaky. He'd just as leave kill you as spit. Wouldn't you, Doan?"

"Sure," said Doan. "Massacres organized any hour of the day

166

or night."

"Yeah," said Amanda Tracy. "And don't think I think you're fooling, either."

"Pardon me," said Captain Perona.

"Here's that man again," Greg observed gloomily.

Captain Perona was standing in the doorway. He was in uniform now, and he looked tall and leanly competent. He crossed the room and stopped beside Doan's table.

"And the stooge," said Greg.

Sergeant Obrian came in the room and said: "I heard you. Do I have to take cracks like that from a lousy tourist, Captain?"

"Yes," said Captain Perona. "Doan, I find that in my haste I neglected a certain formality. Stand up and raise your hands."

Doan sighed and got up.

"Search him," said Captain Perona.

Sergeant Obrian searched fast and expertly. "One .38 caliber Colt Police Positive revolver and—fifteen extra rounds for same. That's all the weapons."

"Look once more. He is reported to carry two."

"Nope," said Sergeant Obrian. "He's clean."

"Where did you hide your other weapon?" Captain Perona asked coldly.

"Nowhere," said Doan. "I didn't have one."

Captain Perona looked speculatively at Carstairs. "Tell your dog to stand up."

"Up-si-daisy," said Doan.

Carstairs lumbered reluctantly to his feet.

"Tell him to open his mouth."

"Say 'ah,' " Doan ordered.

Carstairs lolled out a thick red tongue at him.

"All right," said Captain Perona. "Tell him to lie down again."

"Boom," said Doan.

Carstairs dropped on the floor with a thud and a grunt.

Greg said: "That's a very nice hat you have, Doan. May I see it?" He reached out and picked it up with his good hand. There was a clasp knife lying on the table under the hat. "Oh, excuse me," Greg said.

Doan nodded at him. "Hi, pal."

Captain Perona pounced on the knife. It looked something like a scout knife, except that it was larger and longer. Captain Perona pressed a catch on the haft, and a thick, wide blade snapped suddenly into view.

"Very nice," he said. "Very efficient."

"It isn't mine," said Doan. "I never carry a knife. They give me the creepies."

"Then how did it get under your hat?"

"I'll give you one guess," said Doan, looking at Greg in a speculative way.

"Did you put this under his hat?" Captain Perona asked.

"No," said Greg.

"I'm afraid," said Lepicik, "that you are not telling the truth." He was standing on the stairs, just far enough down them so he could see under the ceiling. "You did put the knife under Mr. Doan's hat."

"You're a liar," said Greg.

"I'm so sorry," said Lepicik politely. "But I saw you do it."

"Well?" said Captain Perona.

Greg shrugged his left shoulder. "Okay. I did. I was afraid you and your stooges were going to search us all, and I didn't want it found on me. I just bought the thing today—for a souvenir."

Captain Perona balanced the knife on his palm. "You bought this in Los Altos?"

"Yes."

"Where?"

"From a street peddler."

"What did he look like?"

"Oh, he was a little guy with a funny face. What's the matter with you, anyway? You don't really think I'd carry a thing like that around with me all the time, do you?"

"Yes," said Captain Perona. "I really think you would—and do."

"Prove it," Greg invited.

"Perhaps I will," said Captain Perona, putting the knife and Doan's revolver in his pocket. "And some other things as well. Colonel Callao, the commandant of this district, is coming to interview you tourists soon. I have some important matters to tell you before he arrives. Are you all here now?"

"Mortimer's upstairs asleep," said Henshaw.

"Don't you dare wake my little darling!" Mrs. Henshaw warned.

"I would not think of it," said Captain Perona. "I would be very pleased if he continued to sleep permanently. Now attend to me, please. You all know that Patricia Van Osdel was killed during the earthquake. You know also, I think, that Doan suspected her death was not an accident. I ask you again, Doan: Why were you so quick to suspect that on the meager evidence available?"

"I've got an evil mind," said Doan. "Can I sit down and rest it?"

"Yes."

"Can I have a drink?"

"Yes."

"Pour me one, too," Greg requested.

Doan looked at him.

"Oh, I'm sorry about the knife," Greg told him. "Forget it. It was just one of those things."

"Some day you're going to pull one too many of those things," Doan said, pouring gin.

"Are you quite comfortable?" Captain Perona asked. "Can you give me your attention now?"

"Go right ahead," Doan said.

"Thank you. As a result of investigation, we have found that your suspicions were justified. Patricia Van Osdel was not killed by accident. She was murdered by being struck on the head by a jagged piece of stone, which was subsequently found in a lane beside her maid, Maria, who was seriously injured by being struck with the same stone."

"How is Maria?" Janet asked.

"Doan was right in his diagnosis there, also. Her skull is

fractured. She is not conscious and probably will not be so for several days. She is under guard at the military hospital, and I do not wish to hear of any of you attempting to visit her. As soon as she recovers she will be able to tell us who murdered Patricia Van Osdel and attacked her, but I do not propose to wait that long to find out."

"Why not?" Doan asked. "You've got lots of time."

"Patricia Van Osdel," said Captain Perona, "was an enormously rich and influential citizen of your country. Your country and mine are now allies in the war. We do not wish any incidents to occur which would disturb our relationship. If it were known that Patricia Van Osdel had been murdered here, it would inevitably arouse suspicions of our ability to protect visitors and tourists, and start demands for investigation of the circumstances surrounding her death and rumors of fifth column activity in military zones and such things. Do I make myself clear?"

"Not yet," said Doan.

"I will proceed. Patricia Van Osdel's death is to be known as an accident until such time as we can find and arrest her murderer and prove that the Mexican Army and Government were in no way responsible or negligent."

"Now I get it," said Doan. "Hush-hush."

"Yes. There is no way for any of you to communicate with anyone outside Los Altos. All exits and entrances are guarded by soldiers. All telephone and telegraph wires went down with the bridge."

"Some bridge," Henshaw remarked. "Couldn't even stand a little shaking up."

Captain Perona eyed him narrowly. "I recall that not so long ago a bridge in the United States—a new one—blew down in a high wind."

"Oh," said Henshaw, subdued. "Yeah, I remember that, now you mention it.... Well, what're we gonna do?"

"Stay here. The bridge supports at either end are intact. We will put cables across as soon as we receive the equipment. We are in touch with Major Nacio by military field wireless now."

"Who's he?" Henshaw asked.

"The man who warned you not to come here."

"Yeah," said Henshaw. "He did at that, didn't he? And was he right!"

"He was," Captain Perona agreed. "Your presence here is a needless complication. However, if you will give me the names of the people concerned, I will see that they are notified that you are safe. You may be forced to remain here for a few days, but there will be no shortage of food or supplies. Now I wish to ask you: Do any of you know why Patricia Van Osdel was so determined to come to Los Altos at this particular time?"

No one answered.

"You," said Captain Perona, pointing at Greg.

"I don't know," said Greg. "I didn't know anything about her business affairs. I was strictly a social acquaintance of hers."

Captain Perona pointed at Doan. "You."

"Now, look," Doan protested. "You're going to have to make a choice here. I can't have killed both Eldridge and the Van Osdel at the same time when they were a half mile apart."

Captain Perona counted on his fingers. "Garcia. Eldridge. Patricia Van Osdel. Maria. A death by shooting, a so-called accidental death, a murder, and a near-fatal attack. All since you came to Los Altos."

"Don't forget the earthquake," Doan suggested. "I had that hidden in my hat along with Greg's knife."

"Captain Perona," Janet said, "I think you're just being silly with your suspicions of Mr. Doan."

Captain Perona turned to look at her. "I asked you earlier this afternoon if you wished to be arrested. You said, no. Have you changed your mind?"

"No," said Janet.

"Then do not meddle in affairs that do not concern you."

"Slap his ugly face, dearie," Amanda Tracy urged. "Kick him in his shins."

"What are you doing here," Captain Perona inquired, "besides making a nuisance of yourself?"

"I'm staying here, fancy-pants, because the roof came off my house. Only Doan, thank God, wasn't around to shove me under it when it started to fall. You'd better pinch him, Perona, before he kills all the rest of us."

"Mind your own business."

"All right," said Amanda Tracy. "How about the earthquake, then? That's my business from now on."

"All rescue work has been organized completely by the military. Property is being guarded, people have been removed from dangerous buildings, and the injured—and others—have been taken care of. There is no disorder of any kind, and there will be none."

"Too bad," Amanda Tracy remarked. "How many people killed?"

"Nine, including Senorita Van Osdel and Senor Eldridge."

"How many hurt?"

"Seventeen severely injured, including Maria. They are in a temporary hospital in charge of Lieutenant Ortega and military nurses and attendants. There were thirty-four others who were injured, but not seriously enough to require more than first aid treatment. Only about five buildings collapsed completely. Many others were damaged badly. We have not had time for a complete survey as yet. The earthquake was sharply localized. Both Mazalar and Santa Lucia felt it only faintly. Is that sufficient information to satisfy you?"

"Yup," said Amanda Tracy.

Doan said casually: "How about witnesses? Did you find anybody who saw what happened to Maria and the Van Osdel?"

"Not yet. There was very great confusion at the time of the earthquake, as you know. People were too interested in their own affairs and their own safety to pay much attention to their surroundings or what other people were doing. We are still investigating."

"I don't get this," said Henshaw. "Why all the argument about Patricia Van Osdel's death and the attack on Maria? It's easy to see what happened. Some of these natives around here noticed how spiffy she was dressed, and one of them just batted her one and Maria, too—and ran off with her dough and stuff. This burg looks to me like it's practically full of thieves."

"Speaking of thieves," said Captain Perona, "it *is* my duty to inform you that unless you make immediate cash retribution for the articles you stole this afternoon, you will be arrested and tried by a military court."

"What?" Henshaw shouted indignantly. "Articles I stole?"

"You were seen and identified by six witnesses."

Henshaw slapped himself on the forehead. "That damned Mortimer! I told him not to lift that junk! Look, Captain. It was the kid took them, not me."

"You are responsible for him."

"Like hell! I'm no more responsible for Mortimer than you are for Hitler!"

"Will you pay, or will you go to jail?"

"Put Mortimer in jail," Henshaw invited.

"Wilbur!" Mrs. Henshaw shrieked.

"One hundred and fifty dollars, please," said Captain Perona evenly.

"What!" Henshaw moaned. "Oh, now wait a minute. It was only some old spurs and a hat. Look, I'll make Mortimer give 'em back!"

"The owner does not want them back. He wants the money to repair his store. And, in this case, he has the choice. I might mention that the jail is very crowded and uncomfortable at this time and that, under military law, the penalty for looting is death."

Henshaw stared. "You said—death?"

"Yes."

"Oh!" said Henshaw. "Oh—oh—oh!" He produced a book of travelers' checks and a fountain pen. "One hundred fifty... Here! Take 'em! Oh, that Mortimer! Oh, just wait!"

"Wilbur," said Mrs. Henshaw, "you won't lay a hand on him—not even a finger. It's all your fault. You tempted him."

"I—I tempted... I never did! I did not! I'll tear him limb from limb! I'll wring his scrawny neck!"

"Enough," said Captain Perona, folding the travelers' checks carefully. "There is another very vital matter. The reason for the trouble with the man, Garcia, and for the presence of a company of soldiers here, and the reason you were warned not to come is that it was suspected that a criminal by the name of Bautiste Bonofile was hiding in disguise in Los Altos. He has now been identified as one Tio Riquez."

"Hey!" Amanda Tracy blurted in amazement. "You don't mean the old drip who had charge of the museum?"

"That old drip," Captain Perona confirmed bitterly. "He had held that position for years, and he had managed to fool everyone. As it was, he was uncovered by accident."

"Well, I like that," said Janet.

"A very attractive accident," Captain Perona corrected, bowing in her direction. "This man is still at large in Los Altos. He cannot—and neither can any of you—possibly escape from the town. We will find him in a short time, but in the meantime I warn you to stay close to this hotel. This man is desperate and very dangerous."

"A public enemy, I bet," said Henshaw. "I've never met one. Bring him around when you catch him."

"I do not think he will be taken alive."

"What was in the museum cellar?" Janet asked curiously.

"We have not been able to determine fully as yet. There were rifles, as he said, as well as a considerable amount of other loot."

"Where'd the old boob steal it?" Amanda Tracy asked.

"That is a military affair," said Captain Perona.

Doan yawned. "He picked it up when he was riding around with, a gent named Zapata."

Captain Perona spun on his heel. "How did you know that?"

"Eldridge told me."

"What else did he tell you?"

"Nothing," Doan answered warily.

Captain Perona leaned over the table. "If you knew—if you even suspected—that Tio Riquez was Bautiste Bonofile and did not inform the military authorities, you are going to find yourself in some serious trouble. Very serious, indeed."

"Why don't I keep my big mouth shut?" Doan asked, sighing. "I didn't know. Eldridge didn't, either. Honest."

"Ah-lou," said a thick, wheezing voice, and an incredibly fat man in a rumpled uniform that was too loose for him everywhere except across his paunch and too tight there rolled himself through the door and peered at them glassily through eyes that were yellowish, bloodshot marbles pouched in bluish puffs of flesh.

Captain Perona saluted stiffly. "This is Colonel Callao. He is a filthy, stupid swine, as you can plainly see. He thinks he understands and speaks English, but he does not. Nevertheless, he will be insulted if you attempt to speak to him in Spanish. Speak English, and he will grin like the fool he is and pretend to understand you. Am I not correct, Colonel?"

"Yuzz," said Colonel Callao, grinning proudly. "Ah-lou. Goom-by."

"He is not," said Captain Perona, nodding politely to him, "representative of the Mexican Army. He is a holdover from the old days. He is slightly drunk now but not enough, I do not think, to collapse or vomit on the floor or to perform any of the other antics such pigs usually indulge in when they are intoxicated to a sufficient degree."

Concha burst through the door like an explosion, her short skirt swirling, her magnificent eyes shooting sparks.

"I heard you! I heard every words you say! And I tell him, too!"

"I would not advise you to," Captain Perona warned smoothly. "For your own —safety. This one, ladies and gentlemen, calls herself Senora Eldridge."

"I am!" Concha shrilled furiously. "I have the papers to prove!"

"Forged, no doubt," said Captain Perona.

"Sure! Forged absolutely genuine!" Concha jerked at Colonel Callao' s arm. "There! That one! The little fats with the big, dumb dog! He's killing my husband!"

"Goom-by," said Colonel Callao helpfully.

"He is! Give him the pinch! Puts him in jail! Shoot him!"

"Bang-bang," said Doan.

"Stop that screaming," Captain Perona said to Concha, "and tell us why you think Doan killed your husband."

"Think! I never think! I see him with these eyes. I see him say to my husband he is going to bury him in Mexico! Then comes the earthquake! Grrrrumble-boom-boom! Right away the fats jumps on my husband and beats him and kicks him and hits him on the head and chokes him and bites him with the big, dumb dog!"

"I'm so sorry," said Lepicik, "but you really didn't see any of that."

Concha glared at him. "You are a little, skinny, big liar!"

"No," said Lepicik, "because I saw you on the Avenida Revolution going away from the house toward the market square just before the earthquake. I noticed you particularly because you are so beautiful."

"Hah?" said Concha, startled.

"Beautiful," Lepicik repeated. "Very. And photogenic, too."

"What's does that mean?" Concha demanded suspiciously.

"It means you would photograph well. Your features are superbly proportioned, and —if you will pardon me —you have a lovely figure. I trunk you would be an outstanding success in motion pictures."

"Why you think that?"

Lepicik smiled apologetically. "I'm a motion picture director."

"Hah! You? Where you work?"

"I'm temporarily at liberty, but I think I can arrange for you to have a screen test, if you wish."

Concha's eyes glistened. "I wish lots!"

"Senora Eldridge," said Captain Perona, "did you see Doan kill your husband?"

"Me?" Concha asked. "No. I am in the streets being beautiful where the skinny one sees me."

"You were lying, then."

"Sure," said Concha. "I don't like the fats. We got no troubles until he comes and kills my husband, I guess."

"Get out of here!" Captain Perona snarled. "And stay out!"

Concha put her thumbs in her ears and wiggled her fingers at him. "Pah! Pooey!" She stuck out her tongue and made a horrid face.

Captain Perona made a move toward her, and she whirled and ran gracefully out the door.

"Goom-by," said Colonel Callao placidly.

"You are right for once, you drooling donkey," said Captain Perona in his smoothest tones. "We are leaving. You tourists, remember what I have told you and govern yourselves accordingly. You will hear from me again soon."

"Not too soon, I hope," Greg told him.

Captain Perona ignored him. He and Sergeant Obrian escorted Colonel Callao politely out the door.

"I got to go get some more of my junk," Amanda Tracy stated. "See you later, kids."

"If you will pardon me," said Lepicik, "I think I will continue my nap."

He went back up the stairs, and Henshaw followed him quietly and purposefully.

"Wilbur," said Mrs. Henshaw. "Where are you going?"

Henshaw didn't answer.

"Wilbur!" Mrs. Henshaw shouted. "Don't you dare sneak in and strike Mortimer! Wilbur!" She got up and ran up the stairs after Henshaw.

"I think I'm drunk enough for the present," Greg said. "I'm a little short of cash. I'll let you pay for the gin."

"Well, thanks," said Doan. "You're too good to me." He waited until Greg had gone upstairs and then nodded to Janet. "Have you got your purse with you?"

"Yes " said Janet, picking it up from the chair beside her. "Here."

"Let me see it, will you? Just throw it over."

She tossed the purse to him. It was a large one made of composition leather, and Doan opened it and fumbled around in its interior while Janet stared at him in amazement. He finally came up with a .25 caliber automatic hardly larger than a package of cigarettes.

"You'd be a sucker for a pickpocket," he said.

"Did you—did you put that in there?" Janet asked.

Doan nodded. "Yeah. I was afraid I might be met by a welcoming committee here and searched like I was just now." He searched in the purse again and found an extra magazine for the automatic.

"Mr. Doan," said Janet, "you lied to Captain Perona. You did have another weapon, and you should have given it to him when he asked you to."

"He doesn't need it. He's got lots of guns." Doan put the automatic and the extra magazine in the breast pocket of his coat. It made no noticeable bulge. "Have a drink?"

"I don't drink."

"What a pity," said Doan, having one himself.

Carstairs growled at him.

"Mr. Doan," said Janet, "I think he's right. I don't think you should impair your faculties when everyone suspects you of—of everything."

"I don't have any faculties to impair," Doan answered. He leaned down and blew his breath at Carstairs.

Carstairs looked at him with a martyred air and then got up and walked over to Janet. He sat down beside her and put his head in her lap.

"Sissy," said Doan. He beat time in the air with his forefinger and sang hoarsely: "'Oh, it's a great day for the Irish!' "

Carstairs mumbled to himself in disgust.

"I'd like to hear you do better," Doan told him. "Janet, did you ever hear of a painter named Predilip?"

"Yes," Janet said. "I don't know much about art, but I've read about him. I believe he's a sort of a modernist, on the order of Van Gogh."

"Is he dead?"

"Oh, yes. I think he died about 1911. He used to live here in Los Altos, you know. His pictures are one of the reasons why the town is famous."

"Yeah. Are his pictures worth much?"

"In money? Yes, they are. I read in a newspaper a little while ago that one had been sold at auction in New York for nine thousand dollars, and that wasn't a good one. His best ones were painted here just before he died."

"Oh," said Doan, taking another drink.

"Mr. Doan," Janet said, worried, "are you sure you feel all right?"

"Marvelous," Doan answered.

"Well, I've never had much experience with intoxicants. I've never seen anyone just sit down and—and get drunk."

"Stick around, kid," Doan told her. "Stick around."

CHAPTER 10

J ANET AWOKE AND FOUND SHE WAS sitting bolt upright in bed with terror like a cold hand clutching at her throat. For what seemed like eons her faculties fought to free themselves of numbing layers of sleep and exhaustion.

She couldn't remember where she was, and the bare room looked enormous and shadowy with the windows like heavy-lidded eyes in their deep niches in the opposite wall and the high, ugly head of the bed looming over her in silent menace.

And then the yell came again. It was choked and half muffled, but the unadorned terror in it was like an electric shock. Janet threw the covers aside and thrust herself to the edge of the bed, ready to flee somewhere, anywhere.

The bedroom door thundered under a series of heavy blows, and Captain Perona's voice said sharply:

"Open this! Open it at once!"

The door thundered again, jumping against its hinges.

"Wait!" Janet cried. "I'm coming!"

She stumbled against a chair and then felt the twist of the iron latch under her groping hand. She turned the big key, and the lock creaked. Instantly the door slammed back against her, knocking her into the corner, and then Captain Perona gripped her arm with fingers like metal hooks.

"Is there anyone in here with you?" he demanded.

"Wha—what?" Janet said dazedly.

Two soldiers thrust past them. One carried a big flashlight, and its brilliant round eye flicked questioningly through the darkness. The second soldier had a carbine, and the steel of its bayonet flashed savagely as he prodded under the bed and into the cubbyhole closet.

"Let go of me!" Janet cried. "What do you mean—coming in this way... Stop that!"

Captain Perona released her. "Senorita, is it your custom to greet visitors unclothed?"

Janet looked down at herself. "Oh! Oh, my!" She turned her back and then turned around again and crouched down protectively.

Captain Perona picked up her dress from a chair and dropped it on top of her as though it were something unclean. "Please put this on and stop offending my modesty."

Janet fought with the dress. "I can't... It's caught... Don't you touch me!"

Captain Perona yanked the dress down over her head. "Please, senorita! This is no time to be flirtatious!"

Janet's head emerged from the dress. "Oh! You—you—You know very well I had no nightclothes with me, and I had to wash out my underthings, and I didn't have anything—"

"No doubt," said Captain Perona.

He shoved her at the soldier with the carbine. The soldier took her arm and hustled her out into the hall. It was a flickering nightmare tunnel with flashlights reflecting from the cold blue of gun barrels, from gleaming brass buttons. There were more soldiers, crowded so close Janet had no chance to count them, their faces dark and tense, excitedly eager.

The one who had hold of her hurried her along, steered her down the stairs at a stumbling run. The big kerosene pressure lamp was lighted, swinging violently on its chain, and its shadows chased and jumped crazily over more soldiers. There were three of them at the door, peering in, and more at the window and the door into the kitchen. The one who was escorting Janet let go of her and ran upstairs again.

"Pardon me," said Doan, "while I put on my pants." He hopped industriously on one leg and then the other.

Carstairs sat on the floor looking rumpled and sleepily indignant. Lepicik was sitting at a table beside the staircase. He was fully dressed and as neat as ever. He was even carrying his green umbrella. He was not at all concerned by the uproar. His expression was one of vaguely polite interest.

"My dress!" Janet exclaimed, pulling at it frantically. "And— and I haven't got any shoes on!"

"Neither have I," said Doan cheerfully. He sat down and put

181

his bare feet up on a chair. "The Captain seemed to be in a bit of a rush."

"What is it?" Janet demanded. "What's the matter?" She looked at the soldiers. *"Querasa?"*

One soldier shrugged. The others shook their heads at her.

"That clears everything up," Doan observed.

"Are you sober now?" Janet asked him suspiciously.

Doan nodded. "Just about."

"Well, do you feel—awfully bad?"

"No," said Doan.

"I thought people always felt bad after they got drunk."

"You have to have brains to get a hangover," Doan told her. "I'm never troubled."

"You *were* very drunk, you know. You sang questionable songs and beat on the table and told jokes that had no point and spilled three drinks."

"That's me," Doan agreed. "That's your old pal, Drunken Doan, when he gets curled."

"Carstairs was very angry with you."

"He's an evil-tempered brute," Doan said. "He's always mad at something."

The Henshaws, all three of them, came rumbling down the stairs like a group of frightened sheep with a soldier herding them along with judicious thrusts of his carbine butt.

"Say!" Henshaw said, struggling with his suspenders. "What gives here, anyway? Are we invaded?"

Mrs. Henshaw screamed: "I'll tell the President! I'll write him a letter! He'll send a battleship right down here and blow you all up!"

"Yeow!" Mortimer screeched. "Maw!"

Mrs. Henshaw enveloped him in a stranglehold. "Don't cry, baby! I won't let the beasts shoot you!"

Henshaw was tucking in his shirttail. "This is sure a fine way to treat tourists and allies. Just wait until I talk before the Rotary Club. I'll sure put the blister on these birds."

"What were you yelling about a minute ago?" Doan asked him.

Henshaw looked sheepish. "You hear me? Well, I was havin' a nightmare. A lulu, too. You know this mountain range is supposed to be a sleeping woman. I dreamed she was lying there all peaceful when a big mouse that looked like Carstairs came sneaking along, and she jumped up and let out a screech and shook her skirts, and the whole damned town fell into the canyon. And then six soldiers started to shake my bed to wake me up! I woke up, all right! Out loud!"

Heels made a quick, crisp clatter on the stairs, and Captain Perona came down and looked at them. His eyes were narrowed, gleaming slits.

"Quiet!" he barked. "Quiet, all of you! Where is the man, Greg?"

No one answered until Janet snapped suddenly: "Was that who you thought was in my room? Why, I'll—"

Captain Perona took a step toward her. "Will you be quiet?"

"Yes," said Janet, scared.

There was a sudden uproar of voices in the kitchen and the metallic clangor of a pan rolling on the floor. Timpkins was thrust headlong into the room. He was wearing a long white nightshirt, and his nutcracker face was contorted and red with rage above it.

"Here now! What's all this? I'm a British subject, I'll have you know! I'll protest—"

"Silence!" Captain Perona ordered. "Where is the man, Greg?"

"Arr?" said Timpkins blankly. "Greg? In his bed, I suppose."

"No! His bed has not been slept in!"

"Why all the sudden interest in Greg?" Doan asked.

Captain Perona watched him narrowly. "Tonight the maid of Patricia Van Osdel—the woman, Maria—was stabbed and killed in her hospital bed. The soldier guarding her was also killed. Three hand grenades were stolen from the armory."

"Don't blame me," said Doan. "I didn't have any grudge against Maria, and besides I was so drunk I wouldn't have known a hand grenade from a howitzer. Ask anybody. Those hand grenades sound like our old pal, Bautiste Bonofile, is out and about again."

"No," said Captain Perona. "He would not need to steal explosives. He has plenty of his own."

"That's nice to know, too," Doan commented. "Looks like, what with this and that, we're going to have a quiet weekend among the peaceful peasants."

"As I may have mentioned before," said Captain Perona, "I do not appreciate your humor. Kindly be quiet. I do not believe that the absence of the man, Greg, at the time of the murderous attack on Maria can be a coincidence."

"Pardon me," said Lepicik. "Please. But it might be."

"Why?" Captain Perona demanded.

"I'm so sorry, but I think perhaps I frightened him."

"How?"

"I believe he recognized me."

"Why would that frighten him?" Captain Perona asked skeptically.

Lepicik smiled. "He would know, of course, that I came here to kill him."

"So?" said Captain Perona. "You came here to kill him. Did you?"

Lepicik shook his head regretfully. "No. I haven't as yet had a good opportunity. Now I'm afraid he has eluded me again. He is so very clever. I had no idea that he knew what I looked like, and he gave no sign that he recognized me. But perhaps he had a description or a picture of me. I have, after all, been hunting him for quite some time."

"This is very interesting," said Captain Perona icily. "Tell me why you have been hunting him."

"Greg is not a refugee from anything except the law in a dozen countries and his own conscience, if he has one. He was a member of a Balkan terrorist group that specialized in political assassination for pay. My brother was a government official before the invasion. A minor official. He had a wife and a very beautiful daughter. One Sunday morning when they were all on their way to church, Greg or one of five other men—I was never able to narrow it down more closely than that—tossed a hand grenade into their small automobile."

There was a heavy little silence.

"And your relatives?" Captain Perona inquired softly.

"My brother and his wife were killed instantly. Both of my niece's legs were blown off. She was seventeen."

"Oh," said Janet, sickened.

"Fortunately," said Lepicik in his mild way, "she did not live. She died three weeks later. I sat beside her hospital bed all that time. She was in great pain."

"The other five men," said Captain Perona. "The ones, besides Greg, who were involved. What happened to them?"

"They died," said Lepicik. "Now, if you will excuse me, I will go find Adolfo Morales and his burro, Carmencita."

"And then what do you propose to do?" asked Captain Perona.

Lepicik looked faintly surprised. "Continue to hunt for Greg, of course."

"He cannot possibly have gotten out of Los Altos."

"I'm so sorry," Lepicik contradicted. "But I'm afraid he has. He is very clever."

"No," said Captain Perona. "He is here somewhere, no matter how clever he is." He hesitated. "I can understand how you feel, and I sympathize with you, but I cannot allow you to remain at large unless you give me your word you will not attempt to find Greg or to harm him."

Lepicik merely smiled.

Captain Perona shrugged. "Then I am forced to place you under technical arrest."

"It will be quite useless for you to do that," Lepicik told him. "I will find Greg sooner or later."

"But not in this district while I am in charge of his safety. You will be placed in my quarters under guard. You will be comfortable there."

"Thank you," said Lepicik.

Sergeant Obrian came part way down the stairs. "Captain, didn't that old artist doll say she was gonna flop here? She ain't around now."

185

"Amanda Tracy!" Captain Perona exploded. "Where is she?"

"Now how do I know?" Timpkins asked drearily. "I was sleepin' peaceful as a baby—"

"Somebody want me?" a hoarse, wheezing voice asked. "Well, here I am. What's left of me."

The soldiers shoved and squeezed in the doorway, and Amanda Tracy staggered past them. One side of her frizzed hair was matted into a crusted tangle, and blood lay like a red, glistening hand across her cheek. She braced herself on thickly muscular legs and swayed back and forth, staring blearily at Captain Perona.

"That fella Greg," she said. "You wait until I get my mitts..." She groped out vaguely with bloodstained hands. "Goes and socks a lady with a rock just because she says hello.... You wait—."

She fell forward as swiftly and suddenly as a tree toppling, and her head clunked solidly against the floor.

Mrs. Henshaw decided to scream and did so, frantically and senselessly, holding on to Mortimer so tightly that his eyes popped.

Captain Perona barked an order over his shoulder, and one of the soldiers in the doorway ducked away into the darkness. Captain Perona dropped to his knee beside Amanda Tracy and felt for the pulse in one of her thick, tanned wrists.

"She is alive," he said, breathing deeply in relief. Carefully he parted the matted, blood-soaked hair. "Ah! It is here! A blow like the one that killed Senorita Van Osdel, only this one glanced and cut instead of striking deep." He looked up. "Do any of you know anything of this?"

"Greg did it," said Henshaw. "Didn't you hear her? Greg smacked down Patricia Van Osdel and Maria and this one, too. Just find him and everything is solved."

"How do you know?"

"I deduced it," said Henshaw.

"Keep your deductions to yourself after this."

"Okay," said Henshaw. "But don't come around and say I didn't tell you—"

"Be quiet!"

Timpkins cleared his throat. "I was kind of muzzy-like from sleep first off... Seems like I remember—"

"What!" Captain Perona barked angrily.

"Here now," said Timpkins indignantly. "Not so rough, if you please. All I was gonna say was that she was complaining about the bedding I gave her—without no reason at all, you may be sure and she said something about goin' over to her place and diggin' some of her own out of the wreckage."

"Why didn't you stop her?"

"Arr?" said Timpkins. "Me? Stop her? Oh, no. I've had a brush or two with her before this."

"I warned you all to stay in the hotel!"

"Now, Captain," said Timpkins. "Naturally, she thought that just applied to these here tourists—not to old residents like me and her."

The soldier came back, panting heavily, with a rolled-up stretcher over his shoulder. He and an other soldier unfastened the straps, opened it out, and put it on the floor beside Amanda Tracy.

"*Cuidado!*" Captain Perona warned.

The soldiers lifted Amanda Tracy's thick body gently and put her down on the stretcher.

Captain Perona stood up. "You see now—from this—that it pays to give attention to my warnings. I do not talk to you merely for the pleasure it gives me. The rest of the night you will all stay in this hotel. I will leave soldiers to see that you do. If the man, Greg, returns he will be arrested. If he does not return, we will find his hiding place and very soon. I will take Senorita Tracy to the hospital now. Senor Lepicik, you will come with me, please."

"Certainly," said Lepicik. "Mr. Doan, will you take care of my umbrella for me, please?"

"Sure, pal," said Doan.

"You will be careful of it?"

"Indeed, yes," said Doan.

Lepicik and Captain Perona followed the soldiers carrying the stretcher out the door. Sergeant Obrian came down the stairs

ahead of more soldiers.

"Don't none of you birds try to fly this coop," he warned. "Some of us will be outside, and we're feelin' nasty." He counted the soldiers as they filed through the door, nodded once meaningly, and followed them.

"Now I don't care for this!" Timpkins snarled. "Not a little bit! Turning my hotel into a jail and a slaughterhouse. I'm tellin' you, and you all hear me say it, no more of this hanky-panky or out you go. Right into the street. Captain Perona or no Captain Perona, I know my rights. I'm a British subject, and I'll protest to the ambassador."

He marched out the back way, his bony bare feet slapping on the floor and his nightshirt fluttering indignantly behind him.

"I'm going to bed," said Henshaw. "I got to snag old Timpkins for a bathroom tomorrow, and I can't sell good unless I get my sleep."

He went upstairs, and Mrs. Henshaw, trailing Mortimer, followed him.

Doan was examining Lepicik's green umbrella cautiously. "I wonder how this works."

"Why, just like any umbrella," Janet told him. "Let me show you."

"Ah-ah," said Doan. "No. Get away. I've got it now."

There was a sudden loud pop.

"Reminds me of champagne," said Doan.

"Did the umbrella make that noise?" Janet asked curiously.

Doan nodded. "Yeah. It also made that." He pointed toward the bar.

There was a bright sliver of steel, about the size and half the length of a knitting needle, stuck deep in the hard wood.

Janet stared. "It—it shot that?"

"Yes. It's an air-gun. A dandy, too. I'd hate to have somebody pop one of those pins into my eye. I bet it wouldn't be very healthy. Let's see. It should pump up here somewhere... Ah!"

The crooked handle turned and slid out six inches, revealing an inner sheathing of oiled metal.

"Sure," said Doan, working it experimentally. "Just like a bicycle pump. Throws air pressure into this cylinder and holds it until you release this catch and then blows it—and the steel pin— out through the length of the barrel. Very neat. I'll bet it's damned accurate at close range, too."

While Janet watched him he went over and started to work the steel needle loose from the bar.

"I thought air-guns were toys," Janet said.

"What do you think now?" Doan asked.

"Why—why, that's a murderous thing!"

"I'll bet it is, at that," said Doan. "This needle is stuck in here two inches. It's got a leather washer here on the reverse end to hold the air pressure..." He stopped working at the dart and looked over the bar. "I think it's about time Doan should have another drink."

Carstairs sat back on his haunches and yelled. There was no other word to express the sound. It was a cry of sheer animal frustration so loud that its reverberations rattled the lamp chain and set the shadows to dancing again.

"All right!" Doan said, when he could make himself heard. "You spoil-sport! You blue-nose! If you feel that badly about it, we'll go to bed instead!"

I T WAS MORNING, AND THE SUN WAS gleaming and grinning generously, regardless of earthquakes, murders, or even Hitler. Janet sat on the parapet that circled the roof of the Hacienda Nueva Inglesa and kicked her heels against the rough plaster, relaxing luxuriously. There was just a slight breeze, and the air felt dry and gentle touching her face.

Los Altos spread away under her—crooked little streets jogging between red, scarred roofs—each detail clear and perfect in miniature. People were splotches of color—serapes and rebozos and white sombreros—moving busily about their affairs like jerky, self-satisfied bugs. Occasionally she could hear the faint overtones of their voices—the thin chittering of words in the mass.

Far on down below, beyond the borders of the town, the Canyon of Black Shadow was like a blue, crooked vein laid against the pink flesh of the earth. So clear was the air that Janet could see the toylike soldiers working around the jagged needle of the bridge support on the far side. A heliograph near them blinked a constant barrage of bright signals at other soldiers on the near side.

Janet breathed deeply, enjoying it all. She turned after a little to look the other way, up the slope of the mountain. The houses above frowned down on her like white, dull faces.

Off to her right, west of the town, the slope stretched upward in a brown, tangled sweep, and Janet looked across its waste absently until her eyes caught and came back to an upthrust of queerly shaped rock. She studied it casually until she could make out a blocky, rough-cut profile. It was as though some giant had taken an oversize ax and cut out nose and mouth and bulge of brows with three expert blows.

Janet turned to her left, still lazily indifferent, and looked up the east slope. They were there—three square, stone monuments in a line like the three bears, big and then medium and then small. Janet smiled a vague greeting at them and wondered how she knew they were where they were. She decided she would have to think about the matter some time when she was more industrious and less comfortable.

From somewhere far off there came a faint, humming buzz. It had no direction at first. It resounded in the whole limitless vault of the sky. Janet stared, shielding her eyes against the glare with a cupped hand.

The buzz deepened to a drone. It localized itself toward the north, faded away, and then swept down with redoubled strength, coming closer with incredible rapidity.

At last Janet's eyes found it—a blurred, black dot moving across the blue of the sky. The drone blended into deep, smooth thunder, and the dot picked up stubby little crossbars on either side.

Heels made a sudden racket on the rickety steps that led up to the roof's trapdoor, and Captain Perona popped breathlessly into sight.

"Pardon, senorita. But this is the best place... Where is it—the plane?"

Janet pointed. "There."

The black dot heeled over and became a stubby cross as the plane swerved and dipped down toward the canyon. The heliograph flickered at it.

The engine roared in a sudden blast of power, and the plane climbed steeply and then came down over the town in a smooth, careful glide with the engine punctuating it in nervous blurps. Janet could see now that it was a short-winged, short-bodied military pursuit ship with an enormous barrel of an engine.

"Yes!" Captain Perona shouted triumphantly. "It is Enrique!"

"Who?" Janet asked.

"My brother. He is a lieutenant—a pilot. He is bringing medicine—anti-tetanus vaccine for Lieutenant Ortega. Watch! Watch now!"

The plane dipped over the plaza, very low, like a swiftly dangerous bird of prey, and blurred little blobs fell out behind it— one, two, three. They jerked and skittered in the slipstream, and then suddenly blossomed out. They were small green parachutes, and they settled down toward the ground, swaying dignifiedly, while soldiers ran and shouted under them, trying to plot their course.

The plane bored upward into the air in tight spirals.

"Your scarf!" Captain Perona begged. "Give me your scarf, please!"

Janet pulled it from her neck. "But why——"

Captain Perona jumped up on the parapet and balanced there, waving the scarf in wild circles around his head.

"He can't see you," Janet said.

"But, yes! He knows I am here! He will be looking!"

The plane suddenly flattened out. The stubby wings waggled up and down, reflecting the sun in dazzling streaks.

Captain Perona waltzed precariously on the parapet. "You see? That Enrique! He has eyes like a hawk!"

Janet caught one booted leg. "Come down off that parapet! You'll fall!"

Captain Perona landed beside her breathlessly. "He saw me! Watch, now! Look!"

The plane rolled over with a sort of deadly precision and then dove straight down at them. The power was full on, and the sound deepened and bellowed until it was like a giant drum in Janet's head. The plane came down and down like an enormous bullet, and Janet could feel her knees trembling with the vibration, and then it flipped up and away, and its black shadow touched them and was gone.

Captain Perona laughed gleefully. "That Enrique! He tried to scare us!"

"He—he did?" Janet asked, swallowing.

Captain Perona grinned. "Enrique is the best pilot in Mexico. Watch him!"

The plane found altitude incredibly fast, and now it came slanting down again, sideslipping. It went past the roof so close that Janet thought she could have reached up and touched it. It was canted over at an impossible angle, and she caught one flashing glimpse of the opened, bonnet-like glassine that covered the cockpit. The pilot was leaning out, pointing with one stiff, black-clad arm.

"Yes!" Captain Perona shouted, making wildly affirmative gestures with his arms and head. "Stand up on the parapet, senorita!"

"Wh—what?" said Janet.

"Quick! So he can see you more plainly!"

Before Janet could move, he caught her around the waist with both hands and swung her up on the parapet. Janet opened her mouth to shout, and then the plane was back again, going much faster now, but closer and lower. She swayed dizzily in the tempest of its passage, and she had an eye-wink sight of the pilot's sinisterly helmeted head peering at her.

Captain Perona swung her down off the parapet again. "Now watch!"

The plane flipped over and roared at them, and as it went by Janet saw the pilot's arms sticking up straight out of the cockpit. He was shaking hands with himself like the victor in a prizefight.

Captain Perona laughed. "That Enrique! He is congratulating me!"

"What for?" Janet asked dizzily.

"Because he agrees with what I said about you."

"What you said... When did you tell him anything about me?"

"Over the military wireless—before he started on this trip."

The plane engine growled ominously.

Janet cringed. "Please tell him to go away!"

"He is going now. See?"

The plane came over the roof, much higher, and then scooted down over the soldiers on the far side of the canyon and waggled its wings at the heliograph. It climbed very rapidly and changed back into a black dot and disappeared over the mountain.

"He would have shown us more tricks," Captain Perona said, "only he is very busy now, and that is one of our newest pursuit ships, and he is not supposed to stunt needlessly with it. Here is your scarf, senorita. Thank you."

"What did you tell him about me?" Janet asked suspiciously, taking the scarf.

"I told him that you were very pretty and very silly."

"Silly!" Janet echoed.

"Oh, that is nothing personal, and besides he would know you were even if I had not told him."

"Well, why would he?"

"He knows all about young ladies from the United States, because be went to school there."

"Where?" Janet demanded. "What school?"

"A place called Harvard. It was very unfortunate, but we could do nothing about it,"

"Unfortunate?" Janet repeated. "Why?"

"He is the third son, you see, and we could not afford to give him a good education."

"Good... Why, Harvard is one of the finest universities in the United States!"

"As you say—in the United States."

Janet glared at him. "Well, where did you go to school?"

"I was very lucky. My family could afford to give me the best education. I studied in Mexico and Spain and Peru at the finest universities in the world. I know a great deal about everything, which is why I found your pretensions to learning so ridiculous."

"Oh, you did, did you? I'll have you know that the school system in the United States is the best there is anywhere!"

"You are mistaken."

"I am not!"

"Then why are there so many stupid people in the United States?"

"Why are there so many stupid people here?"

"Where?" asked Captain Perona politely.

"Very—near—here!"

"You are referring to me, no doubt?" said Captain Perona.

"Yes!"

"You think I am stupid?"

"Yes!"

"You see? Now you are being silly. You do not have the capability to appreciate true learning. And it was silly of you to tell me that falsehood about your being a professor."

"Now you look here!" said Janet. "Now you just look here! I studied nights and weekends and summers and all the rest of the time, and I have an A.B. and a M.A., and I have qualified for an associate professorship in two different colleges!"

"In what field?" Captain Perona inquired.

"Romance languages!"

Captain Perona raised his eyebrows. "Romance?"

"And it's not what you think, either!"

"I trust not. Have you anything more to say to me at this time, senorita?"

"You just bet I have!"

"Then do you mind if I sit down, please, while I give you my full attention? I am very tired."

"Oh," said Janet. "Haven't you had any sleep?"

"None," Captain Perona admitted ruefully. "I was sitting up all the night waiting for Senorita Tracy to regain consciousness, and then at dawn I started the searching parties and laid out territories and areas for each of them to cover."

"How is Miss Tracy?" Janet asked.

"She is all right now. She can leave the hospital this evening. The blow was painful but not serious."

"And Mr. Lepicik?"

"When I last saw him, he was sleeping on my bed. He looked as though he were enjoying himself thoroughly."

"I feel so sorry for him," Janet said. "That terrible tragedy..."

"Save your sympathy for Greg," Captain Perona advised. "I think he will need it."

"Have you found him yet?"

"No."

"What did Miss Tracy tell you about him?"

"It was as Timpkins suggested. She did not think my warning applied to her, and besides she is very sure of her ability to take care of herself. She went to her house to get some bedding and some clothes after dark last night. On her way back she saw Greg near the back of the hospital, and she spoke to him in the bold way she has. He struck her with a stone he was carrying."

195

"But why?"

"He was waiting to sneak in the hospital, then, I think. So he could find and kill Maria before she could give evidence that he was the one who had murdered Patricia Van Osdel and attacked Maria."

"Have you found Bautiste Bonofile?"

"No!" said Captain Perona. He made an angrily frustrated gesture. "And it is a thing that is not possible! Look, senorita. One can see the whole of this small town from this roof. Every house in it. And there is no way that either Bautiste Bonofile or Greg could get out of town. All exits and trails are guarded. And my men can see the whole of the country for many miles around from a number of sentry posts near here. We have searched everywhere thoroughly, and now we are searching a second time. Greg and Bautiste Bonofile are not here, and yet they could not be anywhere else!"

Doan cleared his throat. He was standing on the stairway with his head and shoulders protruding up through the trapdoor. He smiled at them benignly and said:

"Sorry to interrupt, but I wondered if I could send a wireless message through your soldier setup."

"You could not," said Captain Perona definitely. "I have already sent a message to your agency, telling them that you are safe—at the moment."

"Oh now, be reasonable," Doan requested. "I'm not trying to sneak out any information or anything you wouldn't want me to send. I just want to reassure my wife and kids."

Janet looked surprised. "I didn't know you were married."

"Sure. Didn't I tell you? I've got three kids. Little girls. Cute as bugs' ears. They'll be worried about me if they don't get a personal message, and so will my wife. See, I send the kids a telegram every couple of days when I'm away from home. It goes on my agency expense account, of course. But they'll know that if I don't send them a message after this earthquake it's because I'm not able to do it, and they'll imagine I'm at death's door or something. Please, Captain. The seven-year-old is sick with the measles, and the whole joint is quarantined, and they're pretty lonesome."

"Oh, let him!" Janet begged.

Captain Perona stared narrowly at Doan. "What kind of a message do you want to send?"

"Just dopey stuff that kids like. How Papa and Carstairs are okay and thinking of them and loving them. I mean, your man will see that it's addressed to the kids."

"Well..." said Captain Perona doubtfully. "All right."

Doan looked embarrassed. "Well, would it be okay if I sent it in pig-Latin?"

"What?" said Captain Perona. "Pigs?"

Janet said: "It's a sort of a schoolchild language. Switching the syllables of words around."

"For the kids," Doan explained. "They dote on that stuff. I always send them telegrams that way. Anybody can read it, of course, but they think it's a code all for them, and they get a big kick out of it."

"You give me your word you will not give them any information about the murders here or about Bautiste Bonofile?"

"Absolutely," said Doan. "I promise."

Captain Perona took a notebook from his pocket, scribbled on a page, and tore it out. "Here. The transmitting set is at headquarters. Give this to the sergeant in charge. He will send your message—if it is addressed to your children."

"Thanks a lot," said Doan. He kicked backwards. "Get off the ladder, Carstairs. Go on. Back down, you big goop." His head disappeared through the trapdoor.

"I think he's nice," Janet said.

"I wish I thought so," Captain Perona stated gloomily. "I really think Eldridge's death was accidental, and I do not believe Doan could possibly be concerned in the murders of Patricia Van Osdel and Maria, and I am sure that I know more about this affair than he can know. But still he worries me. I wish he were anywhere but here. He is too quick and too clever and too experienced, and this whole thing can be very bad for me unless it is cleared up at once."

"Why?" Janet asked. "It isn't your fault."

Captain Perona spoke slowly: "It is like this. Major Nacio is in charge of the search for Bautiste Bonofile. I am his second-in-command. I am not under the authority of Colonel Callao, although I must defer to him to a certain extent because of his rank. He is merely the district officer here. Major Nacio and his troops are specialists in anti-espionage—in work against subversive elements and spies as well as bandits. I asked to serve with them. It is an honor."

"Of course," said Janet.

"When we trailed the man Doan shot—Garcia—to Los Altos, then we knew that Bautiste Bonofile must be here somewhere close, because we knew that Bautiste Bonofile had some contact with Garcia, although we did not—and do not now—know what it was. Then Major Nacio's plan was put into effect. Every exit and entrance was watched day and night. Lepicik got through as he did only because of the excitement caused by the pursuit of Garcia. He would have been reported very soon if he had not reported himself. We watched Garcia continuously—to see whom he spoke to, whom he met, whom he even looked at. But Bautiste Bonofile managed to warn him anyway. After that, we chased Garcia back and forth through the town, blocking him off each time he tried to get out, hoping that Bautiste Bonofile would attempt to help him. It was a very small chance, I admit. Bautiste Bonofile is too cold-blooded to risk betraying himself to help anyone. However, had your tourists tried to get back out of Los Altos, you would have had a great deal more difficulty than you did coming in."

Janet shivered. "No wonder!"

"So then," said Captain Perona, "Garcia was shot by Doan. Major Nacio had planned for even a contingency like that. The town had been separated into small area units and soldiers assigned to each area. They went to work instantly, searching, questioning each person. You see, I was not neglecting my duties when I took you to the museum. There was nothing for me to do, then. The men are experts. They knew just what to do and how to do it. I had only to wait and sift any evidence which they found. Then came the earthquake."

"Even Major Nacio couldn't foresee that," Janet observed.

"No. Not even he. But since I am isolated here for the moment, I must handle what happens quickly and efficiently. The murders of Patricia Van Osdel and Maria... they must be solved at once, or it will reflect on me and on Major Nacio, too. I must find Greg. I have uncovered Bautiste Bonofile, due to your help, and I must find him, also. It is directly my responsibility, and it is a very grave one."

"Perhaps I could help you," Janet suggested.

Captain Perona looked at her. "Senorita, do you think this is some children's game? Do you realize the type and kind of men I am seeking? Do you realize that Greg and Bautiste Bonofile are murderers and would not hesitate for a second to strike again?"

"Of course I realize it."

"Then kindly occupy yourself with your ludicrous sight-seeing and leave serious matters to those who understand them. I must go now. Excuse me, please."

"Good-by!" Janet said definitely.

CHAPTER 12

J ANET FELL IN WITH LOCAL CUSTOM AND took a
siesta, and it was early in the afternoon when she came sleepily
down the stairs into the bar-restaurant of the Hacienda
Nueva Inglesa. The room was warm and shadowy, and the odors
of spilled wine and tobacco hung comfortably close in the air.

"This one!" said Mrs. Henshaw enthusiastically. She was holding
up one of Amanda Tracy's paintings. "This is the one I want. It'll
look wonderful in the living room."

"Relax," Henshaw advised. He was sitting in front of the door
into the kitchen like a cat waiting at a mousehole. "You ain't gonna
buy any pictures."

"In the living room," Mrs. Henshaw repeated, staring at the
picture raptly. "Right over the mantel."

"Over my dead body," Henshaw corrected.

Timpkins came in from the kitchen. "Dinner'll be served at six
sharp, if you please. It ain't gonna be fancy, and them as don't like
it don't need to eat it."

"Mr. Timpkins," Janet said. "Has my room been cleaned
today?"

"No," Timpkins answered.

"Well—who cleans it?"

"You do," Timpkins informed her. "If it gets cleaned."

"Haven't you any help at the hotel?"

"No. I don't need none."

"Timpkins," said Henshaw.

Timpkins looked at him. "What, now?"

"Sit down," Henshaw invited, crooking his finger and smiling
enticingly. "Right here in this nice chair. Rest yourself, Timpkins.
You've been working too hard all day."

Timpkins sat down slowly and suspiciously.

"I've been spending a lot of time thinking about your business
problems," Henshaw told him.

"I ain't got no business problems."

"That's just it," said Henshaw. "That's your trouble right there. Now you've got a swell setup here. You could make this hotel a gold mine."

"How?" Timpkins inquired skeptically.

"Think of your situation. Analyze it, Timpkins. That's the first step, always. Los Altos, with its scenery, with its quaintness, with its artistic history. It's a sure tourist-puller. And you're on the ground floor. I envy you, Timpkins. I see you as independently rich in the near future."

"Arr?" said Timpkins.

"Yes, indeed. Now consider the international situation. After this war, Europe is going to be a mess. Take my word for it, Timpkins. I know. People aren't going to want to go there any more. Besides that, they won't be able to afford it. They'll want to see new and different things closer to home. They'll want the atmosphere and adventure of foreign lands. Where will they go to get that, Timpkins?".

"Where?" said Timpkins.

"Here. In Los Altos. They'll come by the hundreds with money in their pockets. And when they come to Los Altos, they'll come here to this hotel—naturally. You'll coin dough. The place could be a mint for you. For instance, how much do you charge for rooms now?"

"Five dollars a day."

"You robber—I mean to say, that goes to prove what I'm telling you. You could charge much more—if you were progressive."

"Progressive?" Timpkins repeated.

"Yes. For instance, take the matter of a bathroom. Now I'm not trying to sell you a bathroom, Timpkins. Don't think that for a minute. I'm just using it for an illustration. Suppose tourists come in here after sight-seeing in the town—tired, dirty, discouraged— and they step into the hotel bathroom and they see something like this." Henshaw flipped out the shiny folder like a magician producing a rabbit. "4A, right here. A beautiful setup. Lavish and luxurious. Yellow and black tile with a guaranteed imitation marble trim and plastic streamlined fixtures."

"Naw!" said Timpkins.

"Wait, now. I'm not suggesting you should buy it. Maybe something else would be more suitable. But the tourists would be impressed, Timpkins. In the United States people judge you by your bathroom. It's the most important part of your house. These tourists, after they'd seen 4-A, would go away feeling impressed and refreshed. They'd advertise you by word-of-mouth to other tourists. Now just look through this folder. Pick out something to your own taste."

"Naw!" said Timpkins.

Doan was sitting in the corner near the end of the bar with his hat down over his eyes. Carstairs lay in front of him, snoring in pleasantly deep gurgles.

"Timpkins," said Doan, pushing his hat up. "What part of England do you come from?"

"I'm a British subject," said Timpkins.

"Also a Canadian, I'll bet."

"Arr," said Timpkins. "What's it to you?"

"Nothing. Ever been in England?"

"Yes!"

"For how long?"

"Two weeks," said Timpkins sullenly. He got up. "Now I don't want none of you botherin' me any more. I'm busy."

He went back into the kitchen and slammed the door.

"Thanks, Doan," Henshaw said. "That gives me a new lead. I don't know what kind of bathrooms they got in England, but I've been in Canada once. I went to Niagara Falls and walked across the bridge. I'll run in some references to that the next time I catch him. Always establish some common ground with a prospect. You notice how I sneaked up on him, then? I'm gonna sell him. You watch."

"Mr. Doan," said Janet, "did you get your message off all right?"

"Yes, thanks," Doan told her. "My little girls will get a great kick out of it."

"How old are they?"

"Five and seven and nine. Two brunettes and a blonde."

"What color is your wife's hair?"

"It changes. It's red now."

"Hi-yo, Silver!" Mortimer yelled. He came galloping in through the front door. He had strapped the spurs on over his tennis shoes, and he had to run both bowlegged and pigeon-toed to keep from tripping over them. He had stuffed paper in the band of the sombrero, and it waggled precariously on his head, the enormous brim extending far out beyond his puny shoulders.

"Whoa, Silver," he commanded belligerently, prancing and kicking out with the spurs. He had a braided leather quirt in his hand, and he slashed furiously at the air around him.

"Where'd you get that whip?" Henshaw demanded.

"Just picked it up," Mortimer answered.

"Well, you just pick it back again. Do you wanna get me shot or something, you little rummy?"

"Go dive for a pearl," Mortimer invited. He pranced over to Doan. "Hey, puffy, can I ride the flea-trap?"

"Carstairs?" Doan asked. "Oh, sure. Go right ahead, Mortimer."

Mortimer straddled the sleeping Carstairs. "Get up!" he yelled, punching Carstairs with the quirt.

Carstairs got up—and fast. Mortimer did a neat back-flip in the air and landed flat on his face on the floor. Carstairs sat down on him.

"I figured that would be it," said Doan.

Mortimer yelled in a choked, wheezing gasp. Mrs. Henshaw screamed and ran for him. One of Mortimer's arms stuck out from under Carstairs, and she grabbed that and tugged with all her might.

"Get off, Carstairs," Doan said. "You'll squash the little dope."

Carstairs looked interested but not cooperative. Doan sighed and got up. He took hold of Carstairs' spiked collar and heaved. Mrs. Henshaw pulled at Mortimer. Nothing happened.

"Quit it, Carstairs," Doan ordered. He spat on his hands, took a

new grip on the collar, and heaved back with all his might.

Carstairs stood up. Doan sat down hard, and so did Mrs. Henshaw. Mortimer's face was blue, and his mouth was wide open, and his eyes were popped like grapes. He drew in his breath in a strangled gulp and promptly let it go again.

"Yeow! Maw!"

Mrs. Henshaw blubbered over him. "Mama's poor, poor baby! Don't you cry! We'll have the soldiers shoot the nasty, dirty, old dog!"

"The hell we will," said Henshaw. "We'll buy him a medal or a beefsteak or something."

Doan got up and brushed himself off tenderly. "Damn you," he said to Carstairs. "That floor has got slivers in it."

Carstairs yawned and walked to the door. He stood there looking back over his shoulder at Doan.

"Well, go on out," Doan said. "The soldiers are gone now. Nobody will stop you."

Carstairs mumbled deep in his throat.

"Listen," said Doan, "you're a big dog now. You can go out and attend to your private affairs without me supervising you or them."

Carstairs barked once and made the kerosene lamp jump and jingle on its chain.

"All right," Doan said. "All right!" He went to the door and bunted Carstairs in the rear with his knee. "Get going then, stupid."

Mortimer sat up and wiped his nose on his sleeve.

Mrs. Henshaw dabbed and cooed at him in her worried, futile way.

Timpkins opened the kitchen door. "What's all this noise, now? I ain't gonna have no riots in my hotel!"

"Timpkins," said Henshaw quickly, "I didn't know you were from Canada. That's a beautiful country, and I've always admired it. I went across from Niagara Falls, and that reminds me of our new waterfall flushing system. If you'll just sit down I'll explain—"

"Naw!" said Timpkins, and slammed the door.

"He's weakening," Henshaw said in a satisfied tone. "I'll get him."

Running footsteps made a crisply angry tattoo on the paving outside, and Captain Perona burst through the door.

"Where is he?" he demanded. "Where is that Doan?"

"He just stepped out a second ago to walk his dog," Janet answered. "What's the matter?"

Captain Perona had a slip of yellow paper in his hand, and he waved it in front of her face. "Look! Look at this!"

Janet caught at the paper. "It's a message addressed to Mr. Doan."

"Read it!" Captain Perona snarled.

The message was printed in block letters in pencil, evidently just as the military wireless operator had taken it down. It said in English:

WHY THE PIG LATIN IT TOOK ME AN HOUR TO FIGURE OUT YOU WERENT DRUNK AND DROOLING BUT YOU HIT THE JACKPOT ALL RIGHT I CALLED VAN OSDEL LAWYERS AND THEY HAD NO IDEA THAT PATRICIAS DEATH WAS MURDER AND HIRED US AT ONCE AT FLAT RATE WITH BONUS IF SOLVED AND OPTION ALL FUTURE FLY GOO BUSINESS CONGRATULATIONS AND HIT THIS ONE HARD WITH NO SHARP SHOOTING OR CHISELING.

The signature, written out in the same block letters, was:

**A. TRUEGOLD
PRESIDENT
SEVERN INTERNATIONAL DETECTIVES.**

Janet looked up. "But—but what—"

"Children!" Captain Perona exploded. "Pig's Latin! That criminal sent a message to his detective agency and got them hired

205

to solve the murder of Patricia Van Osdel!"

"How could he have done that?"

"The names of his children are nothing but a code address—an accommodation address! As soon as the message was received there, it was sent to the agency!"

"But your operator—"

"He understands and reads English, but not well. And Doan deceived him. He gave the operator the message a word at a time, constantly correcting and changing it, until the operator was confused. Doan showed him how to transpose the words, or pretended to, but the operator could not do that in a strange language and send them with corrections all at once."

"Doesn't Doan have any children?"

"No! He is not even married!"

"Why, he—he told me—"

"Yes!" Captain Perona agreed fiercely. "He told you! And you told me! You, if you recall, begged me to let him reassure his family! You!"

"Well, I didn't know—"

Captain Perona leaned close to her. "Senorita, the number of things you do not know constantly amazes me!"

"Is that so?"

"Yes! After this kindly keep your ignorance to yourself and cease annoying me!"

Captain Perona whirled around and ran out the door.

"Acts like he was mad or something," Henshaw observed.

"He is," Janet agreed. "And I really don't blame him." She started for the door.

"Where you going?" Henshaw asked.

"I'm just tired of people!" Janet said. "I'm going to talk to a stone image!"

"There are sure a lot of whacks around this joint," Henshaw observed. "I hope it ain't catching."

CHAPTER 13

DOAN AND CARSTAIRS WERE ON A NARROW LITTLE street high on the mountainside above the main part of the town. They had arrived there by easy stages, wandering back and forth aimlessly among the crooked lanes, and now Doan stopped and gazed curiously at a ten-foot wall with broken glass making a faint, sinister glimmer along its top. The wall ran for a good hundred yards along the street. There were some fresh cracks in it, mementos of the earthquake, but it still looked formidably solid.

"Hoo!" said a voice suddenly.

Doan looked around and saw a little boy about ten feet behind him.

"Beeg," said the little boy, pointing at Carstairs. He grinned at Doan. He had three front teeth missing.

"Big and dumb," Doan agreed. "Haven't I seen you before somewhere?"

"Gimme dime."

"I thought so." Doan took a dime out of his pocket and held it up. "But let's you earn it this time. Ever hear of a guy named Predilip?"

"Ah?"

"An artist named Predilip."

The little boy nodded triumphantly. "Boo yet."

"Boo yet," Doan repeated thoughtfully. "Boo yet... You bet?"

The little boy nodded again. "Boo yet."

"Have it your way, then. Where did he live?"

The little boy made flapping motions with his arms and rolled his eyes piously skyward.

"Flying," said Doan. "Up. Angels in heaven?"

"Boo yet."

"I know he's dead," said Doan. "Where did he live before he got dead?"

"Live?"

207

"Home. House. Shack. Domicile."

"Los Altos."

Doan sighed. "I know he lived in Los Altos. But where?"

"Los Altos."

"Okay," said Doan. "Did you ever see any of his paintings?"

"Ah?"

"Paintings. Pictures."

The little boy looked around cautiously. "You wanna buy feelthy picture?"

"No!"

"My uncle, he sell. Very good. Very joocy. Oooh, my!"

"I don't want to buy any dirty pictures. I'm talking about an artist named Predilip."

"Gimme dime."

Doan gave him the dime.

"Denk goo," said the little boy, putting the dime carefully in his shirt pocket. He spun around like a top and ran headlong down the street.

"Hey, you!" Doan called. "Wait a minute! What's behind this wall here?"

The little boy shrilled over his shoulder. *"Casa del Coronel Callao! Muy malo!"*

"I got part of that, anyway," Doan said to Carstairs. "It seems that our pal, Colonel Callao, lives back of this Maginot Line somewhere. Let's go have a chat with him."

CHAPTER 14

T HE WEST SLOPE ABOVE LOS ALTOS WAS MUCH steeper than it looked from the safe distance of the hotel roof, and Janet began to regret her impulse to climb it before she was halfway to the rock-face. The tough, stunted brush tore at her skirt with stubborn, clinging fingers, and there was no breeze to disturb the gleeful jiggle of the heat waves.

A loose pebble got into her shoe, and she had to stop and shake it out. She breathed deeply, and the air was so thin and hot in her lungs that it was not refreshing at all. She almost gave it up then, but she thought of Captain Perona and Doan and his three nonexistent children and man's deceit to woman in general and put her head down and plodded on.

She reached the stone face at last and leaned against it, puffing. The rock pedestal, too, was much larger than it had seemed from the hotel. She looked despairingly up at the overhang that marked its brows, and then she found a series of weatherworn niches on one side.

She climbed up laboriously, flattened against the rock, fingers clutching frantically at the warm, rough stone, until her face was even with the brow. Now all she had to do was to turn around and look in the direction the stone face was looking. That wasn't easy. It took her ten minutes and a broken fingernail, and her neck began to ache abominably.

Finally she got the angle. The stone face was looking at the east slope, and Janet did, too, sighting professionally with one eye squinted shut. Miraculously the three pillars lined up for her—the big one, the medium one, and the small one. Their tops made a neat, down-slanting diagonal.

Janet sighted and calculated and figured, trying to fix the point where the line of that diagonal would hit the slope on beyond the three pillars. She thought she had it finally, and she crawled down the pedestal again and started to work her way across the slope.

The heat seemed to have redoubled, and the warmth of the sun was a sharp-edged weight against the back of her neck. Her mouth felt like it was full of absorbent cotton.

She reached the three pedestals and went on grimly past them. A stubby bush tore a jagged rip in her skirt and left a red, angry mark on the calf of her leg. She stopped and stamped her foot and swore, but she kept her eyes pinned on the spot she had marked ahead.

And then, when she got there, she found she wasn't any place. The spot looked just like the rest of the slope even more so. There was brush, and there was rock, and that was all.

Janet kicked at the brush, and a scorpion scuttled away from her feet. Janet stood still, staring after it, afraid to move. It was an ugly little horror with shiny, jittering legs that clawed at the rock surface and a sting that arched up over its back. Janet swallowed hard and looked longingly down toward the cool shelter of Los Altos.

A voice came hollow and soft from just behind her: "Yes. This is the place."

Janet whirled around. A stunted bush that was like any other bush and the rock under it that was like any other rock had turned out to be something entirely different. The rock had tilted back and up on a pivot, and the shadowed, thin face and liquidly dark eyes of the man who was sometimes Tio Riquez and other times Bautiste Bonofile looked out of the black, square hole underneath it.

"Come here," he said softly.

Janet stood braced and rigid, and she moved one foot back a little.

The long, silvered barrel of Bautiste Bonofile's revolver glinted in the sun. "I won't hesitate to kill you. I have no prejudice against killing women. I've killed a good many at one time and another. Come here."

Janet took a step and then another. Her shoe sole scraped on rock, reluctantly. She drew a deep breath.

"Don't do that," said Bautiste Bonofile. "Don't scream. I'll shoot."

"You—you don't dare—"

"The noise?" said Bautiste Bonofile. "Is that what you're thinking of? That won't stop me. You couldn't find this place, even when you knew where it was and what to look for. No one who didn't know it was here would even suspect such an improbable thing. It would be thought that someone shot you and ran off. Come here."

Janet's feet moved her unwillingly to the black hole, and Bautiste Bonofile drew back and out of sight.

"I can see you," he said. "Very plainly. Come inside. There are steps."

Janet groped down with one foot and found a square, small step cut in the rock. She went down, found another and another. The air felt cool and damp and thick against her face, and she shivered.

There was a little grating noise and a solid thump as the rock door swung shut over her, and the blackness was like a thick cloth over her eyes. She made a little gasping sound.

There was a click, and the bright, round beam of a flashlight moved up and steadied on her face. The dazzling white circle was her whole world, and she could see nothing else and hear nothing until Bautiste Bonofile said in his soft, thoughtful voice:

"How did you know this place was here?"

"I—read about it."

Fingers moved out of the darkness and touched her throat silkily. "Don't lie, please."

Janet pressed her shoulders back hard against cool stone. "I'm not! I did read it—in that same old diary that described the cellar under the church. I remembered it after I noticed the stone face from the roof of the hotel this morning. The diary told how Lieutenant Perona—not the Perona in Los Altos now, but his ancestor—had built another, auxiliary cache above the church. It was a smaller one—for emergencies. It told how to locate it by lining up the rock face with the three pillars."

"I see," said Bautiste Bonofile. "I didn't know all that. I stumbled on the place quite by accident, and I saw that it had possibilities. I didn't know it had a history. Your research must be very interesting,

211

but twice now it has proven to be dangerous for you. Why did you come here?"

"Why, I was just curious... I wanted to see if it was still here—the cache—and if there were any relics..."

"I see," Bautiste Bonofile repeated. "There were several things here when I first found it—some old tools and some boxes that had rotted away to dust. I spent a considerable amount of time improving the place."

The flashlight flicked away from Janet's face and swung around to show a narrow, dark doorway in the opposite wall.

"A—a tunnel?" Janet asked.

"Yes."

The flashlight came back to her face, and the silence grew and lengthened interminably.

Janet swallowed. "What—what are you going to do?"

"With you?" Bautiste Bonofile inquired. "You've caused me quite a lot of trouble."

"I didn't mean—"

"No. Of course not." Bautiste Bonofile chuckled gently. "It's amusing to think that Perona's ancestor is furnishing me a hiding place, isn't it? I would have appreciated it even more all this time if I'd known that. I'm glad you told me. Now as for you. I wonder—"

"Are you going to—to shoot me?"

"That's what I'm wondering," said Bautiste Bonofile.

It was weird and unbelievable, and it was chillingly real. He didn't grit his teeth or snarl or run through any gamut of emotions, but Janet knew with a queer, cold clarity that if he decided it was a good idea to shoot her he would do it right here and now without any further fuss. She waited, holding her breath, and a pulse began to pound in her throat.

"I wonder," said Bautiste Bonofile again, "I think perhaps I could use you. Captain Perona seemed very interested indeed."

Janet tried to keep her voice from quavering. "You know he wouldn't let you go even if—even if—"

"Even if he knew I was holding you for a hostage?" Bautiste

Bonofile finished. "I think it very likely that he might. He knows me, you see. He knows that whatever I promised to do to you, I'd do. And even if he didn't care for you much personally, you are a citizen of the United States, and that might mean diplomatic difficulties for him if you should die in some particularly unpleasant manner in public, as it were.... Go through that door there. Walk straight ahead."

The flashlight moved away and outlined the narrow doorway. Janet moved stiffly toward it, and the rough sides brushed her shoulders. Her body blocked all but stray flickers of the lights, and she groped uncertainly.

"Watch your head," Bautiste Bonofile warned. He made no noise behind her. "Keep going."

The tunnel went on endlessly, and the air grew dust-choked and stifling. Several times Janet bumped her head against projections of rock, and time and the tunnel stretched into nightmare proportions in her dazed mind.

"Slowly now," Bautiste Bonofile said.

And then suddenly there was a scratching, scraping sound right over her head. Janet stopped with a jerk. The barrel of the revolver made a round, dangerous period pressed against her back. Bautiste Bonofile's hand slid over her shoulder and touched her lips warningly.

"Quiet," he whispered.

The fast, irregular scraping stopped, and something snorted loudly. Then Doan's voice, sounding muffled but quite clear, said:

"Don't you think you're a bit too old and too big to dig for field mice?"

There was another snort and a mumbling growl. The scraping sound started again.

"Quit it, stupid," said Doan. "Get away from there and stop playing puppy."

Carstairs bayed angrily, and the sound of it was like a blow against Janet's eardrums.

"Well, what?" Doan demanded. "I don't see anything."

Carstairs bayed again, more loudly.

"Less noise, please," said Doan. "We're trespassers, you know. Do you want to get me an interview with some of Perona's soldiers?"

Bautiste Bonofile moved in the darkness and murmured in Janet's ear: "Reach up over your head. Push the rock."

The rock was counterweighted like the other, and it swung back and up in a solid square. Sunlight bit brilliantly into Janet's eyes.

She was staring up into Doan's surprised face. He made a quick, tentative motion with his right hand that stopped as soon as it started.

"That's right," said Bautiste Bonofile. "I will shoot her unless you do exactly as I say."

Doan smiled blandly. "Well, of course. I'm not hostile. I was just startled. You're Bautiste Bonofile, huh? I've been wanting to have a talk with you."

"Step down into the tunnel," said Bautiste Bonofile. His hand touched Janet's shoulder. "Back up."

She went back three shuffling steps. Doan swung agilely through the square opening and dropped into the tunnel. He kept his hands half raised.

Above them Carstairs barked angrily.

"Make him stop that noise!" Bautiste Bonofile ordered. "Make him come down here!"

Doan turned around and hauled himself half out of the opening. He grabbed Carstairs by the collar. He pulled. So did Carstairs—in the opposite direction.

"Get him in here quickly," Bautiste Bonofile said in a dangerous tone. "Don't play tricks."

"He's afraid of holes," Doan panted. "Come on, damn you! Get in here!"

Carstairs' claws skittered on the edge of the opening. Doan was hanging down from his collar, half suspended.

"He got stuck—in a culvert once," Doan gasped. "Scared—ever since. Come on, Carstairs. Hike!"

He let go and ducked. Carstairs sprang straight over his head with a raging snarl, fangs bared, eyes greenish and savage. His broad chest struck Janet with the weight of a pile driver and knocked her sideways and down, and as she fell she saw Doan spin around as lightly and gracefully as a dancer with the little .25 automatic in his hand. He shot and shot again instantly.

The powder flare burned Janet's face, and the echoing roar of the shots deafened her. The smoky tunnel tipped and swerved dizzily in front of her eyes."

Doan's hands were under her arms, lifting her. "Are you hurt?"

"N-no," Janet gasped. "I guess—"

Carstairs growled in the darkness.

"Let him alone," Doan said. "He's not going anywhere."

Janet swallowed hard, fighting against the numb sickness that was creeping over her. "Is he—hurt?"

"Not a bit," said Doan. "He's just dead. Here! Brace up!"

"I—I think—"

Doan scrambled out of the tunnel and leaned back through the opening. "Here! Grab my hands!"

Janet caught at them, and he swung her lightly upward into fresh, clean air and sunlight.

"Sit down. That's it."

Janet sat down and breathed deeply again and again.

"Feel better now?" Doan asked, watching her.

"Yes," said Janet firmly. "Did you really kill Bautiste Bonofile?"

Doan nodded. "I thought it was a good idea. He might have been carrying another rattlesnake in his pocket, and I'm allergic to them. Carstairs."

Carstairs put his head out of the square opening. Doan caught his collar and heaved. Carstairs grunted and scrambled and came up on to solid ground. He shook himself distastefully, looking at Doan.

"That was nice interference you ran for me," Doan told him. "I thank you very kindly."

Carstairs sat down and looked pleased with himself. He lolled

215

out a tongue that had an ugly little smear of red on it and panted cheerfully at Janet. Doan walked over and kicked the tunnel entrance stone, and it swung on its pivot and thumped shut and became part of the smooth unbroken tile of the patio in which they were sitting.

"Neat," Doan commented.

Janet looked around. A high wall stretched on three sides of them, and the other side was taken up by the long sun veranda of a house. There were chrome easy chairs with gaily colored leather cushions on the veranda and a swing with a striped canopy and tables with glass tops.

"Quite a gaudy dive," said Doan. "The earthquake knocked a piece out of the wall over there." He pointed to a V-shaped notch with a pile of rubble lying below it. "Carstairs and I came in that way. I think that tunnel must have an air-hole or a ventilator in it. Carstairs trailed it clear across the patio. How did you get into it?"

"From the other end. I read about a cache that Lieutenant Perona had dug, and I was looking for it when—"

"That Perona," said Doan, "turned out to be quite a dangerous guy for you to know. And you'd better watch that descendant of his pretty closely, too."

"You lied to him," Janet accused, remembering.

"What about?" Doan asked.

"You're not married!. You don't have any wife and three small girls!"

Doan watched her. "How'd you find that out?"

"From the answer to your message"

"Answer?" said Doan. "Answer! Did that damned, dumb Truegold send me a straight answer through the military wireless setup?"

"Yes, he did."

"What did it say?"

"It said that he had informed the Van Osdel interests about Patricia's murder and that your agency had been hired to solve the mystery."

"All right," said Doan. "But that Truegold is too dumb even for the president of a detective agency. Wait until I see him again."

"That's not the point, Mr. Doan. You appealed to Captain Perona's pity by telling him about your children being quarantined with the measles, and you gave your word that you wouldn't send out information about Patricia Van Osdel."

"I told him I wouldn't tell my kids," Doan corrected. "But that's just a weasel. Yes, I lied to him."

"Well, aren't you ashamed? You involved me, too."

"You shouldn't have believed me," Doan said. "And neither should Perona have."

"Why not?" Janet demanded indignantly.

"Because I'm a detective," Doan said. "I told you something in the same line before. Detectives never tell the truth if they can help it. They lie all the time. It's just business."

"Not all detectives!"

Doan nodded, seriously now. "Yes. Every detective ever born, and every one who ever will be. Honest. Perona should have known that. He lies himself whenever he thinks it's a good idea. I'm sorry, though, if he got mad at you on my account."

"You had no right..." Janet paused. "Oh dear! You just saved my life, and now I'm talking to you this way.... I'm sorry, Mr. Doan!"

Doan chuckled. "Forget it. So many people are mad at me for so many different reasons that one more or less—"

Carstairs growled, and Doan whirled around tensely. *"Aqui!"* a voice shouted.

A soldier was peering at them through the niche in the wall. He climbed over and dropped into the patio. Another soldier and another and another scrambled over after him. They advanced in a raggedly spaced line. Their bayonets glittered, and their brown faces were grimly set.

"Something tells me," said Doan, "that I'm going to have a heart-to-heart chat with Captain Perona in the very near future."

217

I T WAS THE SAME SMALL, SQUARE ROOM in which Doan had been incarcerated before, but now Captain Perona and Colonel Callao and Lieutenant Ortega sat in a solemn, official row behind a table in the center of the floor. None of them spoke when the soldiers ushered Doan and Janet into the room. Carstairs was between Doan and Janet, and he sat down and looked at the three officers for a moment and then yawned in a pointed way. Captain Perona nodded at the soldiers, and they went out and closed the door.

"Senorita Martin," said Captain Perona formally, "I regret to see you in your present company."

"Mr. Doan and Carstairs are my friends!" Janet told him.

"That shows loyalty but also a lamentable lack of brains," said Captain Perona. "Now kindly keep silent until you are addressed. Doan, this is a military court of inquiry. We would have met sooner to consider some of your actions if it had not been for the confusion resulting from the earthquake."

"No need to apologize," Doan said amiably.

Captain Perona's lips tightened. "That was not my intention. By a very contemptible sort of trick, you deceived me and sent a message to the detective agency which employs you informing them of Patricia Van Osdel's murder. As a result—which you intended—you have been hired to solve the mystery of her death, although there is no mystery."

"No?" said Doan.

"No. You will receive no fee from this case. I have solved the murder, and I have no intention of letting you steal the credit for it. We have learned through our own sources of inquiry that Patricia Van Os-del drew twenty-five thousand dollars in United States' currency from her bank in Mexico City four days ago. She made no major purchases subsequent to that time, and it is reasonable to assume, since a search of her possessions at the Hotel Azteca failed to reveal it, that she brought the money to Los Altos with her."

"In her purse," said Doan.

"That is immaterial. The money furnished the motive for her murder. Her companion, Greg, knew she had it. He was looking for an opportunity to steal it. The earthquake gave him an excellent chance. He struck down Patricia Van Osdel and the maid, Maria, and stole the money. But Maria was only wounded. She could identify Greg as the murderer when she recovered consciousness and would certainly do so. He came to the hospital and killed her last night to insure her silence. He was seen by Amanda Tracy, and he struck her down, again to keep from being identified."

"Greg got his arm broken in the earthquake," Doan observed.

"Yes. He fell while he was pursuing Maria. That is why he only wounded her then. He was in great pain and anxious to get away from the scene of his crime. We have not apprehended him as yet, but we will very soon. That ends the matter. Also, it absolves the Mexican government and the army of any responsibility. Patricia Van Osdel virtually caused her own death by her choice in friends and by secretly carrying such a sum of money with her without informing us of the fact so we could take extra precautions to protect her. Now have you anything to say?"

"Oh, a hell of a lot," Doan answered.

"Proceed," said Captain Perona.

"Well," said Doan. "First there's me. You were under a little misapprehension as to why I came to Los Altos. I wasn't hired by any crooked politicians to come down here and persuade Eldridge not to come back to the United States."

"No?" said Captain Perona.

"No. I was hired by a Committee of Good Government to bring him back so they could give the brush-off to the crooked outfit that is running the state. That outfit is slightly on the subversive side, and a lot of people would like to see them go away and not come back any more. If Eldridge testified to what he knew, it would have done the job up brown. But the Committee couldn't get him extradited because he had too much influence here and there."

"This is very interesting," said Captain Perona, "if true."

"It's true. Due to slander, libel, defamation of character, and

219

unfounded rumors I have the reputation of being a little sharp in my business activities."

"Yes, indeed," Captain Perona agreed.

"So they hired me to pretend I was hired by Eldridge's crooked pals to scare him into staying here. That would naturally make him slightly resentful. Then he and I would cook up some sort of a supposed double-cross of his crooked pals, and he would return to the United States voluntarily so the Committee could lay hands on him and throw him in jail until he got talkative. Eldridge actually had no intention of returning, before we started to work on him. He was just talking in the hopes of shaking down his pals."

"You actually expect me to believe this?" Captain Perona asked politely.

"Sure."

Captain Perona watched him. "You forgot to mention the matter of the ten-thousand-dollar bribe."

"No, I didn't. There wasn't any bribe or any ten thousand dollars. That was just a rumor."

"What is in the safety deposit box in Chicago?"

"A well-gnawed steak bone," said Doan. "Carstairs is progressive. He doesn't bury his bones like other dogs. He deposits them in banks."

"Bah!" Captain Perona exploded.

"Honest," said Doan. "I'll sign a power of attorney, and you can have your consular agent go and look in the box."

Captain Perona breathed deeply. "If this fantastic nonsense has the faintest relation to the truth," he said with a certain amount of satisfaction, "you have failed in your mission."

"Oh, no," said Doan. "Eldridge dictated a dying statement to me—signed, sealed, and witnessed in triplicate."

Lieutenant Ortega looked up quickly. "That is impossible. Eldridge could not possibly have dictated a statement after receiving the injuries which caused his death."

"He did, though," Doan maintained.

Captain Perona frowned at him. "You intend to forge a statement."

"Me?" said Doan. "Oh, no. Why, if I did that all those crooked politicians would haul me into court and prove the charges in the statement were false."

Captain Perona opened his mouth and shut it again, helplessly. "Doan," he said at last, "the United States is an ally of this country's, and as such we wish to treat its nationals with all due consideration, but I warn you to get out of Mexico and stay out."

"Wait a minute," said Doan. "I want to set you straight on a couple of other matters first."

"What matters?" Captain Perona inquired icily.

"I want my dough. I want you to give me the official credit for solving the mystery of Patricia Van Osdel's death."

"And what possible reason could I have for doing that?"

"Because if you do, I'll tell you where to find Bautiste Bonofile."

There was a dead, ominous silence.

Captain Perona stirred a little in his chair. "I now retract what I said a moment ago. You are not going to leave Mexico. You are going to stay here for about twenty years, I think."

"It's nice of you to ask me," said Doan. "But no."

"Where—is—Bautiste—Bonofile?"

"Do I get credit on the Van Osdel deal?"

"No! If you do not tell me at once where Bautiste Bonofile is, you are going to regret it."

"Don't get tough," Doan warned, "or I'll dummy up on you, and then you'll never find him. Come on, Perona. Let's make a deal. I get credit for Van Osdel. You get credit for Bautiste Bonofile. That's a nice offer."

Captain Perona rubbed his hand over his face and sighed deeply. "I dislike you, Doan. I dislike you very much, indeed. You are an unscrupulous, cold-blooded criminal, and I think—and hope most fervently—that you will come to a bad end one day soon."

"I can hardly wait," said Doan. "But let's make a deal first."

Captain Perona said: "I have failed to find Bautiste Bonofile, and that is a reflection on me and on Major Nacio's organization. The cables will be in place over the Canyon of Black Shadow by tonight. My failure will then be a matter of public knowledge. You have won, Doan. I must bargain with you because I have no choice. You will be given the credit for solving Patricia Van Osdel's death. Where is Bautiste Bonofile?"

"In a tunnel under Colonel Callao's patio."

"What?" said Captain Perona sharply.

Doan nodded. "Yeah. He is."

Captain Perona turned slowly to look at Colonel Callao. Colonel Callao's face was as loosely blank as ever, and he was smiling, but there was a sheen of perspiration on his forehead.

"Don't let him kid you," said Doan. "He understands English. Enough to get by, anyway. He's got a swell poker face, but he can't control his eyes. I think he's been dealing for and covering Bautiste Bonofile all along."

Colonel Callao stood up very slowly and leaned his weight against the table. His face was darkly leaden now. No one else in the room spoke or moved. Finally Colonel Callao pushed himself away from the table, swaying a little, and walked toward the door, pushing one foot ahead of the other.

Captain Perona looked at Lieutenant Ortega and nodded once. "I assume all responsibility here. I order you to follow Colonel Callao and place him under close arrest."

Lieutenant Ortega got up and saluted stiffly. He walked out of the room behind Colonel Callao. The door boomed shut.

Captain Perona looked at Doan. "I like you even less after this. Colonel Callao is a drunken pig, but he has done some very brave things in his day. I had some suspicion of him. I thought he understood English, and I have been trying to trick him into betraying himself by insulting him in that language, but he was too clever. Explain to me how you knew where to find Bautiste Bonofile."

"I didn't know, and I didn't find him. Janet did."

Captain Perona glared at her. "You! You knew! And you stood there silent and let me compromise my honor by bargaining with this criminal!"

"You told me to keep still until you addressed me," Janet said.

"So! You choose this particular time—the only time since I have met you—to obey my orders!"

"Stop shouting at me."

"I will shout at you if I please!" Captain Perona roared. "You do not have the brains of a two-year-old child! I think I will put you in jail and keep you there until I decide whether or not I want to marry you!"

"What?" Janet said dazedly. "What did you say? Until you decide whether or not you want—"

"Do not be coy," Captain Perona ordered. "I detest that in a woman. I have not made up my mind as yet whether you would be a suitable wife for me, and after this performance I have grave doubts. But I am a just man, and I will give you one final chance to prove you are worthy of the honor. How did you find Bautiste Bonofile?"

Janet stamped her foot. "If you dare to think I would ever even consider—"

"Answer my question!"

"I won't!"

Doan said mildly: "It was that diary again. There was another cache dug by your illustrious ancestor mentioned in it. Janet was looking for it. Bautiste Bonofile had found it. I forgot to tell you that he's dead."

"Dead!"

"Yes," said Doan. "And I'll save you the trouble of asking. It was me again. I shot him."

"So!" said Captain Perona. "You lied about that also! You did have another gun!"

"Don't you *dare* talk to him like that!" Janet shrilled. "Mr. Doan saved my life! That Bautiste had a gun poked right against my back, and Carstairs jumped at him, and Mr. Doan shot him, and it was good enough for him! And if you weren't such an arrogant dumbhead it never would have happened because you would have found Bautiste months ago!"

"I am afraid that is correct," Captain Perona admitted ruefully. "So then, Doan, the matter becomes settled. Now all that is needed

223

is for us to find the man, Greg."

"Oh, I know where he is, too," said Doan.

"What?" said Captain Perona incredulously. "You know... Well, where is he?"

"In his grave."

Captain Perona stared at him. "You said—grave?"

"Sure. I knew that right away when you couldn't find him. Greg couldn't hide in Los Altos for five minutes without being spotted if he was alive. A dead man—a buried one doesn't take up much room. There are lots of fresh ruins around here."

"You are insane," said Captain Perona.

"Nope. Look at it this way. Patricia Van Osdel drew a lot of money out of the bank and made a big point of coming here at this particular time—even bribed the hotel to put on the bus trip after they had canceled it. Why? Because she had an appointment with someone here yesterday. Greg might have known about the money she was carrying, but there was one other person who would be sure to."

"Who?" Captain Perona asked numbly.

"Why, the person she was going to pay it to."

The hinges on the door at the back of the room creaked just slightly, and then a voice said bitterly:

"You dirty little rat. You dirty, stinking crook."

"Hello, Amanda," said Doan. "I was just telling the Captain that if he really wanted to find Greg he could probably uncover what's left of him if he dug around under your house a bit."

Amanda Tracy was wearing a bandage like a lopsided turban over her frizzed hair. Under it the tanned skin of her face looked dry and yellowish.

"No," Janet breathed softly. "Oh, no."

"Yes," said Doan. "Amanda cooked up a deal to do Patricia out of some of her dough. Offhand I'd bet that she told Patricia that she had uncovered some of Predilip's paintings. The reason I say that is because Patricia was careful never to mention Predilip's name, although he's one of the best reasons to come to this town. Patricia was a bit of a chiseler in her refined way, and if she thought she could get an undercover bargain in some previously undiscovered paintings which now are very valuable, she'd come running, and she'd bring cash to overawe the person she was dealing with. How about it, Amanda?"

"You're so damned smart," said Amanda Tracy. "I'll tell you something you don't know. I didn't take anything from Patricia Van Osdel that wasn't mine. Do you know where her old man got his flykiller formula? From my mother. She made it up herself and used it around the farm. Old Van Osdel came along selling phony patent medicine one day, and he saw it work. He got my mother to tell him how she made it and got her to sign a release of all her rights in it for five dollars. Five dollars!"

"Patricia came by her chiseling honestly," Doan commented.

Amanda Tracy made a savage gesture with her clenched fist. "Just five dollars, and Van Osdel made millions out of it! And then later, when my father died and we lost our farm, I asked him to give us just a little to help us out—to keep my mother from dying in the county poor-house. He refused. I told him then that I'd get some of his dirty money whether he gave it to me or not—plenty of it. I waited for a long time before I got a chance. I painted up some damned good imitations of Predilip, and I contacted Patricia when she came back to America. I told her I'd found the pictures in an attic of a house Predilip had lived in. I made a good story of it. I intended to sell her the fakes and then tell everybody about it and laugh like hell when she tried to get her money back."

"Not a bad idea," said Doan. "Why didn't you do that instead of killing her?"

"You should ask, little man. Because of some others like you, and that's why I've always hated the whole breed. When I threatened old Van Osdel, he lured some private detectives to follow me around for awhile. I knew that, but I didn't know they had taken pictures of me—candid shots. I knew Patricia had never seen me, but she *had* seen those pictures. She recognized me right away. She knew then that the whole deal must be a gyp, and she just laughed at me. She didn't laugh long, though."

"*Dios mio,*" Captain Perona whispered.

225

Amanda Tracy laughed at him. "The earthquake was just what the doctor ordered. Patricia was walking away from me when it happened. I picked up a rock and slammed her and grabbed her purse. Maria started running and squawking, but so was everyone else right then. I chased her and hit her with the rock. I thought I'd finished her. No one noticed me before or afterward. They're used to me in this town."

"What about Greg?" Doan asked.

"He followed me from the hotel last night. He knew why Patricia had come here, and he guessed what had happened. He wanted the twenty-five thousand. All of it, if you can imagine the nerve of him. He was a nasty one, that boy. But I knew he didn't have his knife with him. I did have mine. He slammed me with a rock once. That was all he had time for."

Janet made a little gulping sound.

"Brace up, dearie," Amanda Tracy said. "I've got a surprise for the three of you." She held out her right hand. "Isn't it pretty?"

"Mother of God—a hand grenade!" Captain Perona exclaimed.

"One of yours," Amanda Tracy agreed. "You should really keep better track of them." She reached behind her with her left hand. "I'm going to leave this little iron egg with you. There'll be quite a dust-up when it lets go, and after it's all over I'll be in my little hospital bed looking very surprised and innocent, and I don't think any of you will tell stories about what I've just said."

"Wait!" Captain Perona shouted. "You can't—"

"Good-by, now," said Amanda Tracy. Her left hand had found the latch, and she pulled the door open behind her.

Lepicik was standing in the doorway looking politely interested. He nodded casually to Doan and then hit Amanda Tracy in the back of the neck with the edge of his palm. Her head snapped forward, and Doan dove for her. He caught her right hand in both of his and held it rigid while her thick body twirled and slumped loosely down.

"Get it!" Doan gasped. "Get the grenade! Look out! She's got her finger through the firing pin ring!"

Captain Perona knelt down beside him, breathing hard. With infinite care he untwisted the thick fingers. He had the grenade then, and he shifted it from one hand to the other uneasily and then put it down on the desk.

Doan let go of Amanda Tracy and stood up and wiped his forehead thoughtfully.

"Mr. Doan," said Lepicik. "Excuse me, but I have a message here that came through the military wireless. It's a little confusing, and I thought perhaps you could explain it. It's from a man named Carpenhyer, who is a motion picture agent in Hollywood, California. Have you ever heard of the man?"

"Yes," said Doan. "He's one of the best. Are you really a director?"

"Certainly," said Lepicik. "I have directed many cinema productions—in London, Rome, Stockholm, Berlin, Paris, Vienna, Moscow. Before the war, of course. But this Carpenhyer says he can get me a job at—" Lepicik stopped to verify the figure "—one thousand seven hundred and fifty dollars a week. Could that be correct?"

Doan nodded, wincing. "I'm afraid so, if Carpenhyer says it is. Take it. But quick."

"You!" said Captain Perona, suddenly recovering himself. "How did you get out of my quarters? Where is the soldier who was guarding you?"

"He had a headache," Lepicik said. "So I gave him some opium."

"Opium!" Captain Perona repeated wildly.

Lepicik looked surprised. "Just a small pill. It is very good for headaches. But it put him to sleep."

Sergeant Obrian burst in the room through the front door. "Say, that old artist doll has scrammed out of the hospital, and I can't find—" His mouth stayed open.

"You," said Captain Perona dangerously, "have arrived, as usual, in the nick of time. There is the artist doll. She has just been frustrated in an attempt to massacre us all. Put her in jail and make sure before you do that she does not have any hand grenades or other deadly weapons concealed about her person."

Amanda Tracy stirred and moaned.

"Oh!" said Janet. "I can't stand to see... I've got to get out of here!"

She dodged nimbly around Sergeant Obrian and ran headlong out the door and across a neat, graveled plot of parade ground toward the plaza. Behind her she could hear both Doan and Captain Perona shouting at her anxiously, but she couldn't stop. And then she saw something that did make her stop.

"Yes!" said Bartolome proudly. "Is it not a wonder of wonders most incredible?"

It was the bus. It had dents in it as big as footballs. It was lopsided and swaybacked, and both the rear tires were flat. But it was out from under the debris and up on its own wheels.

Carstairs and Doan and Captain Perona pulled up beside Janet and stared, too.

"The engine," said Bartolome, "has fallen out and broken itself lamentably, but that is only a matter of the most minor."

Henshaw came pacing gloomily up to them. His head was bowed, and his hands were folded behind him.

"Observe!" Bartolome commanded him. "The bus of scenic magnificence resumes itself!"

"It ain't gonna do me no good," Henshaw said.

"What's the matter?" Doan asked him. "Didn't you sell Timpkins the bathroom?"

"No," said Henshaw. "I didn't sell him the bathroom." His voice rose to a wail. "Timpkins sold me his damned old hotel!"

THE END

www.ingramcontent.com/pod-product-compliance
Lightning Source LLC
Chambersburg PA
CBHW032142020726
47496CB00003B/681